HAVEN

KRISTI COOK

Simon Pulse
New York London Toronto Sydney

SIMON PULSE
An imprint of Simon & Schuster Children's Publishing Division
1230 Avenue of the Americas, New York, NY 10020
First Simon Pulse hardcover edition February 2011

For information about special discounts for bulk purchases, please contact Simon & Schuster Special Sales at 1-866-506-1949 or business@simonandschuster.com.
The Simon & Schuster Speakers Bureau can bring authors to your live event. For more information or to book an event contact the Simon & Schuster Speakers Bureau at 1-866-248-3049 or visit our website at www.simonspeakers.com.
Designed by Mike Rosamilia
The text of this book was set in Berling LT Std.
Manufactured in the United States of America
2 4 6 8 10 9 7 5 3 1
Library of Congress Cataloging-in-Publication Data
Cook, Kristi.
Haven / by Kristi Cook. — 1st Simon Pulse hardcover ed.
p. cm.
Summary: Violet McKenna's life started falling apart when a premonition of her father's murder came true, but at a new school, Winterhaven, she finds friends with psychic gifts and an alluring boy whose destiny is entwined with hers in a critical—and deadly—way.
ISBN 978-1-4424-0760-2 (hardcover)
[1. Psychic ability—Fiction. 2. Supernatural—Fiction. 3. Boarding schools—Fiction. 4. Schools—Fiction. 5. Orphans—Fiction. 6. New York (State)—Fiction.] I. Title.
PZ7.C76984Hav 2011 [Fic]—dc22 2010021803
ISBN 978-1-4424-0762-6 (eBook)

For Vivian and Eleanor,
the coolest kids ever.
Seriously.

HAVEN

1 ~ A New Beginning

I'll never forget that first glimpse of Winterhaven as we pulled up the long, curving drive—gray stones bathed in the lavender haze of dusk, looking like an old European university, all flying buttresses and stone spires reaching toward the sky. Leaves in every shade of the autumn spectrum—red, yellow, orange, brown—littered the ground at my feet, crunching beneath my boots as I stepped out of the car and looked around. This was it—my new home, my new life.

Typically, I had just been dumped there as unceremoniously as had the luggage at my feet. My mom hadn't even bothered to come along for the ride. Okay, technically Patsy is my stepmother, but since my real mom died when I was four and my dad married Patsy about, oh, two seconds later, she's all I've got. She was always clear about her priorities, though—my dad, and her career, in that order. I think I made the list somewhere between the Junior League and Jimmy Choo shoes.

To give Patsy credit, though, she *had* made an effort to spend more time with me after my dad died. I thought we were making progress when she took an entire Saturday afternoon off and invited me out to lunch. But that's when she dropped the bomb—she'd been offered a job in New York, a once-in-a-lifetime opportunity, she called it. So less than a month into my junior year, Patsy gave me a choice: stay in Atlanta with Gran, or move to New York with her.

There were no other options, no one else to foist me off on. No living relatives except for Gran, my real mom's mother. And as much as I adore Gran, I just wasn't sure that she was up to having me move in with her and Lupe, her companion/housekeeper. After all, Gran was old, set in her ways. I didn't want to be a burden.

And, okay . . . I'll admit that there was more to it than that. *Way* more. I can't really explain it, but once I saw that Winterhaven brochure in the pile that Patsy had dumped in my lap, I somehow *knew* that this was the place for me. I'd been so sure of it that I'd actually refused to apply anywhere else.

And so . . . here I was. Time to see if my instincts had

been correct. I made my way up the stairs toward the largest of the buildings, the one marked ADMINISTRATION. Taking a deep breath, I pushed open a set of double doors at the top of the stairs and stepped inside, looking around a huge rotunda. On either side of me, two staircases curved up, like a swan's wings. Up above was a stained-glass-tiled dome, a huge chandelier hanging from its center. Directly below it stood a bronze statue cordoned off by red velvet ropes. WASHINGTON IRVING, the plaque read. The school's founder. Which, I had to admit, was pretty cool.

Letting out a low whistle of appreciation, I turned in slow circles, admiring the view. *Wow.* The glossy brochure hadn't done this place justice. I hoped it was costing Patsy a fortune.

At the sound of approaching footsteps, I froze, my heart thumping loudly against my ribs. A tall woman with graying auburn hair came into view, smiling as she hurried toward me, her high heels clicking noisily against the black-and-white checkerboard marble tiles.

"You must be Miss McKenna," she called out. "Welcome to Winterhaven, *chérie*. I'm Nicole Girard. Are these all of your belongings?" She nodded toward the two trunks the driver had left at my side before disappearing without a word.

"That's it," I answered, my voice a bit rusty. "I had the rest of my stuff shipped."

"Very good. Just leave them there, and I'll take you right up to the headmaster's office. Dr. Blackwell is looking forward to welcoming you."

"Great." I tried to sound enthusiastic. Glancing back one last time at my trunks, I followed Mrs. Girard up the stairs on my left and down a long hall lined with portraits of stern-looking old men in suits. Former headmasters, I guessed.

Finally we stopped in front of a large, arched wooden door that looked like it belonged in a medieval castle. Mrs. Girard knocked three times before turning the brass handle. "Dr. Blackwell?" she called out, stepping inside with me trailing behind. "The new student has arrived."

A leather chair swiveled around, startling me so badly that I took a step back and nearly tripped over my own feet. A man sat behind the massive desk, watching me. His hair was totally silver, but his skin was surprisingly smooth except for crinkles at the corners of his eyes—eyes as silver as his hair. With his wire-rimmed spectacles and a pipe between his teeth, he looked just like I imagined a headmaster should.

"Welcome, Miss McKenna. What a pleasure to meet you."

"Th-thank you, sir," I stammered.

"And how was your journey?"

"I think I slept through most of it," I answered truthfully.

"I do hope you were able to explore the city a bit before

coming here. I told your stepmother there was no rush."

"I did, thanks." I had spent two weeks helping Patsy settle into her new apartment on the Upper East Side.

"Very good." He nodded. "Thank you, Nicole. I'll ring the bell when I'm ready for you to show Miss McKenna to her room."

"Very well, sir," the woman replied, then took her leave with one last smile in my direction.

Dr. Blackwell motioned for me to take a seat opposite him, so I settled myself into the chair across from his desk.

"Well, then," he said, laying down his pipe and shuffling a stack of papers. "I have your transcripts right here. Quite impressive. Windsor Day School, advanced classes, honor roll. A fencer." He took off his glasses and looked up at me. "Hmm, on the state championship team, it says."

"Yes, sir. I'm recovering from an injury, though." Almost out of habit, I reached across to rub my right shoulder.

"Well, you'll be pleased to know that we've quite a fencing program here at Winterhaven. Our instructor is an Olympic gold medalist. I'm sure there will be a place for you on the girls team."

I shifted in my seat. At Windsor we'd had just one team—and I had been the only girl on it.

"As to your schedule, we've made some placements based

upon your credits, but you'll find our class offerings a little different here from those at Windsor Day. If anything doesn't appeal to you, let us know at the end of the day tomorrow and we'll make the necessary adjustments."

"I'm sure it'll be fine." I took the page he pushed across the desk.

"Breakfast is served in the dining hall from seven till eight thirty, lunch at noon, and dinner from five to six thirty." He shuffled through some more papers on his desk. "Let's see, you'll be in the East Hall dormitory. Mrs. Girard is house-mistress there, and her word is law. I'm sure I needn't tell you that smoking and alcoholic beverages are strictly forbidden. Mrs. Girard will inform you of the remaining dormitory rules when she shows you to your room."

I must have looked panicked, because he smiled a gentle, grandfatherly smile. "I assure you, they are nothing too strict. Now then, have you any questions for me?"

"Um, a roommate?" I asked hopefully.

"Ah, yes. You do have a roommate, and she's eagerly awaiting your arrival. Miss Cecilia Bradford. I believe you'll get on famously."

I nodded, hoping he was right. I wanted to fit in. To *blend* in.

Dr. Blackwell steepled his hands beneath his chin, silently

watching me for a moment. "I'm very sorry about your father's death, Miss McKenna," he said, startling me.

My stomach rolled over in my gut. Was that information there in the papers on his desk? It had happened two years ago, but it still felt like yesterday. I couldn't stand to think about it, even now. Especially now. *What doesn't break us only makes us stronger,* Gran liked to say, but it never did make me feel any better.

"Quite tragic," the headmaster added. "Not something one can easily forget, is it?"

"No," I muttered, dropping my gaze to my lap. It wasn't easy to forget, especially when people kept bringing it up.

"I imagine that tomorrow will be a day of discovery for you. You might find yourself somewhat . . . surprised by what you find here at Winterhaven. If you have any questions or simply need to talk to someone, my door is always open. Figuratively speaking, of course."

I only nodded in reply.

"Well, then." He tipped his head toward the door. "Shall I ring the bell for Mrs. Girard?"

"That'd be great," I said, standing on shaky legs.

"I hope your first night at Winterhaven is a pleasant one, Miss McKenna." He extended one hand toward me as Mrs. Girard bustled back in.

"Thank you, sir." As I took his hand, a shudder ran up my arm. His hand was cold—like ice—despite the fire crackling away in the fireplace behind him.

"Come now, Miss McKenna," Mrs. Girard said. "If we go quickly, we might catch Miss Bradford before she heads down to dinner."

With a nod, I picked up my bag and stuffed my class schedule inside, then followed her out. We seemed to walk forever, one corridor leading to the next, up one staircase and down another. How in the world was I ever going to find my way around this place?

Finally we entered what looked like an oversize, paneled study with a stone fireplace on one side, a wall-mounted television in the corner, and bookshelves taking up the opposite wall. Brown leather couches and chairs were scattered about.

"This is the East Hall lounge," Mrs. Girard explained, "where you'll have study hour after dinner each night. Other than that, it's to use as you please. Vending machines are just over there, beside the mailboxes. Girls' rooms are this way." She motioned to the right, and I followed her into yet another hall, this one lined with group photos of girls, all wearing blue velvet gowns. About halfway down the hall we stopped in front of a door with the number 217 on it, and she knocked sharply. When no one answered, she produced a key from her pocket and turned it in the lock.

"Here we are," she said.

Stepping inside, I quickly surveyed the place. The room was surprisingly big, with two white wooden beds on either side of a window. The required desk and dresser were there beside each bed, and an open doorway on one side of the room led to what looked like a little sitting area, complete with love seat, chair, and coffee table. *Not bad*, I thought. It was actually pretty nice.

Mrs. Girard cocked her head toward the bare side of the room. "I'll send the housekeeper right up with some clean linens for your bed."

"Thank you," I said, setting my bag on the empty desk.

"I see your trunks made it up here already, and your course books are there on the shelves." With a nod, she rubbed her hands together. "Now, then. House rules. No boys on the girls' floor, and vice versa. No smoking, no alcoholic beverages. You will find snacks and beverages in the lounge and the café. The housekeepers come on Tuesdays and Fridays, so I ask that you have your clutter cleared away on those mornings. No cell phones in the lounge, or anywhere else on campus, for that matter. They must remain here in your room at all times. No music so loud as to disturb your neighbors. Lights out by eleven on school nights, midnight curfew on weekends. I suppose that's it for now. The rest can wait."

There was more? I wasn't what you'd call a party animal—not at all—but lights out at eleven seemed a little harsh, and so did the cell phone thing. I wasn't used to going anywhere without my cell.

"Oh, and the restrooms and showers are just next door, on your right." Just then the door was flung open, and a girl about my height wearing a pink robe and bunny slippers burst in, her hair wrapped in a towel.

"Oh!" She stepped back in surprise when she saw us standing there. "You're here!"

"Good evening, Miss Bradford," Mrs. Girard said. "I've brought you your new roommate."

"You must be Violet," she said brightly.

"And you must be Cecilia." Deep brown skin, dark eyes, curly hair peeking out of her towel. She was beautiful, and I felt like a pale plain Jane in comparison.

She waved one hand in dismissal. "Oh, everyone calls me Cece. You have *no* idea how glad I am you're here."

Mrs. Girard moved toward the door. "Well then, I think we're done going over the rules, Miss McKenna. Here's your key"—she laid it on my desk—"and I'll leave you two to get acquainted. You have your class schedule?"

I nodded. "Yes, ma'am."

"Very good. You'll find a campus map on the back. Have a wonderful evening, then. And don't forget, Dr. Blackwell and myself are available to answer any questions that might arise over the course of the day tomorrow."

After she left, I turned my attention to Cece. She was standing by her bed, watching me curiously. "I cleaned out the closet and made sure your half was empty," she offered.

"Thanks. The room is much nicer than I expected. Big."

"Yeah, it's not too bad, except for the shared bath. But you get used to it. And hey, at least it's right next door."

I cleared my throat, trying to think of something to say. "You've been here since freshman year?" I asked at last, knowing it sounded lame.

"Yup. Home sweet home." She removed the towel from her head, revealing dark curls that fell just past her shoulders. "So you're from Atlanta?"

"Lived there my whole life," I said with a shrug. Same neighborhood, same house—just down the block from Gran, who'd live there *her* whole life. God, we were a boring bunch.

Still, it had been comfortable. If only Patsy had left well enough alone, hadn't forced me to choose between her—the closest thing I had to a parent—and the only place I'd ever called home.

But she *had* made me choose, and I'd chosen Winterhaven. I tried to think of this as a new beginning, a fresh start. I'd reinvent myself—the new-and-improved Violet McKenna. No one here would know the names I'd been called—freak, weirdo. Half-jokingly, of course, but my friends had no idea how close to the truth they'd been, and how much that scared me. I *was* a freak, and I'd do just about anything to make sure no one here noticed it.

"Well, I've lived *here* my whole life," Cece said. "The city, I mean. My mom's family is from New Orleans, though, so we spend a lot of time down there. I think I've got some voodoo queen in my blood!"

"Now *that* sounds interesting." I sat down on my bed, watching as Cece walked over to the sitting area and started picking up magazines that were scattered about.

"Just don't let my mother hear you say that," she called back over one shoulder. "So, what is it that you do?"

"You mean, like, fencing?"

"You're a fencer?" she asked, carrying the magazines over to her desk and leaving them in a pile that looked in serious danger of toppling over. "You mean swords and all that stuff?"

"Yeah. I hear the program here is pretty good."

"Oh. Yeah, sure. But I meant . . . you know . . ." Cece trailed off, shaking her head when I said nothing. "Never mind," she said with a shrug, glancing up at the clock above her desk. "Crap, when did it get so late? I've got a student council meeting tonight."

She hurried over to her dresser, pulling open drawers and haphazardly pulling things out. Minutes later she was dressed in jeans and a pink T-shirt, a touch of gloss on her lips. Very low maintenance—I liked that.

"So, you're on student council?" I asked, just trying to make conversation.

"Yep, you're looking at the newly elected junior class president," she said with a grin, grabbing her keys off her desk and stuffing them into a pocket.

"Cool," I said.

She shrugged. "I don't know. Is it cool? I swear, sometimes I think I'm headed toward total dorkdom."

"No, it really *is* cool." Actually, everything about Cece seemed cool, which made me feel like an even bigger loser.

She paused by the door. "I feel terrible just leaving you here, fifteen minutes after you walk through the door. Want me to call some of my friends, ask them to come over and show you around?"

I shook my head. "No, I swear I'll be fine. By the time you get back, I'll have everything all unpacked and organized."

She bit her lower lip, then nodded. "Okay. I guess I'll go, then."

"Go," I answered with a laugh, shooing her out.

As soon as the door closed behind her, I looked around with a sigh, surveying the blank side of the room—my new digs, such as they were. I'd never shared a room with anyone before, much less a bathroom. It was definitely going to take some getting used to, but I had a really good feeling about Cece.

I couldn't resist the urge to go over to her desk and straighten the magazines, though. *Vogue, Entertainment Weekly, Rolling Stone*. Yeah, we were going to get along just fine.

Across the room, my cell phone made a chirping sound. Hurrying back to my own desk, I dug around in my bag till I found it. I expected a message from Patsy, checking to make sure that I'd arrived safely and all that. Instead I found a text from Whitney, my best friend since the very first day of kindergarten, when we'd trooped into our classroom and found our cubbies, conveniently alphabetized by first name, right next to each other. We'd sort of started to drift apart lately, mostly because she'd left Windsor for a performing arts school freshman year. She had new friends, new interests, and I had gotten increasingly busy with fencing. Still, she'd always been a phone call away. *She still is,* I reminded myself.

I scanned her message—asking how it was going so far—

and smiled. At least *someone* cared. I sent her a quick text back, promising to e-mail her as soon as I got my laptop set up.

If I could find my laptop, that is. I glanced down at the trunks that held nearly all my earthly possessions, and sighed. Time to start unpacking.

Morning came far too quickly. Still in my pajamas, I winced at the sight of my bloodshot eyes staring back at me in the mirror.

"You're going to miss breakfast if you don't hurry and get dressed," Cece said, eyeing me from across the room as she pulled on her shoes.

"I know. I just . . . I didn't get much sleep last night. New bed and all." I'd actually lain awake most of the night, only drifting off somewhere near dawn.

"I'll wait for you," she offered.

I weighed my options. I could go down now and face the crowd—get it over with. Or I could enjoy some quiet time alone and pull myself together. Ultimately I took the coward's way out. "It's okay, you go on ahead. I just need some coffee."

"There's a coffee machine in the lounge. At least, they call it coffee. Personally, I think they're using the term a little too loosely."

I had to laugh at that. "The way I feel right now, just about anything will do. What time's first period?"

"Eight forty-five. What's your first class?"

I hadn't even glanced at my schedule yet. "Let me see." I grabbed my bag and rummaged through it till I found the sheet Dr. Blackwell had given me. "First period, Hackley Hall, Corridor A, Room 312. Culture and Society in Nineteenth-Century Britain." Wow, that *was* a sophisticated-sounding course for high school.

"That's an advanced-level class," Cece said, wrinkling her nose. "You must be a brainiac or something."

I just shrugged. I'd been called worse.

"Anyway," she continued, "Hackley Hall is where all the junior- and senior-level classes are held, and it's the building just behind us. Here, give me your schedule and I'll show you on the map."

I handed it over along with a pen and watched as she scanned my class list, turned it over and circled a big rectangle on the map, then drew a line from what must be the dorms to the circled building. "There you go," she said, handing it back to me. "After that, you're on your own. Your classes are all more advanced than mine. But I'll save you a seat in the dining hall at lunch, okay?"

"That'd be great. Will I get lost trying to find my way there?"

"Nope. Just follow the hungry crowd."

"Gotcha."

Grinning, she stuffed some notebooks into a pale pink backpack. "I just know you're going to love it here," she said, pausing by the doorway.

God, I hoped she was right.

2 ~ The Eyes Have It

Taking a deep, fortifying breath, I stepped into the classroom, my schedule still clutched in one clammy hand. Left and right, kids elbowed past me and took their seats. I glanced down at the page I held, reminding myself that it was totally normal to be a little nervous. New school, new kids . . . it was going to take some getting used to. Corridor A, my schedule said. Room 312. This was it. My gaze shot back up, toward the rows of seats before me.

And then I saw him. Second row, third seat back. Gorgeous eyes. He looked at me strangely, as if he were surprised to see me, a steady gaze beneath a baseball cap pulled low over his brow. Whoever he was, he was watching me so intently that I could barely breathe. For the briefest of moments I felt a flicker of fear. The hum of voices receded and all I could hear was the steady pounding of my own heart. My schedule slipped through my fingers and fluttered to the ground beside my feet in slow, swooping arcs.

Great. I hadn't even been at Winterhaven a full twenty-four hours and already I was making an idiot of myself. My cheeks burning, I knelt to retrieve the page. And then they were there, not inches from my face—those eyes. Not quite blue, but not quite gray, either.

"I think you dropped this," he said, completely derailing my train of thought. My gosh, that voice . . . deep and soft, with the hint of an accent. British, maybe? I was definitely a sucker for accents.

My heart skipped a beat as I stared at the rumpled page he held in his outstretched hand. For some unknown reason, I took a step back, wanting to increase the distance between us. Reluctantly, I raised my gaze to meet his.

The first thing I noticed was that his face was pale, his skin perfect except for dark smudges beneath his eyes. His lips were full, his nose slightly crooked, as if it had been broken years ago and not quite set right. Beneath the baseball cap, wavy golden-blond hair peeked out, curling against his collar. And his eyes . . . I forcibly suppressed a sigh. More blue than gray, I realized, with thick, dark eyelashes. Most girls would kill for eyelashes like that.

My mouth went dry. I cleared my throat, afraid that if I met his stare I'd never be able to look away. "Thanks," I managed to say, holding out one trembling hand for my schedule.

He placed it in my palm, somehow managing to brush my fingers with his own. "I'm Aidan Gray," he said. "Welcome to Winterhaven."

Before I even had a chance to reply, he was gone, slipping back through the aisles to his seat. Shaking my head, I found an empty seat in the front row and set my bag down beside the desk.

Sliding into the molded plastic seat, I pulled out a notebook and pen from my bag, keeping my gaze fixed on my desk while the whispers buzzed around me.

Aidan Gray. I fought the urge to say it aloud, to hear it slip off my own tongue. My God, I was losing my mind. Either that, or I'd suddenly become really shallow. I wasn't sure which was worse.

I looked up just as a tall, balding man in a tweed jacket strode in, carrying a briefcase and whistling to himself. The teacher. At least I hoped he was, because another few minutes of sitting there waiting for class to start and I was sure to turn around and look for *him*. Aidan Gray.

The room got silent as the man in tweed took his place behind the desk, looking every bit the absentminded professor as he fumbled with a stack of papers. He pulled out a pair of glasses—wire-rimmed, of course—and put them on while he studied a small slip of paper. With a nod to himself, he looked up, his eyes quickly scanning the room before settling on me.

I swallowed hard, nervously fiddling with my pen.

"We have a new student," he said, inclining his head toward me. "You must be Violet McKenna."

I cleared my throat, my cheeks suddenly hot. "Yes, sir."

"It says here your mother was just appointed assistant secretary-general for Legal Affairs at the UN. Hmm, impressive," he grunted. He eyed me over the top of the page, his bushy brows raised in what looked like disbelief. "And you've moved here from . . . ?"

"From Atlanta," I answered, wishing a hole would open in the floor and swallow me up.

"Well, we're glad to have you, Miss McKenna. I'm Dr. Penworth," he said, removing his glasses. "Miss Patterson, will you see that Miss McKenna finds her way to her next class?"

"Sure," the girl sitting to my immediate right chirped out, startling me. "Hi," she whispered, leaning across her desk toward me. "I'm Sophie."

I mouthed "hi" back and tried to smile.

Apparently done humiliating me, Dr. Penworth finally got on with business. "Shall we pick up where we left off? I believe we were discussing the laws of primogeniture, were we not?"

His voice settled into a lecture-mode steady drone, and I opened my notebook, realizing I had a lot of reading to do to catch up with the class.

The hour passed quickly. My hand was cramped from taking so many notes, but it kept me focused.

Suddenly what sounded like church bells ringing startled me so badly that I dropped my pen. Everyone else snapped shut their notebooks and began to stuff their things back into their bags, so I retrieved my pen and did the same. Standing up, I looked entreatingly to my neighbor, ready to follow her around like a lost puppy. But then I sensed *him*, standing just behind my right shoulder.

"Mr. Gray," Dr. Penworth called out, his voice jolly. "You've a firm grasp of the class material. Would you see that our new student gets caught up?"

Oh, please, no. I almost groaned aloud. Never had a guy made me feel so flustered, so completely tongue-tied, so . . . so hyperaware and self-conscious as this one did. I didn't want to be alone with him, afraid I would humiliate myself, afraid—

"Of course, sir," he answered, and I felt my stomach drop.

He was so close now that I could feel his breath against my neck, and I was sure he saw me shiver in response.

"Very good." Dr. Penworth nodded to himself and began the task of returning his sheaf of papers to his briefcase.

Summoning my courage, I turned around to tell him—*Aidan*—that I really didn't need any help, but he was gone. I spun toward the door, my eyes quickly scanning the emptying room.

"Amazing how he does that, isn't it?" the girl beside me asked.

Amazing? How about freaky? "I guess you could call it that," I muttered.

"It's Violet, right?"

"Yep." I nodded, realizing I had no idea what her name was. It had gone in one ear and out the other.

"I guess you're Cece's new roommate? She's been moping around since Allison left."

"Allison was her old roommate?"

She nodded.

I couldn't stanch my curiosity. "Why'd she leave?"

She looked around, as if to make sure no one was listening. "Last spring, she *told*. Her parents, I mean. You know, about the school."

"Told what?" I asked.

"Put it this way—they think she's nuts. Locked her up somewhere, from what I heard. I mean, c'mon, everyone knows that's why you don't tell. Anyway, let me see your schedule or we'll both be late."

Totally confused, I handed her the piece of paper. Her eyes quickly scanned it, and then she grinned. "Feminism in British Lit. Same as me. C'mon, let's go. Ackerman's great; you'll like her."

With an uneasy feeling in the pit of my stomach, I followed her down a long corridor, out a set of double doors, and into a wide stone courtyard. There was a fountain in the center, complete with gargoyles and a spray of water rising high in the air. Gray stone arches framed the courtyard on all four sides, and double doors just like the ones we'd come from led toward corridors in every direction.

I whistled in appreciation, all my doubts forgotten. "Wow! It's like . . . like something out of Harry Potter."

"I know. It's beautiful, isn't it? What was your school in Atlanta like?"

"Nothing like this," I answered, shaking my head in amazement. "It was just a day school, anyway."

"So this is your first time at boarding school?"

"Yeah." I followed her through the arch directly opposite the one we'd come from.

"So, how do you feel about it? Boarding school, I mean?"

I shrugged. "It seemed like a good idea."

"Well, Winterhaven has a way of finding us, doesn't it?" She paused as the crowd pushed by.

Sophie. That was her name. Sophie Patterson. It popped into my head, just like that. "The rules seem a little . . . outdated, though, don't they?" I asked, trying to ignore the curious stares as I fell back into step beside Sophie. "I mean, no cell phones?"

"Well, they like to call the rules 'traditional.' Have you met Dr. Blackwell yet? The headmaster?"

"Yep, last night. He seemed okay."

"A little odd, yeah, but he's cool. Everyone likes him."

I couldn't resist. "Speaking of odd, what's the deal with Aidan Gray?"

Sophie sighed dramatically. "He's pretty hot, isn't he?"

That was an understatement. "I guess," I lied, not wanting to be too obvious. "What's he, like, the star quarterback or something?"

"No way! Aidan's an intellectual—the smartest kid at Winterhaven, and that's saying a lot. He was definitely checking you out, though, wasn't he? Weird."

I shrugged, trying not to look too offended.

"Oh, I didn't mean it like that!" she said, reaching out to

give my hand a friendly squeeze. "It's only . . . well, he doesn't really pay much attention to anyone. Kind of a loner, you know? Some people think he's gay, but I'm not sure. . . ." She trailed off, shaking her head.

"He's definitely not gay," I said with absolute assurance, though I couldn't say how I knew.

"You think?" she asked, sounding hopeful.

"Pretty sure," I murmured. Because freak that I was, my instincts were usually right.

"Here," Sophie said, motioning to her left. "It's right down this hall. So, what is it you do?"

That same question again. I guess extracurriculars were pretty important at Winterhaven. "I, uh, I'm a fencer. You know, fencing team and all that."

For a moment Sophie looked puzzled. "I think we have a pretty good fencing program here," she finally said with a shrug.

"That's what they keep telling me. I guess I'll find out sixth period."

"It doesn't bother your shoulder?"

"My . . . my shoulder?" I stuttered. How did she know about my shoulder? Had I been rubbing it?

"Yeah, when I touched your hand . . . well, never mind. At least it's healing nicely."

I could only nod. It *was* healing pretty well, but how did she know that? My nerves on edge, I silently followed Sophie into a classroom similar to the one we were in before. Everyone turned to stare as we walked in and made our way to two empty seats in the third row.

Steeling myself with a deep breath, I followed the crowd into the cafeteria—the dining hall, they called it—and scanned the room for a familiar face. Cece had promised to save me a seat, and so had Sophie, before we'd parted after second period. I figured I'd take up whomever I happened to see first.

I hitched my bag higher on my shoulder and stood on tiptoe, my palms dampening nervously. Sitting alone in the cafeteria would just scream "I'm the new girl. Everyone stare at me while I eat."

After what felt like an hour but was probably only a minute or two, I spied Sophie's strawberry-blond head poke up above the crowd as she waved me over. I let out my breath in a rush and hurried over to the table. As I drew near, I saw that Cece was also there, sitting across from Sophie. Good, they were friends. That spared me from having to choose who to sit with.

"Hey," Cece called out cheerily. "You found us. I was about to send out a search party." She pulled out the chair next to her. "So, how's it going?"

"Not bad, I guess," I said, sinking gratefully into the chair. "Seems like the same kids are in most of my classes, so the initial curiosity is beginning to wear off."

"Yeah, the brainiacs," Cece said.

"Hey, I resemble that remark," Sophie launched back.

"You said it, not me. Anyway, shut up and let me make the introductions. Everyone," Cece said, "this is Violet McKenna, my new roommate."

Two girls I'd never seen before stared at me.

"This is Kate Spencer," Cece said, pointing to a perky-looking blonde. "Kate is Sophie's roommate. And this is Marissa Tate." An exotic-looking girl with long, straight black hair eyed me warily. "Marissa somehow got one of the single rooms. No roommate, so we let her hang with us."

"Hey, I can't help it if I like my privacy," Marissa shot back.

"It's great to meet you both," I said, sounding way more confident than I felt.

Marissa reached out to touch my bag. "Ooh, Prada. Nice."

"Thanks," I murmured. I'd gotten it last year at Patsy's Junior League tag sale.

"So . . . Sophie says Aidan Gray was checking you out," Kate said, her chin propped in the palm of one hand.

"Really?" Cece asked, her eyes widening. "You're kidding, right?"

Sophie shook her head. "I kid you not. His head snapped up the second she walked in the room, and next thing you know, he was over there whispering sweet nothings in her ear."

"He was just picking up my schedule, that's all," I countered.

"And now, get this," Sophie continued on, completely ignoring me. "Dr. Penworth asked him to tutor her, and he actually agreed."

I swallowed hard. "Well, not really tutor me. Just help me catch up is all."

"Wow." Kate sat back in her seat, her arms folded over her chest. "You better milk it for all it's worth—take your sweet time catching up, if you know what I mean."

I shook my head. "He makes me kind of . . . nervous." No, that wasn't the right word. Not nervous, just . . . self-conscious. I couldn't explain it, really. I knew I was being silly—I'd only exchanged a couple of words with him, after all.

"Nah, it's not nerves you're feeling." Kate shrugged. "It's just the Aidan effect."

"The Aidan effect?" I asked, curious.

Kate smiled, her cheeks dimpling. "Yeah, he makes us all a little gooey and speechless. Come on, girls, back me up here."

"Sad, but true," Sophie said, nodding gravely.

"Embarrassing as hell," Marissa added. "Jenna Holley seems

to be the only one immune to it. He pretty much ignores her, though."

Kate nodded in agreement. "Even though she looks like a model."

"I think she *is* a model," Cece put in. "Isn't that what she does during summer break? In Europe, or something like that?"

Kate shrugged. "As *if* I would know."

"Um, I don't mean to interrupt," I said, looking around at the long tables filled with students, all eating. "But I'm starving."

"Oh my God, I'm so sorry." Cece stood up, and the other girls followed suit. "We were so busy yapping, I forgot you skipped breakfast. C'mon, let's get some food."

We left our bags sitting there at the table and hurried across the packed room. At the far side of the dining hall, several lines snaked out of open doorways.

"Okay," Cece said, "you've got hot lunch there. I think it's spaghetti and meatballs today. Soup and salad bar that way. Sandwiches this way. What'll it be?"

Everyone looked at me expectantly. "A sandwich, I guess?"

Minutes later I was back at the table, a chicken salad sandwich on my tray along with a bottle of iced tea. My stomach grumbled as I sat back down and attacked my food.

"Sophie says your mom's a hotshot lawyer at the UN,"

Cece said, then took a bite out of her own sandwich.

"Yeah, something like that," I answered around a mouthful of chicken salad, wishing Sophie hadn't been quite so forthcoming. "But she's . . . um, she's really my stepmom. My real mom died when I was little."

"What about your dad?" Marissa asked. "A lawyer, too?"

That bite of sandwich suddenly felt like a rock in my stomach. "No, he's a . . . um, he was a journalist, but he passed away too. A couple of years ago." *Might as well get it over with.*

"Oh my God, I'm so sorry," Cece said, giving Marissa a dirty look.

"No, it's okay," I said, even though it was anything but.

"Was he sick?" Sophie asked.

My throat constricted. "No. It was . . . an accident."

"An accident? Like a car accident?"

"C'mon, Soph, stop," Cece said. "This isn't the Inquisition. Let Violet eat, will you?"

"What about your parents?" I asked, my voice wavering only slightly.

"Both doctors," Cece answered. "Dad's a psychiatrist and Mom's an ob-gyn. Boring as hell."

"Not as boring as mine." Marissa pushed her long, straight hair behind one ear. "My dad's a professor at Columbia, and my mom's a fund-raiser. Nowhere near as interesting as Kate's mom."

"It's not really as interesting as it sounds." Kate wrinkled her nose at Marissa, then turned toward me. "My mom's an actress, mostly Broadway, though she's done some TV, too. You know, *Law and Order,* stuff like that. No dad, though."

"Yeah, it was an immaculate conception." Sophie laughed, and her friends joined in.

Kate scowled at her. "I'm sure it wasn't that innocent." She turned her attention to me. "He dumped my mom when he found out she was pregnant."

Cece shrugged. "His loss."

"Douche," Sophie said.

Kate took a swig of her Coke. "But hey, get this. I've done the math, and it looks like I was conceived while my mom was in *Phantom of the Opera*. Maybe my dad was the Phantom. How cool is that?"

Cece grimaced. "I guess you could call that cool."

"Or creepy," Sophie put in. "You think he wore the mask while they were doing it?"

Marissa choked, spitting out her drink as she did so. "Blech," she sputtered. "Don't even go there."

For a moment, no one said anything. I could feel Marissa's eyes watching me as I took another bite of my sandwich. It was as if she was trying to figure me out, trying to decide . . . something. *If she can trust me or not,* my mind supplied. Which seemed a little silly, considering she'd just met me. All we were doing was making small talk, anyway.

"How about your parents, Sophie?" I asked, trying not to look in Marissa's direction. Her steady gaze was getting unnerving.

"My dad's in finance—manages a hedge fund—and my mom's what I call a professional volunteer," Sophie answered. "You know, committees, foundation boards, stuff like that."

"And they have a house in Saint Bart's," Cece added, smiling broadly. "That's the best part. If we're all real nice to her, we might get invited there for spring break."

"Cece likes to celebrity-watch. It's disgusting," Sophie said, tossing her hair.

Cece narrowed her eyes. "Yeah, you didn't think it was so disgusting last year when we were following Leonardo DiCaprio around, now, did you?"

Everyone laughed, and I joined in. *I think I'm going to like it here,* I told myself. These girls were nice, all of them. Even Marissa, who clearly would take a bit more effort to win over than the rest of them.

That they were accepting me as easily as they were was a miracle in itself, and I wasn't going to complain if Marissa was a little standoffish at first. With a smile I watched them all chattering happily. Yeah, I'd made the right choice when I'd picked Winterhaven. Definitely.

Suddenly the girls went entirely silent, all of them looking over my left shoulder. The hair on the nape of my neck rose, and for a moment I didn't move. And then, as if in slow motion, I turned around and found myself looking up into the face of Aidan Gray. I swallowed hard, unable to utter a single syllable.

"It's Violet, right?" he asked.

I cleared my throat before attempting to answer. "Yeah" was all I could say.

His eyes regarded me for a moment, and I noticed a coldness there that I hadn't noticed before. Finally, he spoke. "I thought maybe we could meet after sixth period. To go over the history material," he added.

"Um, okay." Why was I tripping over my tongue?

"What class do you have sixth period?"

I just sat there, my mind spinning. I came up completely blank.

"Fencing," Sophie piped up. "Didn't you say you had fencing sixth period?"

I sighed my relief. "Oh, that's right. Fencing."

"I'll meet you outside the gym, then, and we'll try to get you caught up."

"Okay, great. Thanks," I added, feeling a bit woozy.

His gaze traveled over my face, making me incredibly self-conscious. "See you then," he said at last, and then he was gone.

Slowly, I turned back to my tablemates, who all looked as stunned as I felt. What was with this guy?

"The Aidan effect," Sophie said with a sigh.

3 ~ Tea for Two

The afternoon sped by. Right after lunch I followed Sophie and Kate to fourth-period trig. It felt comfortable sitting there between them, chatting while we waited for class to begin. I was more at ease than I had been all day, and I was beginning to recognize several kids from my morning classes. Some even managed to smile at me rather than stare.

Fifth period I was back on my own again. Cultural Anthropology: Folklore and Legend, which sounded much more promising than the plain old anthropology course taught at Windsor. Even more interesting, the headmaster was listed as the instructor. After double-checking the room number to make sure I was in the right place, I hurried inside. The classroom was much smaller than any other I'd been in so far, with the desks arranged in a semicircle. Seeing no one I recognized, I found an empty seat and slid into it.

I dug out my notebook and pen and started doodling while I waited for class to begin. After a minute or two, a strange awareness shot through me, and I looked up to see Aidan Gray slip into the seat directly across the room, facing me. *Great.* There went my concentration, especially since he sat there watching me, studying me like some interesting bug under a microscope.

Still waiting for Dr. Blackwell, I decided to study Aidan right back. He was tall, close to six feet, I'd say. More long and lean than muscular, but not skinny. He wore dark jeans with combat boots and a black hooded sweatshirt, a multicolored striped scarf hanging around his neck. The ball cap from earlier was gone, and his hair shone like gold in the afternoon sun that streamed in through the bank of windows behind him.

Suddenly he swung his head toward the door, and a second later Dr. Blackwell walked in. The headmaster smiled when he saw me sitting there, and I could swear he actually winked when he passed my desk.

"Has everyone met our new student?" he asked, moving to

stand in front of his desk. For perhaps, oh, the twentieth time that day, everyone turned to stare at me.

"No?" Dr. Blackwell asked in response to the unintelligible murmurs. "Well, then, Miss McKenna, if you'll stand up, please."

Stand up? *Oh, please, no*. Why did teachers insist on doing this? Didn't they realize how cruel it was? Feeling as if I were going to barf right then and there, I stood, my legs a little shaky.

"Class, please welcome Miss Violet McKenna. I am confident that you will all do your best to make her feel right at home."

No one said a word.

"Thank you," the headmaster said. "You may sit, Miss McKenna. Now, I believe we left off yesterday with a discussion about tribal folk dance in West Africa, correct?"

Everyone nodded, flipping open notebooks and pulling caps off their pens. I chewed on the end of my own pen, fully aware that Aidan continued to stare at me across the width of the room rather than take notes as Dr. Blackwell began his lecture. It was almost as if he was trying to distract me. Or annoy me, I wasn't sure which. *Don't look up*, I reminded myself, trying unsuccessfully to concentrate on Dr. Blackwell's voice. What was he talking about, anyway? Tribal dances? In Africa?

Instead of listening to the lecture, I concentrated on the sound of pens scratching paper, on the scent of chalk lingering in the air. Reaching up to stifle a sneeze, I let my gaze drift to the windows, where wide beams of sunlight cast long stripes across the green speckled carpet. Dust motes floated in the air, looking like insects. I knew I should be listening, paying attention to what Dr. Blackwell was saying, not allowing my mind to wander aimlessly. I also knew that Aidan was still watching me; I could feel his gaze, unrelenting.

This was ridiculous. Straightening in my seat, I willed myself to concentrate. ". . . in an effort to ward off evil spirits and preternatural creatures," Dr. Blackwell was saying, and my waning attention immediately snapped into focus.

The girl sitting to my left raised her hand.

"Yes, Miss Anderson?"

"By preternatural creatures, do you mean like, well, like—"

"Good question," he interrupted with a nod. "But no. They call them by different names than we do, but werewolves, vampires. Assorted creatures of the night, and—"

The bells interrupted him, and I let out my breath in a rush. Man, but that had been the longest fifty minutes of my life.

"Please read chapter seven by tomorrow, and be prepared for a quiz," the headmaster called out over the din. At once the class sprang into motion, slapping shut notebooks and retrieving bags. Careful not to raise my gaze, I reached for my own bag and took my sweet time stuffing my things back inside, hoping that Aidan would have done his speedy disappearing act by the time I stood up to leave.

No such luck. "Miss McKenna, Mr. Gray," Dr. Blackwell called out. "A moment, please." I slid out of my chair, my heart thumping against my ribs as I made my way to his desk. Aidan followed two steps behind.

"Mr. Gray, Dr. Penworth tells me he has asked you to help Miss McKenna catch up on your history material."

Aidan nodded. "He did."

"I might ask you to do the same with our class material, then. Would that be too much of an imposition?"

A strange look passed between the headmaster and Aidan, and I shifted my feet uncomfortably. Finally Aidan spoke. "Of course not."

"Very well. Thank you, Mr. Gray." He turned his attention toward me. "Miss McKenna, I vow you will not find a more able tutor here at Winterhaven. Mr. Gray will have you caught up in no time."

"Great," I muttered, casting a sidelong glance at Aidan.

"Off with you both, then." He dismissed us with a nod toward the door.

Sixth period was next, the last of the day. Only problem was, I had no idea where the gym was. Hurrying back to my desk to retrieve my bag, I pulled out my schedule. *Sixth period, Varsity Fencing, Gymnasium Studio A*. That was all it said. I turned back toward Dr. Blackwell's desk, but he was gone. Great. Tossing my bag over my shoulder, I hurried out into the hall, hoping I'd run into someone who looked familiar.

"Above the gym."

"Oh!" I stopped short, my breath catching in my throat. Aidan stood there, leaning against the wall. "You scared me."

"Sorry," he said with a shrug. "Studio A. Above the gym. Come on, I'll walk you there."

"Don't you have a class or something?" I asked, trying to slow my breathing as he pushed off the wall and fell into step beside me.

"Nope. I'm free sixth period. Independent study."

I could only nod.

"It's not far," he said, his tone conversational. "Back through the courtyard, the one with the fountain, and then two buildings behind the dormitory, just up some stairs."

"I'm sure I can find my way," I mumbled, feeling ridiculous. It wasn't that I didn't like being around him—in fact, the opposite was true. It was just that I knew that the more time I spent with him, the more likely I was to embarrass myself. As it was, I could barely form coherent sentences.

"I don't mind walking you," he said with a smile.

The afternoon sun was hidden by thick, gray clouds. The breeze blew some leaves across our path, and I shivered.

"You look cold," Aidan said, his brows drawn together.

"I *am* cold." I rubbed my arms. Maybe I was coming down with something—maybe that was why I felt so funny.

"Here."

Before I knew it, Aidan had taken off his striped scarf and was wrapping it around my neck. "I can't have you dying of hypothermia before I've had the chance to catch you up on your coursework." His mouth curved into a smile, and my heart did a little flip-flop.

Without thinking, I pulled the scarf up over my nose and inhaled. Immediately the sidewalk began to swim before my eyes.

Aidan reached out to steady me, his hand grasping my wrist. I took a deep breath as his face swam back into focus. "You really don't look well," he said.

I shook my head, trying to clear it. I didn't know what was wrong, but I was totally and completely losing it. "I'm fine," I lied. "I haven't eaten much today, that's all. God, your hand is cold."

He snatched it away and headed toward a steep staircase. "C'mon, this is a shortcut."

With a nod, I followed him up, trying my best to stay

focused, to put one foot in front of the other. Finally we reached the top, and I paused to catch my breath. Aidan waited patiently, watching me. I took two deep, calming breaths—and then it happened, like it had so many times in the past.

My vision darkened, tunneled, and I sank to my knees with a groan. Squeezing my eyes shut, I fought to block the vision, but it came anyway, flashing across my mind's eye like a sped-up movie.

It was dark, nighttime, and I was walking down a mostly deserted street. I knew it was New York City, though the street was unfamiliar, more seedy than Patsy's Upper East Side neighborhood. Dark, swirling fog obscured the sidewalk as I hurried on, in pursuit of someone. Something. A flash of movement to my right caught my eye and I sped off in that direction, seemingly unaware of any danger. A flyer on a post, HOW TO WRITE A NOVEL IN A WEEK *spelled out in black type. Up ahead, I saw a figure materialize in the fog, a shadow in black. "Aidan!" I cried out, my hands cupped around my mouth.*

Aidan? And then the vision ended, just like that. No more than a couple of seconds had passed, and I hoped it just looked like I had stumbled.

Aidan was beside me in a flash, reaching for my hands and helping me to my feet. "What happened?"

"Nothing, I . . . I tripped is all." My entire body felt flushed as I swayed against him. Damn it, I hated this. *Hated it.* Why couldn't I be normal? Here it was, my first day at a new school, in a new *state,* for God's sake, and everyone would see right off the bat what it had taken years for my friends at home to notice.

He shook his head. "You didn't trip. I don't know what it was, but you called out my name."

"No, I didn't." Did I? *No.* No, I hadn't said a word. I heard myself call out his name in the vision, but in reality I hadn't said a thing. At least, I didn't *think* I had.

"Forget sixth period," he said. "I'm taking you to the nurse. Now." Without another word, Aidan reached for my hand. He took off toward the building just ahead, pulling me along.

"I'm fine." I tried to pull my hand from his, but he only tightened his grip. I knew he was trying to help, but it was humiliating—he probably thought I'd had some sort of seizure or something. Of course, that was better than him knowing the truth.

For the first time since I'd arrived at Winterhaven, I wished I'd stayed in Atlanta after all.

"You're fit as a fiddle," the school nurse proclaimed in a cheery Irish brogue. Nurse Campbell, she called herself. "No temperature, your blood pressure is fine. Did you eat well today?"

"Not really," I murmured. Just a couple of bites of that chicken salad sandwich.

"Well, there you go. You youngsters are always so busy, rushing from one place to the next and not taking the time to properly nourish your bodies." She peered at me more closely, her brow furrowed. "Not on some crazy fad diet, are you?"

"No, of course not," I said in indignation. I'd just been . . . nervous.

"I'm glad to hear it. Well, off you go, then. I'll send a note around to the office and tell them you're excused from sixth period. Take some time before dinner to rest, dearie." She pushed aside the white curtain, and I followed her out of the exam cubicle.

Aidan was still standing where I'd left him, leaning against the wall beside the reception desk.

"Can I count on you to see her back to the dorms, Mr. Gray?" the nurse asked.

"Sure," he said. "Is everything . . . okay?"

"Nothing a little dinner won't cure," she answered, patting me on the shoulder. "See that she eats, won't you?"

Feeling like a child, I looked up at Aidan and smiled weakly. "I told you I was fine."

"Hmm, if you say so. Come on, I'll walk you back."

I nodded mutely. Aidan held the door open, and I hurried out, wrapping his scarf around my neck as I did so.

"Do you want to go back to your room, or do you feel well enough to go over some of the class material now?"

I looked up at him in surprise. "Sure. I mean, we can go over it now."

"Okay, then, let's go. To the café, where we can get you something to eat."

I fell into step beside him. "The café?"

"Yeah, if you'd like, we can even order a tea service there."

"A tea service? What do you mean, like little cakes and stuff?"

"Yeah, little sandwiches and scones with clotted cream. Just one of Dr. Blackwell's eccentricities," he answered.

Convinced he was teasing me, I followed him through a set of double doors and down a long, carpeted hall that looked vaguely familiar.

"Sixth period hasn't let out yet, so it should be pretty empty. Here we go." We reached the end of the hall and entered a big atrium with glass-fronted stores on both sides. On the left was what looked like a school store—gray fleece sweatshirts with WINTERHAVEN emblazoned across the front were displayed in the window, along with backpacks and notebooks, all with the Winterhaven crest. On the right was the café, with several tables out front and several more inside. Just beyond the café, I spotted a bookstore.

Bells jingled in the door as I followed Aidan inside the café and past a counter filled with sandwiches and pastries. He headed toward a booth in the far corner.

"I'll go and order. You like tea, right?" he asked, and I nodded as I sat down.

A minute or two later, he was back. "Okay, one tea service, coming up," he said. Only then, as Aidan sat back down across from me and pulled out a notebook from the black canvas backpack I hadn't even realized he'd been carrying, did I remember the vision. I hadn't seen anything bad happen—not really. Still, it unsettled me. Why was I following Aidan around New York City in the dead of night? And what was he doing, moving silently through the fog like a shadow?

For a moment I allowed myself to wonder if the vision would eventually come to pass, but in my heart I knew that it would. Of course it would, no matter what I did to try and prevent it. That was my curse, the one I tried to hide from the rest of the world.

And then I could have sworn I heard a voice in my head—Aidan's voice. *We've all got something to hide,* it said, as clearly as if it had been spoken aloud, as if it was replying to my thoughts.

At once my gaze snapped up and met his, and my heart began to pound. He looked startled, surprised. His eyes widened, the irises now as gray as storm clouds, then narrowed as he watched me bite my lower lip.

My head was buzzing, my palms suddenly damp. *What the holy hell just happened?* I was losing my mind, hearing voices. And it wasn't just any voice—it had been Aidan's.

Somehow he knew my secret.

4 ~ Revelations

"There she is," Cece said as I stepped into the room and closed the door. They were all there—Sophie, Kate, and Marissa, sitting on Cece's bed. Waiting for me, obviously.

"So, how was it?" Sophie asked. "Your afternoon, I mean."

"It was okay," I answered, dropping my bag onto my bed and collapsing there myself. "I'm totally beat."

"Kate heard that someone saw you in the café with Aidan," Cece said. "During sixth period."

Word sure traveled fast. "Yeah, he was trying to catch me up on my classes. Dr. Penworth asked him to, remember?"

"And?" Marissa prodded.

I sat up, shrugging. They were all watching me expectantly. "And that's about it."

Cece jumped up and hurried over to my bed, sitting down beside me on the quilt that Lupe had made me, and tucking her bare feet beneath herself. "C'mon, inquiring minds want to know. What did you and Aidan talk about?"

"Just schoolwork," I answered. It was the honest-to-God truth. After that weird moment where I'd imagined his voice in my head, we'd opened our books and gotten busy—all work and no play. A few minutes later, someone had come out from behind the counter and brought us a pot of tea and two dainty teacups on saucers, and then returned with a tiered silver tray holding miniature sandwiches and scones. An old-fashioned tea service, just as Aidan had promised. Weird, but nice.

I'd sat there picking at my food, listening to his hypnotic voice as he'd summarized a full month's worth of lectures. I'd forced myself to concentrate, and I thought I'd done a pretty good job, too, all things considered. Maybe it was really fascinating material, or maybe it was all in the retelling. Either way, I just needed to read through a few more chapters and take some notes, and I'd be set for tomorrow's quiz.

"Just schoolwork?" Marissa looked disappointed. "That's all? You must have talked about something else."

I shook my head, sorry to disappoint them. "Nope, 'fraid not."

"Why did you skip sixth period?" Kate asked.

"Oh. That. I guess I didn't eat enough and I got a little light-headed after anthropology class. I almost passed out, and Aidan had to take me to the nurse's office." I felt the heat rise in my cheeks. As embarrassing as it was, I figured I better tell them the truth. For all I knew, half the school had witnessed the incident, and word would surely get back to them.

Marissa eyed me sharply. "Well, I sure hope you weren't faking it," she said. "Because he'd know if you were. You don't know how to block your thoughts, do you?"

"What do you mean, block my thoughts?" It suddenly felt as if something were strangling me, and I reached a hand up to my throat. Aidan's scarf. I was still wearing his scarf. I loosened it, hoping no one recognized it or I'd never hear the end of the questions.

"He can read minds," Sophie explained. "That's his *thing*. You know, his gift? So you have to know how to block your thoughts around him, if you don't want him to know what you're thinking. It's easy, really."

"Yeah, sure," I said, laughing.

"No, really," Cece said.

"Hey, you never told us what your thing is," Sophie said,

turning toward me. "You're not going to make us guess, are you? I hate it when people do that."

Kate picked up a pillow from Cece's bed and threw it at Sophie. "She has to tell us; it's against the code not to. Have you gotten a copy of the COPA yet?"

"The copa?" I shook my head in frustration. "I have no idea what you're talking about."

Marissa rolled her eyes. "The code. You read it, sign it, and then you destroy it. Usually on your first day."

"Maybe she hasn't gotten it yet," Sophie said. "It's possible that she . . . you know, hasn't figured it out yet."

Marissa shook her head. "Everyone figures it out by the end of the first day, if they didn't already know."

"Guys, I don't know what you're talking about, but I'm tired, I feel like crap, and I almost passed out today. Any chance you could cut me some slack?"

Cece's hand flew to her forehead, her dark eyes as wide as saucers. "Oh my God, she really doesn't know."

"Then she's clueless—"

"Shut up, Marissa," Sophie said, giving her a dirty look. "Just because you were a legacy and knew all along—"

Suddenly they were all arguing at once, about who knew and who didn't know . . . *something.*

"Will you all just shut up and tell me what you're talking

about?" I had to shout to be heard over the commotion.

"Yeah, shut up, guys," Cece said. "Maybe we should go get Mrs. G."

"Just tell her," Marissa said, shaking her head. "We're going to be late for dinner."

"Tell me what?" I asked, my hands beginning to tremble. There was something I didn't know, something about the school . . . I could suddenly sense it, as if I'd been ignoring the feeling gnawing at mind until now. A missing piece of the puzzle. My blood ran cold in my veins, and I shivered.

"I'll do it," Sophie said. "Okay. You must have realized by now that you've got some . . . I don't know what to call it . . . a gift of some sort. A *psychic* gift."

My heart pounding, I just shook my head. *My visions . . . how do they know?*

Marissa looked annoyed. "Oh, c'mon. Think about it. A sixth sense, maybe. Premonitions. Something . . . something out of the ordinary."

Still I said nothing. There was no way in hell I was going to own up to it. "Well, everyone here does," Sophie said. "Every single student at Winterhaven."

No. *No.* It was impossible; it couldn't be true. "You're joking, right?"

"Does she sound like she's joking?" Marissa snapped,

tossing her hair over one shoulder. "C'mon, out with it. You've got to do something special, or you wouldn't be here."

I tried to swallow, but my mouth was too dry. "Maybe I do. But you can't tell me that everyone here—"

"Yes, everyone," Sophie insisted. "Every student, every teacher. Even the headmaster."

"But," I sputtered, "but . . . that's insane. There's no way—"

"Think of it as a school for gifted and talented kids," Kate offered. "Only we've got a different sort of talent, that's all."

"So you're telling me, what? That this is some sort of . . . of magic school?" I asked.

"No, nothing like that," Sophie said, shaking her head. "This is just a regular prep school, where all the kids happen to have psychic abilities. We can't even use them in class, by the way. It's against the COPA."

"Code of Paranormal Activity," Cece clarified. "Basically, it says you're not allowed to use your gifts in class, to manipulate or harm your fellow classmates in any way, or for any sort of personal gain. I forget what else . . ." She trailed off, shaking her head.

"You're lying," I said. They had to be; there was no other explanation. This was a normal school . . . expensive, yes. Elite, maybe. But *normal.*

"Why do you think you're here, then?" Marissa asked, her tone a bit softer.

"Because my stepmother moved to New York, that's why, and this looked like a good school. That's it. No other reason."

"Didn't you feel somehow . . . drawn here?" Sophie asked.

Oh my God. I did. It was true, and I couldn't even explain it. Was it possible that they were telling the truth? Taking a deep breath, I searched my instincts, and my eyes suddenly filled with tears.

She was telling the truth. As crazy as it sounded, she was. Now it all made sense—the strange comments and questions that I hadn't understood. "A day of discovery," Dr. Blackwell had said.

Cece reached for my hand. "See, that's the way it works," she said softly. "Winterhaven somehow finds its students. They apply, they come. No one knows how."

"If you build it, they will come," Kate intoned.

"But . . . but what if someone came who wasn't . . . who didn't . . . you know," I stammered. "Have gifts?"

"They don't," Sophie said with a shrug. "So, are you going to tell us what your gift is now?"

"Yeah, I'll show you mine if you show me yours," Kate said with a laugh.

"Here, I'll go first, if it'll make you feel better," Sophie offered. "Remember this morning, about your shoulder? After I'd touched your hand? Well, all I have to do is touch someone, and I can tell if anything is, you know, wrong. With their body. Illness, injury, stuff like that. It's some rare form of clairsentience. I want to be a doctor someday. I'm really good at the diagnosing part, but as far as treatment goes . . ." She trailed off, shrugging.

"What did you call it?" I asked. "Clair . . . what?"

"Clair-sen-ti-ence." She enunciated each syllable, as if she were talking to a child. "It's when you can sense or see something just from touching a person or an object—like, about the past or future or whatever."

I nodded. "Okay, what about the rest of you?"

"I'm a tellie," Kate volunteered, her voice full of pride.

"A tellie?"

"Yeah, telekinetic. I can move stuff. With my mind. There's a lot of us here at Winterhaven. Wanna see?"

Wow. People could really do that? I mean, having visions was one thing, but actually moving things with your mind? Goose bumps rose on my skin, a shiver working its way down my spine. "Maybe later," I murmured. "What about you?" I asked Cece, silent beside me.

"Astral projection. Thank God for Winterhaven, because I

couldn't really control it before I came here. You know, like it was sort of involuntary? It was getting scary."

"It's still scary," Marissa said with a frown.

Astral projection? I didn't even know what that meant.

"Marissa's just grouchy because her gifts are a little more undefined."

Marissa shot Sophie an icy glare. "I'm just your basic empath is all. Pretty low on the gift-o-meter, as my friends here like to remind me. Whatever you have, it can't be any lamer than that."

"Visions," I blurted out. A sense of relief washed over me, taking me totally by surprise. It felt *good* to say it out loud. "I have visions. About the future. Usually bad stuff."

Cece frowned. "Uh-oh, precognition. That must suck. Can you . . . you know, prevent the bad stuff? Once you've seen it?"

I shuddered, thinking about my dad. "Sometimes. But I . . . I have to be subtle about it. Otherwise people just think I'm psycho."

"Ah, I see the problem there." Cece nodded, squeezing my hand. "That does suck."

Yeah, it did. "So, what else is there?" I asked. "The other kids, I mean."

"Mostly run-of-the-mill stuff, like us," Marissa answered.

"Clairvoyants, clairsentients, telekinetics, a few like Cece here who can project. Aidan can read minds, and I bet he's telepathic, too. And then there are a few freaks who can shift."

"Shift?"

Sophie nodded. "Yeah, shape-shift. I wouldn't have believed it if I hadn't seen it with my own eyes. I had to room with one my freshman year. Pretty creepy. I'll point 'em out in the dining hall; they all stick together."

"Sophie is exaggerating," Kate said. "Yet another of her 'gifts.' They don't really shape-shift, they just . . . go all fuzzy-like or something. It *is* kind of weird, though."

"I swear I once saw Lauren Dwyer shift into . . . I don't know, something like fog," Sophie argued. "Totally creeped me out. I think they can shift into more than they let on, too. Probably why they're always huddled together, whispering. Plotting," she added, and everyone laughed.

"But how . . . how's it all kept a secret?" I asked. "I mean, the school is right here in plain sight."

"Who could tell, looking at us?" Sophie said with a shrug. "We're just . . . you know, normal kids with unusual gifts."

"And none of us are going to tell," Kate added, reaching up to stretch. "We're just happy to have a place where we can be ourselves. Besides, who would believe it?"

The reality was finally sinking in. I'd left behind everything that was familiar to me so that I could go someplace where no one knew I was a freak, where no one would notice that I sometimes acted weird and knew stuff I shouldn't know. And now here I was, at a school filled entirely with freaks.

A bubble of hysteria welled in my chest, and I started laughing so hard that it hurt. I mean, c'mon, how could I *not* laugh? Next thing I knew, tears were running down my face and I was crying so hard I could barely catch my breath.

No one said a word. They just sat there and let me cry it out. Cece rubbed my back; Sophie brought me a glass of water.

At last my sobs were reduced to sniffles. Sophie handed me a clump of tissues, and I blew my nose. Feeling like a total moron, I turned toward Cece. "So that's what happened to your old roommate?" I asked with a hiccup, still all sniffly and hoarse. "Allison? She tried to tell someone about the school?"

Cece nodded. "Yeah, something freaked her out. She wouldn't tell me what, though."

"I think Aidan Gray had something to do with it," Kate said.

"No way," Cece shot back. "Aidan never had anything to do with Allison."

"Aidan never had anything to do with any girls, period."

Marissa looked at me pointedly. "Until now. Hey, isn't that his scarf?"

When I didn't answer, Cece continued on. "Anyway, Allison told her parents and they thought she'd gone nuts."

"Couldn't she just, well . . . *prove* her gift to them?" I asked.

Cece frowned. "Her parents are total nonbelievers. Allison's a clairvoyant and she goes into a trance when she's seeing. She tried to show them, and they had her committed. Just imagine if you didn't believe in psychic powers, and you saw someone do that."

For several seconds we all sat in silence, digesting that.

Finally Kate turned toward me and smiled. "I guess you haven't met your GC yet, huh?"

"GC? I'm almost afraid to ask what that stands for." I grabbed another tissue and blew my nose.

Cece laughed, and her friends joined in. "Guidance counselor," she finally said. "You'll get assigned a guidance counselor is all."

"What, to tell me how to use my gifts to save the world? To benefit humankind? To fight off super-villains?"

Sophie smirked. "Ha-ha. Very funny. Your guidance counselor will do what any guidance counselor does—help you apply to college, decide which careers best fit your talents, that's all."

Cece nodded. "There *are* psychic coaches available, though, if you need one. Like if you're having trouble with control or something like that. Or just want some help strengthening them."

"My powers, you mean?" I asked incredulously.

"We try not to use that word here, Miss McKenna."

I looked up and saw Mrs. Girard standing in the doorway, smiling at me.

"We say 'gifts' or 'talents.' I see you've come to understand Winterhaven's unique situation," she said, moving to stand beside my bed.

I rubbed my temples, desperately trying to wrap my head around everything I'd just learned.

"I'm willing to bet that you'll come to appreciate it much sooner than you think," Mrs. Girard said. "After all, this is a safe haven for people like us, like you." She reached into her pocket and pulled out a folded piece of paper. "I've brought you this."

Warily, I took it. With trembling hands, I unfolded the page. *Code of Paranormal Activity* was written in script across the top, and beneath it was a long list of numbered items. Rules, I supposed, given what the girls had told me. The famous COPA.

"Read it, study it, absorb it. And when you're done, bring

it to Dr. Blackwell's office to be properly disposed of. At that time, he will answer any questions you might have. I trust you girls will help her out in any way necessary through this period of adjustment?"

They all nodded in unison. "Of course," Cece said, reaching over to hug my shoulders. "We'll take good care of her."

5 ~ Nothing to Fear but Fear Itself

"Okay, please tell me I'm not the only dork who freaked when they figured it all out," I said, setting down my dinner tray on the table and sliding into a seat.

Cece sat down beside me. "Of course you're not. It's just that we all came in as freshmen—it was a long time ago, and it was different, anyway. We sort of figured it out together by the second day of orientation. All the upperclassmen have to keep it under wraps until the newbies catch on. But it's different with a transfer student. You were on your own."

Sophie nodded. "I remember being pretty upset when I figured it all out. I mean, my whole family is really into academics, and I'd never met anyone with gifts before."

"Luckily, Marissa was in our orientation group," Cece said, "and she's a legacy. She already knew, and that made it easier on all of us."

I glanced around at the group of girls surrounding me. "So, besides Marissa, do any of you have relatives with . . . you know, gifts?"

Cece nodded. "My grandma does. Remember that voodoo stuff I mentioned? We've never really talked about it, but it's just kind of understood, you know?"

"Nothing in my family," Kate said with a shake of her head. "Unless it came from my dad's side."

"My dad doesn't even know about me and my mom," Marissa put in. "We decided it was probably better that way. Anyway, it's not like we have a gift you can actually *see.*"

I was still a little unclear as to what Marissa's gift was. I wondered if the admission requirements were a little more lax for legacies, but I didn't dare ask.

"What about her?" I asked, tipping my head toward a tall brunette at the table beside ours. "Why is she wearing gloves?"

"Clairsentience," Sophie said. "Like me, but a different form. When she touches stuff, she absorbs all the energy from people who touched it before her. Totally distracting. The gloves protect her from that."

"And the blonde sitting beside her?"

"That's Stacy Dalton, the head cheerleader," Cece answered. "Also some form of clairsentience—same types usually stick together. I'm not sure, but I think Stacy's gifts are weak, though. Kind of vague."

Marissa frowned at her from across the table. "Just because you can leave your body and travel around doesn't make you all that special."

"Give me a break, I don't 'leave my body.' Only my astral self does," she said with a grin.

I still didn't know what it meant, this astral projection thing. I'd have to ask her later. There were so many things I didn't understand. The Hitchhikers at least got a Guide to the Galaxy. I got nothing.

After Mrs. Girard had left, I'd sat there in stunned silence reading the COPA while the other girls got ready for dinner. I felt stupid, totally blindsided by things that I should have picked up on.

It was all just so surreal. I mean, I'd come to New York for one reason—to be normal. To hide my so-called gift from the world. That had been the plan, and I'd been totally committed to it. But the amazing thing was, by Winterhaven's standards I *was* normal. I had nothing to hide.

"What about him?" I nodded toward a tall, blond guy

headed our way. He looked pretty normal, like any high school jock.

"That's Jack Delafield," Kate answered with a smile. "A tellie like me, and hands off, he's mine."

"Hey," he called out, bending down to kiss her cheek. "Coach called a special practice, but I'll be around later if you want to do something."

"Sure. Hey, Jack, this is Violet. Violet, Jack." Kate made the introduction. "She's Cece's new roommate. A precog."

Precog? It was going to take me forever just to learn the lingo.

"Cool. Nice to meet you." Jack smiled warmly, then turned his attention back to Kate. "I'll call you when I'm done, okay?"

"'Kay," she answered, then blew him a kiss as he walked away.

"He seems nice," I said as soon as he was out of earshot. "How long have you two been going out?"

"Almost a year now. He's the star running back on the football team," she added, pride in her voice.

"You said he's tele . . . telegenetic, like you?"

"Telekinetic," she corrected. "Yeah, but we're different types. I'm a macro, he's a micro."

"There's more than one kind?"

"Show her, Kate," Marissa said, gesturing toward the salt shaker on the table between us.

Kate shook her head. "Nah, I shouldn't. We're not really supposed—"

"Oh, just do it." Marissa picked up the shaker and moved it directly in front of Kate.

"Geez, all right." She took a deep breath and focused her gaze on the salt shaker.

My heart began to pound in anticipation, and I clasped my hands together beneath the table. Seconds later, the shaker slid silently down the length of the table, stopping right at the edge. I let out my breath in a rush, my skin tingling all over.

"There, are you happy?" Kate asked. "Anyway, Violet, that's macro. I can move big stuff, stuff you can see. But Jack, he's micro. He can move molecules, atoms, stuff like that. Stuff you need a microscope to see. Apparently it's pretty handy in the chemistry lab."

"But . . . but I thought you couldn't use it in school," I stuttered. "Isn't that against the COPA?"

"He can't use it in chemistry class. But he can do his own stuff in the lab, in his free time. He and Aidan are always working on projects together."

"He and Aidan are friends?" I asked, somehow surprised.

"Well, I wouldn't call them friends, not really. They don't hang out together, except in the chem lab. Oh, look over there. That's the shifters, that group there in the corner."

I turned to watch as five perfectly normal-looking kids sat down and started to eat—three girls and two guys, nothing remarkable about them at all.

"Don't stare," Cece whispered, and I turned back toward the food that sat in front of me, getting cold. Beef stew, and not half-bad, really, though I had zero appetite.

"So, what kind of projects do they work on? Aidan and Jack," I clarified, curious now.

"Research," Kate answered. "Medical stuff. I don't know what Aidan's working on, but Jack . . . well, he's got a little brother who has this really severe type of epilepsy, so that's what he's working on."

"I still don't get the whole brother thing," Sophie said. "It's weird, isn't it?"

"What? That he has epilepsy?" I asked.

Sophie shook her head. "No, the fact that he has a brother at all."

I was completely confused now. What was so weird about having a brother? "I don't get it," I finally said.

Beside me, Cece shrugged. "Most of us here at Winterhaven are only children—at least, everyone I know is."

"Except for Jack," Kate put in.

"But . . . but why?" I stammered, looking around at the other girls, hoping for an explanation. "I mean, why is everyone an only child? It's got to be more than a coincidence, right?"

"I don't know," Sophie said, shaking her head. "No one's ever been able to explain it."

I shifted in my seat, strangely unsettled by this latest revelation. "I should go," I said, pushing back from the table. "I'm supposed to go to Dr. Blackwell's office, if I can find it."

"I'll walk you there," Cece offered, and I nodded gratefully as she stood and picked up her tray.

Minutes later I was following Cece through several maze-like halls, up a flight of stairs, and down another hall that seemed to go on forever. Finally we climbed another flight of stairs and made our way past the old headmasters' portraits before at last reaching the carved wooden door that led to Dr. Blackwell's office.

"Here you go," she said, a little breathlessly. "Do you want me to wait for you?"

"No, I'm fine." I was breathless too. Probably nerves more than anything else. "Thanks, though."

"Okay, I'll see you later, then. Have fun," she added mischievously, then turned and left me there.

I took a deep, calming breath, trying to steady myself before

I faced the headmaster and the truths he'd no doubt tell. Just as I raised my hand to knock, the door swung slowly open, creaking on its hinges. "Come in, Miss McKenna," he called out, and I stepped inside, my palms sweating like crazy.

"Sit down," he said, gesturing to the same chair I'd sat in the night before.

I did as I was told, wiping my hands on my jeans. "Thanks," I murmured.

"Tell me, how was your first day here at Winterhaven?"

"It was . . . good," I said, barely able to speak. Why was I so nervous? He'd never been anything but friendly. Even now he was smiling warmly at me, his silver eyes twinkling in the firelight.

"I'm glad. Mr. Gray assures me that you will have no trouble whatsoever catching up with your coursework. All the classes were to your liking?"

I cleared my throat before speaking. "Yes, sir. I . . . um . . . unfortunately I missed my fencing class, but—"

"That's fine, don't worry," he said, waving one hand in dismissal. "You'll get there tomorrow."

For a full minute he said nothing, and I started to squirm in my chair. Finally he spoke. "Now I suppose you see that Winterhaven is unique in more ways than one. I hope that does not make you uncomfortable."

"No, I . . . I'm a little surprised, that's all." I couldn't help but wonder what his psychic abilities were. After all, my new friends had told me that everyone at Winterhaven had them, even him.

"And you've read the code?"

"Yes, sir." I reached into my back pocket and pulled it out, unfolding the page with damp hands.

"No questions?"

"No, it's pretty straightforward. A lot of it doesn't apply to me anyway, since I don't really have any control over my visions. They just . . . come."

"To the contrary, Miss McKenna. I think you will find that your visions can be harnessed, perhaps put to good use. But all in due time."

A bubble of hope welled in my chest, and I nodded.

"Also, keep in mind that adherence to the code is very important where extracurricular activities are concerned. We want your school experience to be as normal as possible, which is why we allow our teams to participate in the All-Ivy League. When interacting with students from other schools, it is vital that you keep the COPA in mind at all times."

"Of course," I said. I got it—don't let the regular kids see what freaks we were.

"Very well, if you've no questions, I'll take back your copy of the code. You must sign here"—he pushed another piece of paper across the desk toward me—"to acknowledge that you've read it and agree to abide by it. A pact, if you will."

I took the paper and glanced down at it, my eyes quickly scanning the words.

> I, Violet Ashton McKenna, do hereby vow that I have read the Code of Paranormal Activity, herewith referred to as the COPA. My signature certifies that I fully understand the COPA and agree to abide by it at all times, at all costs. I also acknowledge that if I fail to abide by the COPA, I may be duly expelled from Winterhaven. Signed in the presence of Dr. Augustus Blackwell, Headmaster of the Winterhaven School, on this third day of October, in the village of Tarrytown, New York.

Beneath it was a blank line for my signature. Dr. Blackwell handed me a pen, and with shaking hands, I scrawled my name.

There, it was done. I stared at my signature, still a little stunned by the absurdity of the situation.

Dr. Blackwell retrieved the page and folded it in thirds before sealing it with an old-fashioned wax seal. "And into the fire it goes," he said, taking the folded paper along with my copy of the code. He tossed them both into the flames behind him. "Secrecy is a prized thing here at Winterhaven, and we leave no written evidence of that which we wish to keep private. The contract is symbolic—a gentleman's agreement, if you will."

I nodded, watching as the flames began to lap at the pages, curling the edges till they at last burst into flames. A full minute later they scattered to the grate below in charred bits.

"You must understand how important strict adherence to the code is to this school's security, to its very integrity," he said, swiveling back to face me.

"Yes, sir," I said, swallowing hard. "I understand."

"Very well." He drummed his fingers against his desk, watching me. "Some students choose to learn to block their thoughts, if need be, for privacy's sake. If you would like to learn, we can assign you a coach."

"Sure," I said with a nod. It seemed like everyone else already knew how to do it, so I figured I should learn too. Particularly since Aidan could read minds, and I definitely didn't want him knowing my thoughts when I was with him.

"I'll have Mrs. Girard make the arrangements. I suppose our business here is done, then." He rose from his chair and reached across the desk to shake my hand. "But do not hesitate to return, if any questions arise that Mrs. Girard cannot answer to your satisfaction."

"Thanks." Just as before, his hand was cold as ice.

"Can you find your way back to the dormitory?" he asked.

"Sure," I said, though in reality, I had no clue how to get back.

"Hmmm, perhaps I should send for someone to see you back safely," he said with a chuckle, reaching for the telephone that sat on his desk.

"I can find it, really," I said. How hard could it possibly be? Down a hall, up some stairs . . .

He released the phone with a shrug. "If you're sure, then. I might remind you that you are to be in your bed by eleven." His silver eyes were twinkling again. "Good night, my dear. And good luck." I could still hear him laughing softly as I closed the door and set off.

A quarter hour later, I was ready to admit that I was totally and hopelessly lost. I'd gone down the same hall—the one with the headmasters' portraits—at least three times, and up the same staircase twice. I was beginning to panic when I spied a door I hadn't remembered seeing before.

I hurried over, hoping I'd finally found a means of escape. It led outside; I could see the moon in the square panes of glass at the top. For a minute or so I stared at the door, considering my options. I might get just as lost outside, but at least I wouldn't be wandering these same halls.

Please don't let it be locked, I thought, giving it a hard push. Thankfully it wasn't, and I found myself out in the cool, clear night.

With no clue where to go.

A grassy lawn stretched out before me, maybe for a hundred yards. I could make out the faint outline of buildings beyond the grass, but I had no idea which building housed the dorms. I had always traveled indoors between the administration building and the dorms, in connecting corridors of some sort. If I could just find the courtyard, maybe I could find my way from—

"Need some help?" a voice called out behind me, and I nearly screamed in fright.

My heart beating wildly, I turned to find Aidan standing there, leaning against the side of the building.

"Are you trying to give me a heart attack?" I asked, running a hand through my hair. It was the second time in one day that he'd scared the living daylights out of me. Still, I had to admit I was glad to see him—so glad I was almost giddy.

With his hands shoved into his pockets, he walked over to where I stood. "Sorry about that. Happy to see me, huh?" He grinned at me in the moonlight.

It was a good thing it was dark out, because I was sure my face was scarlet. "You're not allowed to do that, you know," I scolded. "It's against the code."

"What, sneak up on you, or read your mind?"

"Both. I guess I'm going to have to learn how to do that blocking thing."

"I wish you wouldn't," he said. "Your thoughts are pretty interesting." Suddenly his smile disappeared. "You heard me today, didn't you?"

My breath came faster, making puffs of smoke in the air. "What do you mean?" I asked, tripping over my tongue.

"You know exactly what I mean, Violet. You heard me. In your head. That makes you telepathic, by the way."

"Really?" I wasn't sure I wanted to be telepathic.

"Yeah, but you know what's really weird?" he asked, taking two steps toward me. I couldn't answer—I just stood there like an idiot. "What's really weird," he continued, "is that no one else can. Hear my thoughts, I mean."

"That . . . that can't be right," I stammered. "I'm sure other people can. This school is supposedly full of kids who can do stuff like that."

His gaze pierced mine. "Oh, there's plenty of kids who can hear telepathically. They just can't hear *me*."

Instinctively I took another step backward. My vision had finally adjusted to the dark, and I could clearly see his face, his eyes. They looked silver now, reflecting the moon. The longer I stared into them, the harder it was to look away.

"You're afraid of me, aren't you?" he asked.

I swallowed hard. "Should I be?"

"You tell me."

"Um, I guess you look pretty harmless," I said with a shrug. I was trying really hard to not think—about him, at least. How on earth did one block their thoughts?

Without warning, he reached out and trailed a finger down the side of my face. Oh, man, but the Aidan effect was in full force—I couldn't breathe, couldn't speak, and my legs felt like Jell-O. How was it possible that I was scared of him and attracted to him, all at once?

Perhaps I should be afraid of you instead, he said, his voice a whisper in my mind. His lips hadn't moved, and yet I'd heard him, as clear as could be, the words accompanied by a weird electrical buzz in my head.

Fear settled in the pit of my stomach, and yet I wanted to kiss those pale lips of his. And the worst part? *He knew.*

"I have to get back to the dorm," I blurted out.

"I'll walk you," he said, and I let out my breath in a rush. Without another word, I followed him.

6 ~ The Great Wall of China

"Forget it," I said, dropping my head into my hands. "I'm never going to get the hang of it."

My new "psychic coach" just sighed. Her name was Sandra and she showed up for our appointment wearing a blue Juicy tracksuit, as if she were a personal trainer or something. And she was *way* too perky, besides. Mrs. Girard told me that Sandra was a gifted mind reader, and I suppose she was, considering how easily she was reading mine no matter how hard I tried to stop her. I really *was* trying, but it was no use.

"Come on, Violet. One more try. You can do this, if you'd just concentrate. Visualize a wall, a barrier of some sort. Something thick and impenetrable. Do you see it?"

"Yeah," I muttered, doing everything she'd told me to do. Concentrate. Focus. Think in images, not words. A wall. A stone wall, around my mind. It was there; I could see it in my mind's eye, like the Great Wall of China, encircling my brain. My stomach grumbled, and all I could think about was lunch.

"A tuna salad sandwich and a Diet Coke," Sandra said, sounding exasperated. "Okay, let's call it a day."

I nodded, desperate to escape the confines of my room. It was Saturday, after all. My first Saturday at Winterhaven, and I was exhausted. It had been a long week of tough lectures and awkward "getting to know the new kid" moments. I was still behind in most of my classes, even though Aidan had met with me each day after sixth period and patiently gone over everything I'd missed. Though I'd never admit it, those tutoring sessions had quickly become the highlight of my week.

Anyway, right now I just wanted to eat some lunch, take a nap, and maybe spend an hour or so in the gym, working on my parry.

"We'll try again next week," Sandra said.

I looked up, surprised to see her still standing there by the door. "Sure. Same time?" I asked.

"Same time. And practice, okay? You didn't learn those fencing moves in one day, did you?"

I couldn't help but smile at that. "Good point. Okay, I'll practice."

"Great. Enjoy your weekend."

"Wait!" I called out, just as she reached for the door. I had to know. . . . "How close do you have to be to read my mind? I mean, can you do it from across campus?"

The idea of Aidan reading my mind whenever he wanted—from wherever he happened to be—made me want to heave, considering how often I was thinking about him. *Way* more than I should be.

She turned back toward me with a grin. "Don't worry. He'd—I mean, *I'd* have to be pretty close by, at least within sight of you. A physical wall might not stop me if you were just on the other side of it, but even so, it would take some effort."

"Thanks," I murmured, my cheeks burning.

"Anytime. Bye!" She opened the door and trotted out, her blond ponytail swinging behind her. *Way* too perky.

I let out a sigh, then walked to the window and looked down at the lawn below. If I moved fast, I might catch up with Cece and the rest of them in the quad before they headed over to the dining hall. The sky was clear and blue and students milled about in short sleeves. I pressed my hand against the glass, surprised at the warmth. It felt more like late August than early October, not that I was complaining.

I glanced down at my clothes, a black short-sleeved cable-knit sweater and jeans, and shrugged. Just a little lip gloss and I was ready to go.

Sitting down at my desk, I reached for the shiny pink tube and took off the cap. Just as I touched it to my lips, my vision began to tunnel, the eerie hum in my head growing louder and louder. The tube of gloss clattered to the desk. *No, not again.*

But I was gone, no longer in my cozy little dorm room, but somewhere outside instead.

Back in Manhattan, that same dark, foggy street as before. Following Aidan. He turned down a dark alley, and I could sense the danger. I called out his name, just as before, and this time I saw him turn toward me—and there was blood on his face, his mouth. I screamed, an ear-piercing scream, terrified that he was hurt, that . . .

And then, just as quickly as it had begun, it was over. I was back at my desk, staring at my own ashen face in the mirror above my desk.

"No," I said aloud, surprised to find my voice hoarse, my throat tight and scratchy. As if I'd really screamed in terror, and I realized that maybe I had. Thank God no one had been around to witness it.

Two visions in such a short time—and both of them about Aidan. It was odd. Usually my visions were months apart, and they always—*always*—involved people I knew well, people I really cared about. Which mostly limited my visions to my dad, Patsy, Gran, Lupe, and Whitney.

When I was younger I'd do really stupid things, like attempt to warn them. "Don't ride your bike anymore," I told Whitney once, trying not to cry. She was going to fall and break her wrist. I didn't know when, just knew it was going to happen at some point. She'd ignored me, of course, and broken her wrist two weeks later.

It weirded people out when I tried to warn them about stuff. Not because they truly *believed* that I knew things before they happened, but because it made me seem like a freak—a crazy, hysterical freak—even when my predictions came true. People were uncomfortable with things they didn't understand, and no one understood me. So I'd learned to keep my mouth shut—most of the time, at least. Until my dad . . .

Forget lunch, I had to get over to the gym now. It was the only way I knew to clear my head, to push away the unpleasant thoughts and memories and concentrate on the foil instead.

In minutes I'd pulled my hair into a ponytail. Rising on unsteady legs, I grabbed my bag and dashed out. Only when I'd gotten halfway down the hall did I realize I hadn't even locked the door, and I ran back and fumbled with the key until I heard the bolt click into place.

Hurrying through the East Hall lounge, I kept my head down, focusing on the floor as I made my way past the tables and chairs toward the far side of the room. *Please don't let me run into anyone I know,* I thought, increasing my pace. The last thing I wanted was to have to stop and chat. But just when I thought I'd made it through safely, I heard someone call out my name. A hand reached for my shoulder and I spun around, surprised to find Aidan standing there.

"We need to talk," he said.

A shudder ran through me. "Not right now."

"Yes, right now. Come on, follow me," he commanded, and I didn't even think to refuse. Instead I simply followed him, down a flight of stairs and into a long hallway.

"Where are you taking me?"

"To a study room. Here, come on." He opened a door to our right, and I followed him inside. The light flickered on, humming noisily, and it occurred to me that he hadn't even touched the switch.

"How did you—"

"What happened?" he asked brusquely, interrupting me.

"What do you mean, what happened?"

"I sensed your fear, heard you call out my name."

"I . . . no, I didn't." *Stone wall,* I told myself. Great Wall of China, around my thoughts.

"The Great Wall of China isn't going to do it, Violet. Come on, tell me what happened."

Feeling slightly woozy, I dropped my bag to the floor beside my feet. No way was I telling him what I'd seen—not till I had more to go on. The vision had been too quick, too vague. I needed specifics before I could consider warning him. "Why were you listening to my thoughts?" I finally asked.

"I wasn't. You called my name—telepathically," he clarified. "Several times, actually, and you sounded terrified. Tell me what you saw."

"What are you talking about?" I asked, hedging.

"You know about things before they happen, don't you?"

I felt the blood drain from my face, and my heart skipped a beat. "No, I don't."

"Yes, you do. Call it whatever you want—premonitions, dreams, flashes of the future. Somehow you *see*. And you just saw something—something about *me*."

"No." I shook my head wildly. "No, it's just intuition, that's all." My vision began to narrow, and for a split second I thought I was going to faint—or even worse, have another episode. I took several gulping breaths of air, and before I knew it, Aidan had crossed the small space and taken me into his arms, my face pressed against his chest.

"Hey, it's okay. Shhh. Just tell me what you saw."

"It was you, in some dark alley, and there was blood," I said, my voice breaking pathetically. "That's all."

"Blood?" he asked, his voice rising. "On you?"

"No, on you. I think. Anyway, it's not like it means anything."

"I know you don't believe that."

"Maybe I want to believe that. Can't you understand? I don't want to be a . . . a freak. A sideshow act," I said, choking on the words. *Oh no, not the tears*. I pulled away from him in humiliation as my eyes began to spill over.

He reached for my hand and pulled me back toward him. "You're not a freak, Violet. Hasn't this place taught you that? The true freaks are the ones who don't believe, the narrow-minded people who have no faith, who can't see what's right in front of their eyes."

I sniffled, wiping my eyes with the back of my hand. "You have no idea how much I wish that were true," I murmured, hoping I hadn't gotten snot on the front of his shirt.

"I'm just glad you're okay," he said. "I heard you scream, and I ran right over."

Well, that's one way to get a guy's attention, I thought.

"Trust me," he said, his voice tinged with amusement, "you don't need to go to such extremes. I have a tough enough time as it is, trying to figure out what it all means."

I swallowed hard before raising my gaze to his. Big mistake, because as soon as our eyes met, every rational thought flew out of my head. I was frozen, almost paralyzed.

"Your eyes are beautiful—the color of emeralds." His voice was a husky whisper.

My heart began to race. No one had *ever* said anything like that to me before, and it made my knees a little weak, my insides gooey.

And then I remembered that he could hear what I was thinking. Averting my gaze, I stepped away from him in embarrassment.

"What are you doing tonight?" he asked, retrieving my bag from the floor.

I cleared my throat before I answered. "Um, nothing really."

"Good. I'd like to show you something. Will you meet me in the East Hall lounge after dinner? Around eight? Actually, you better make it nine."

"Sure," I murmured. Was he asking me out? On a date?

You could call it a date. His voice, in my head.

Would I ever get used to all the weird stuff here at Winterhaven?

"You'll get used to it soon enough," he answered aloud. "Everyone does. Come on, I'll walk you to the gym."

7 ~ Anticipation

"Oh. My. God. Aidan Gray asked you out?" Cece didn't even attempt to hide her surprise as she plopped down on the bed across from me. "On, like, a *date*?"

"I don't know. I guess. He said he wanted to show me something."

Cece's eyes suddenly twinkled with mischief. "Hmm, now *that* could be interesting."

"Get your mind out of the gutter," I chastised.

"Wait till I tell everyone. They're not going to believe it, especially Marissa."

"I wish you wouldn't. It's kind of . . . I don't know. Embarrassing."

"You're only here a week and the hottest guy at Winterhaven asks you out, and you want to keep it a secret? Are you crazy?" She tugged off her boots and tossed them toward the closet.

"You really think he's the hottest guy here?"

"Well, yeah. Duh. Don't you?"

"Yeah, but I guess he's not, you know, good-looking in the normal way. I mean, he's so pale and his nose is a little crooked. His eyes are gorgeous, but there's something . . . I don't know, something kind of strange about them, don't you think?"

"Hah! I can't think *anything* when he's around."

"Me either." At least, not when I got too close to him.

"What time are you meeting him?" Cece asked.

I glanced down at my watch. "Not till nine."

"And?" she prodded. "What are you going to wear?"

I shook my head. "I have no idea. I don't know what we're going to be doing. Jeans, I guess? And a sweater."

Cece nodded enthusiastically. "Yeah, that green cashmere one in the closet."

Patsy had gotten it for me at a little boutique in SoHo. I think it still had the tags on. "Boots?" I asked her.

"Yeah, but not those sheepskin ones. Do you have any knee boots, maybe?"

I jumped off the bed and hurried to the closet. In seconds I returned carrying a black leather pair with high wedge heels and silver buckles.

Sitting there cross-legged on the bed, Cece squealed. "Oooh, perfect! God, why have you been hiding these?" She stroked the leather appreciatively. "Now, what about your hair?"

"What about it?" I asked with a shrug.

"Well, it's just that maybe you could, you know, try something a little more . . . um, sophisticated?"

Okay, so my hair wasn't the height of fashion. I kept it long, since it was easier to put into a ponytail. "Unless there's a salon here at school, I'm pretty much screwed," I said.

"Oh, no, you're not!" Cece jumped up and reached for her cell.

"Wait! Who are you calling?" She was already pressing buttons.

"Kate. She's great with hair! I mean it, you'll look like you stepped out of a magazine and—oh, hey, Kate. What're you doing right now? Oh, good. Yeah, maybe. Hey, can you come over and bring your hair scissors? Violet has a date tonight and she desperately needs you to do something with her hair. Nah,

I'll let her tell you. Trust me, you're not going to believe it." She flashed me a grin. "And bring Sophie—we'll give Violet a makeover. Sure, call Marissa. I know . . . that's exactly what I was thinking. Okay, bye."

I let my breath out in a rush. Well, there went my privacy. I didn't know why it mattered; they'd have found out anyway. I knew Cece and her friends well enough by now to know that there were no secrets between them.

And a makeover sounded kind of fun. It was one of those things that normal girlfriends did together—if they weren't busy with fencing tournaments, or generally avoiding large groups of people who might become friends and therefore star in their depressing visions.

Hanging out with the girls, going on a date . . . a week at Winterhaven, and already my life was changing—for the better, I hoped. Not bad, I thought, smiling happily to myself.

Not bad at all.

"Okay, open your eyes."

I did, and just sat there blinking at my own reflection. Sophie had lined my eyes with some dark, smoky liner and brushed my lids with plum-colored shadow. My eyes had never looked so bright green, so exotic. I don't know what else she did to my face, but my cheeks shimmered and my lips looked almost pouty. I could have easily passed for nineteen.

And my hair . . . it was still the same boring light brown, but now angled bangs hung across one eye and the bottom of my hair flipped up and out just below my shoulders.

"Wow!" Marissa said, behind me.

"Wow is right," Cece agreed. "So, what do you think?"

Everyone looked at me anxiously. A slow smile spread across my face. "I like it."

Kate's eyes met mine in the mirror. "I can't wait to see everyone's expression when you walk into the dining hall!" she said with a grin.

Sophie nodded enthusiastically. "We'll have to touch up everything after dinner, though. Before you go out. Where are you going, anyway? There's a movie tonight, a seven and a nine fifteen. Or maybe to the café?"

I shrugged, unable to look away from my own reflection. "I don't know. He didn't say."

"But he told her he wants to show her something," Cece said with a giggle.

"Hey, no fair. I want to see too." Marissa actually smiled at me. Thank God. I was finally breaking down that barrier of hers. "You think he'll at least buy you a coffee before he whips it out?" she added, wiggling her dark eyebrows suggestively, and everyone burst out laughing.

"Hey, have you heard from Allison?" Kate asked Cece once the laughter died down. "Can she write from wherever they're keeping her?"

The playful mood in the room sobered at once. "I haven't heard from her at all," Cece said. "Not once. Not a letter, not a phone call. It's like she dropped off the face of the earth."

"Well, have you considered, you know"—Kate waved a hand in the air—"going to her? Just to see if she's okay?"

Cece wrinkled her nose. "I don't know. I guess I could. What do you guys think?"

"Do you even know where she is?" I asked, sitting down on my bed and reaching for my boots. It was almost time for dinner. Nine o'clock seemed forever away.

"I don't have to know where she is," Cece answered, shaking her head. "I just have to will myself to her. That's the way it works."

It took me a minute to catch on, to realize that they weren't suggesting that Cece actually *visit* her; they were suggesting that her astral self do it.

"I think you should," Marissa said, putting on her own shoes. "Why not?"

"Yeah, I guess I could. I'd feel better knowing exactly what happened to her. I just always feel so bad, like I'm invading someone's privacy or something."

Sophie shrugged. "Well, her parents are jerks. I wouldn't worry about *them*. Why don't you go tonight?"

"Nah, it's easier in the morning. I can't do it when I'm tired. At least, not on purpose."

Summoning the courage, I finally asked, "How exactly *do* you do it?"

She sat down on the bed beside me. "Well, it sometimes happens spontaneously, when I'm not even trying. But . . . it's kind of hard to explain. I have to really relax, get my body to sleep even though my mind stays awake. Sometimes I just focus on a sound—like a humming in my head. Next thing I know, there are these awful vibrations. Scared me to death the first couple of times. And then I just pop out. Usually my hands and feet first. Sometimes my head sticks, and that's kind of weird. And then I have to get away from my body, or the cord will just jerk me back in."

"The cord?" I was still a little fuzzy on the details.

"Yeah, that's kind of hard to explain too. The astral cord—it keeps me tethered to my physical body. But it's really disorienting when you're too close to your body, so I get away as fast as I can."

I had to ask, even though I felt stupid doing so. "Where exactly do you go?"

"Anywhere I want," she answered with a shrug.

"But . . . but what if someone sees you?"

"No one can see me. They might hear me, if I wanted them to, but they probably wouldn't remember it. Hey, Kate, throw me my bag, will you?"

Kate was standing by the door, nowhere near Cece's bag. I didn't even flinch when the bag lifted itself off the desk and flew right into Cece's lap.

"Show-off," Marissa called out.

"So what's everyone else doing tonight?" I asked.

"Something with Jack," Kate said, smiling coyly. "Clothing is optional."

Marissa made a face. "Gag. What about you, Sophie?"

"Studying," she answered with a sigh. "I'm getting a little behind in trig."

"Don't be such a square, Soph." Marissa rolled her eyes. "It's Saturday night. C'mon, live a little. Go to the movie with me and Cece."

"Hey, some of us want to go Ivy," she answered with a scowl.

Marissa's eyes narrowed. "That excuse is starting to get real old, real fast."

"Why do you care?" Sophie shot back. "I think you and Cece can survive a Saturday night without me."

Suddenly the air felt thick, heavy with Marissa's disapproval. It was like a living, breathing thing, "C'mon, Marissa,"

Cece scolded. "Seriously. You're sucking all the fun right out of the room."

"Sorry," Marissa muttered. "Didn't mean to harsh your squee. I can't help it, you know."

I felt it lift then, like a breath of fresh air had swept across us all. I shook my head, amazed.

"That's better." Sophie favored Marissa with a smile. "Anyway, I'm sorry I snapped like that. It's just . . . well, I really want to do well this semester."

"S'okay," Marissa said with a shrug.

Kate swallowed noisily, one hand rising to her throat. "Hey, Soph, tell me if I'm coming down with something, will you? My throat's a little sore, and I don't want to swap spit with Jack if I'm getting strep."

Sophie hurried to her side and reached for both her hands, clasping them in her own. She closed her eyes for a moment and took a deep breath, while the rest of us waited expectantly.

After a few seconds, she opened her eyes and dropped Kate's hands. "Nah, you're fine. It's not strep, tonsils are healthy and your lymph nodes are good. C'mon, are we going to go eat, or what?"

8 ~ A Room with a View

I tried my best to look nonchalant as I sat on one of the brown leather couches in the lounge, staring at the TV on the wall, waiting for Aidan. I had no idea what show was on—it was just a blur to me. I suddenly wished I'd thought to bring a book. Not that I would have read it, but I could have at least pretended to. I think by now everyone in the East Hall dorm had heard about my date, because the lounge was surprisingly full, and everyone turned toward the door with a hush every time someone came in.

The suspense was killing me. Why had he asked me out? I mean, okay, apparently the fact that he even noticed my existence seemed to prove interest on his part, according to Cece and her friends. *My* friends too, I realized with a smile.

Anyway, there had definitely been a . . . a moment of some sort between us that first night, when he'd helped me find my way back to the dorm. And he had studied me pretty closely the first couple of days, but it had seemed more like curiosity than actual interest. Besides, he'd kept a polite distance during our tutoring sessions, and I had assumed that my infatuation was entirely one-sided. But, I don't know, the way he'd held me earlier, comforting me, was pretty promising, and then there was that thing he said about my eyes.

I'd only known him for five days, so why did it feel like ten times that? Like I'd known him forever? Like we were . . . meant to be together. Probably just wishful thinking, I decided.

I'd never had a boyfriend before. Sure, I'd dated a few guys, gone with them to homecoming dances and the movies or the mall to hang out. But nothing serious had ever come of it—couldn't, really, because I knew that if I started to care, I'd start seeing all kinds of bad things happening to them in my visions. I didn't want to go there.

Anyway, the guys I knew best were my fencing teammates, and how could they possibly think of me romantically when they faced me, day after day, across the piste—and usually found themselves on the losing end of my foil?

I glanced down at my watch, a stainless-steel Movado that Gran had given me for my sixteenth birthday. Two minutes till nine. Drumming my fingers against the couch's curved arm, I suddenly wished I had waited in my room. I looked way too eager sitting here, watching the minutes drag by.

Just then awareness shot through me and I turned toward the door as Aidan strode in, ignoring the curious glances and excited whispers that seemed to follow him wherever he went.

"Hey," he called out, and I stood up, nervously smoothing down my sweater.

As usual I couldn't even speak—all I could do was stare at him. He looked great, wearing jeans and a blue button-down shirt left undone over a vintage rock T-shirt. There was a cut on his forehead, above his right eye, that hadn't been there earlier in the day.

Wow, you look amazing, came his voice in my head.

I blushed, realizing that maybe he'd been checking me out while I'd been busy doing the same to him.

I took a deep breath, deciding to give it a try. Why not? *You look great, yourself.*

His smile let me know he'd heard me. He reached for my hand, and I let him take it.

Only then did I realize that the lounge had grown silent. Everyone was staring at us.

"You ready?" he asked, aloud this time.

"Sure," I managed to mumble, dropping his hand so I could reach for my jacket.

"Great, let's go."

I followed him out, barely aware that he had taken my hand again, his fingers intertwined with mine. "So, where are we going?" I asked as soon as we left the crowded lounge behind.

"You'll see. Here, you better put your jacket on."

I shrugged into it as we paused by the door leading out.

Leaves crunched beneath my boots as we made our way silently across the quadrangle, lit by a full harvest moon. Kids milled about, some sitting on blankets beneath a sprawling old oak; others hurrying toward the theater. Their voices carried on the breeze—young, carefree voices, calling out to one another in greeting, laughing, chatting. Everything about it seemed perfectly normal, like any boarding school. It was easy to forget that everyone I saw had psychic powers of some kind, and that the gorgeous guy holding my hand could read my mind.

"I'll stop doing it, if it'll make you feel better."

I rolled my eyes in frustration. "That's really not fair," I said, hurrying my pace to keep up with him.

"How are the blocking lessons going, by the way?"

An owl hooted in the distance. "Horrible. I've only had one lesson, but I can't seem to get the hang of it."

"Well, it takes practice. Okay, this is it, this path right here."

I followed him toward a stone building up ahead, all silvery in the moonlight. "What is it?"

"An exact replica of the King's College Chapel at Cambridge, only smaller. Can you climb a ladder in those boots?"

"A ladder?"

"Trust me, it's worth it."

As we drew closer to the building, I saw twin spires reaching up toward the night sky above a soaring arch of stained glass. I couldn't wait to get inside.

I almost expected the big wooden doors to be locked, but they weren't. We slipped inside without saying a word, and stopped in what I supposed was a small vestibule. It took a moment for my eyes to adjust to the dark.

Aidan led me farther into the chapel, toward the rearmost pew. As my eyes continued to adjust, the details came slowly into focus, stealing away my breath.

Tipping my head back, I marveled at the sight of the vaulted ceiling, the intricate design looking almost like lace. With only the moon casting its light through the rows of floor-to-ceiling stained-glass windows, the stonework glittered like jewels.

In a split second, sconces lining both walls flickered to life, filling the space with soft, yellow-tinted candlelight. I gasped, taking a step backward in fright, prepared to flee. But Aidan held my hand tightly, preventing my escape. "It's okay," he whispered, his breath warm against my cheek.

My fear was soon replaced by wonder. The light of the candles made everything look different—eerily beautiful, and, I don't know . . . somehow mystical.

"Come on, you haven't seen the best of it," Aidan urged, moving down the aisle, past the rows of wooden pews and toward the altar at the end. I followed alongside him, a death-grip on his hand. I was scared yet fascinated, all at once. How had he lit the candles? I mean, obviously he had done it with his mind, but *how*?

We passed the altar and moved toward the very back of the chapel, through a door, and up a dark spiral staircase. I trailed one hand across the rough stones as we climbed higher and higher. Finally we reached a wide landing, a wooden railing running across the front of it. I stopped and leaned against it, looking out. I could see the entire chapel below us, straight across to the entrance and the arched window above it. In the flickering candlelight it all looked surreal, like something out of a dream.

"This is amazing," I said, letting out my breath in a rush as I drank in the view.

"We're not there yet." He reached for my hand and pulled me back to his side. "This is where the ladder comes in. You sure you're okay in those boots?"

"Yeah, I think so."

"Don't worry, I won't let you fall," he promised. "Okay, right here. You go on, hold tightly with both hands. It's ten rungs."

He was right; I counted.

"Now reach for the railing, there to your right. Got it?"

I nodded as I felt around for the railing I was supposed to find. There it was—smooth wood, against the wall. "Yep, I've got it."

"Okay, move as far away from the ladder as you can, still holding on to the railing. It's okay, I'm right here behind you."

As if he needed to tell me. I was totally aware of his presence. I could have sworn that I felt it physically, like a . . . a string or something, connecting us. It made me think of Cece and her astral cord. Taking a deep, steadying breath, I did what he asked and moved away from the ladder, my boots shuffling noisily against the floor.

About twenty steps away, I felt a wall, and stopped.

"Give me a minute," he said.

I felt him move away from me, heard a rustling over in the corner. I wondered how it was that he could see well enough to do whatever it was he was doing.

"Close your eyes," he said, and I felt his hand take mine. As always, a shudder ran up my arm, then down my back. "Sit down, right here." He pulled me down beside him, onto a soft, fluffy blanket of some sort. It felt like velvet—soft, worn velvet. "Okay, just lie back."

I kept my eyes squeezed shut; his voice was like a ghost's beside me. But I did just as he said, and felt my head settle onto something soft.

"Now open your eyes," he said.

I did—and sucked in my breath sharply. Directly above us was a square window, framing the full moon. Wispy, featherlike clouds cloaked the lower half, drifting across in slow motion. It looked so close, the moon—so bright and clear that I felt like I could reach up and touch it. I raised one arm, my hand stretched out toward the sight, and for a second I could have sworn that the clouds brushed against my skin, feeling somehow cool and damp against my fingers.

"It's wonderful!" I breathed, squeezing his hand. My focus shifted then, and I was totally aware of him, his body next to mine, touching me from shoulder to heel.

"I knew you'd like it. This is my favorite place on campus; I come here every full moon. Before now I've always come alone."

"Thank you," I said, knowing that it wasn't enough, not really.

"It's plenty, Violet. And you're welcome."

I smiled in the dark, imagining his face. "How did you get the blanket and pillows up here?" I asked at last. "I can't imagine carrying it all up that steep ladder."

I felt him shrug beside me. "How else would I get it up here?"

Good question. "So, this is what you do in your spare time?" I teased. "Climb things? Interesting."

"Yeah, if the view's worth it. What about you? In your spare time? Fencing, right?"

"Yeah. My dad . . . he believed strongly that a girl should know how to take care of herself. So, when I was little, he wanted to start me in some kind of martial arts. You know, karate or something. I tried it, but I never liked it. It's just too . . . I don't know, too personal," I said with a shrug. "So I tried fencing lessons instead. Right away I loved it. I was good, too. Really good," I added proudly.

"And fencing's not as personal?" I could hear the amusement in his voice, and it made me smile.

"No way. Your opponent's on the other end of a weapon, for one. And being inside the protective gear, the gloves, the mask . . . I don't know, I can't really explain it. It's like a cocoon or something."

"Interesting," he murmured. "I've never thought about it that way before."

"And anyway, after my dad died . . . well, it somehow makes me feel closer to him."

"So it's just you and your mom now?"

"Stepmom," I corrected. "Long story. Anyway, it's my turn."

"What is it you want to know?"

So much, I realized. I knew almost nothing about him. "For starters, how about where you're from."

"From Dorset, England," he answered. "At least, originally."

"Huh. I guess that explains the little bit of an accent."

"You've got a good ear," he said with a laugh. "I thought I'd lost it entirely by now."

"Where are your parents now? Here in the States?"

"No, they're long dead," he said, sounding strangely dispassionate.

"I'm sorry." We had that in common, then. Both of us orphans. "No brothers or sisters?" I assumed he was like the rest of us—an only child.

"Actually, I had two younger sisters. But they're dead as well."

"That's terrible." I didn't know what else to say. His whole family, gone?

He shrugged. "It was a very long time ago."

Still, I felt badly for prying. I knew how it felt to lose a family member and then have people prod you for details.

"You loved your father very much, didn't you?" he asked, his voice soft.

I swallowed hard, amazed that I was even considering talking about it. "Yeah, I did. I still can't believe he's gone. I mean, he used to be gone for months at a time, on assignment. But he always came back." My throat tightened, and I forced myself to continue. "Until the one time he didn't."

"He was a journalist?"

I blinked up at the night sky, watching as the last wisps of clouds drifted away from the moon, leaving it entirely exposed. "Yeah," I answered at last. "A correspondent for a cable news network."

"Where did it happen?"

"Afghanistan. We didn't hear from him for nearly a month and the network had no idea where he was or who had him. And then the kidnappers . . . they released a . . . a videotape."

"But you already knew, didn't you?"

"Yes," I said, shuddering at the memory of the horrific vision.

"There are some things in this world that are worse than monsters, aren't there?"

I nodded. It was a strange thing to say, but he was right. "He was so mad at me when he left; he thought I was being selfish. I had seen everything—his kidnapping, his murder. I tried to tell him, tried to convince Patsy to make him stay, but he was furious. Said I shouldn't scare Patsy like that, that she had enough to worry about with him away."

"You can't blame yourself, Violet."

Tears burned behind my eyes. "I should have done more to stop him."

"What could you possibly have done to stop him? Some people don't want to believe anything beyond the ordinary. They walk right into danger with their eyes wide open, refusing to see what's right in front of them."

I knew he was right, but that didn't make it any easier. "I should have *made* him see."

"He loved his job, didn't he?" Aidan asked.

"He did. Maybe more than he loved me." As I said it, I realized that *that* was what was really bothering me, what was eating away at my insides.

He shook his head. "C'mon, Vi, do you really believe that?"

A single tear slipped down my cheek, and I wiped it away with the back of one hand. "I guess not."

"What about your stepmother?" he asked. "What did she say when she realized that you had been right?"

"Are you kidding? She never believed it. I tried to tell her, tried to explain about the visions, but all that got me was a visit to the shrink. I guess she convinced herself it was just a coincidence. It's not like it's unheard of, what happened. Something like that was always a possibility, whether I had foreseen it or not."

"I suppose so. But I saw what happened to you when you had a vision your first day here. You stumbled, and sort of zoned out or something. How did you explain that all those years?"

"Trust me, they dragged me to a ton of doctors. Never could find a medical explanation, so they just called it a mild seizure disorder and left it at that."

"And you were okay with them thinking that?"

"It was either that or a padded cell. The rest of the world isn't like Winterhaven, you know," I said sharply.

"You're right," he said. "I'm sorry. I guess I've been here long enough that I sometimes forget."

I took a deep breath.

"So, where do you live now?" I finally asked. "When you're not here, I mean."

"I have a place in Manhattan," he answered.

"Alone?" He wasn't an adult; he had to have some sort of legal guardian or something.

"I've got Trevors," he clarified, and I could hear a trace of amusement in his voice.

He rolled onto his side, facing me. "Trevors is . . . like family."

Next thing I knew, his cool fingers were on my face, tracing a line from my temple down to my chin. I just held my breath, not moving a muscle, waiting for him to say something. I could feel my own heart beating fast and furious, and I wondered if his was doing the same.

Finally he spoke. "I don't understand it, Violet. You're both a part of my past and a part of my future. You feel it too, don't you?"

"I think so," I murmured. I was definitely feeling . . . *something*. I reached out and touched the cut on his forehead, my fingertip barely brushing the wound. "How'd you get this?" I asked, sensing his body tense beneath my touch.

There was a trace of amusement in his voice when he answered. "You wouldn't believe me if I told you."

"Well, I hope the other guy looks worse," I teased.

"You don't know the half of it."

"You're really good at avoiding questions, aren't you?" I said with a laugh.

"Hey, I'm not the only one who dodges questions. You never really told me what you saw in your vision today."

"Do I have to?" I didn't really want to think about it, much less discuss it.

He nodded. "It's kind of . . . important."

With a sigh, I relented. "Okay, fine. You were walking down

a foggy street in Manhattan. A dark, seedy street, and I was following you. That's about it," I said, hedging.

"No, there's more. You have to tell me exactly what you saw that frightened you so badly."

I shook my head, trying to tamp down my rising panic. "No, I can't. Besides, you can read my mind. You tell *me* what I saw."

"I can't see your visions," he snapped, sounding frustrated.

My breath hitched in my chest. "Is that the real reason you brought me here tonight? To hear about my visions?"

His hand found mine. "No. I brought you here because I knew you would appreciate this place as much as I do, and because I wanted to spend some time with you. Still, I wish you would tell me exactly what you saw." His fingers were on my face again, and I felt myself relenting. I knew he was somehow manipulating me, and yet I was powerless to stop it.

I sighed in defeat. "Like I said, I was following you down some seedy street. And then, I don't know, there was a flash of movement, or something. I called out your name and you turned around. There was . . . blood." I swallowed hard, unable to go on.

"Blood where?"

I shrugged, not really wanting to remember. "I don't know, your face, I think. That's it, that's all I saw."

"Don't worry about it," he said, his voice firm.

And just like that, my fear evaporated. Disappeared. I sat up, shaking my head in frustration. "Stop it, Aidan. Stop manipulating me like that."

He sat up too. "I don't know what you're talking about."

"Yes, you do. I don't know exactly what it is you do, what powers you have, but—"

"We don't like to call them that here at Winterhaven," he said, doing a perfect impression of Mrs. Girard.

"I'm serious," I said, and I meant it.

"I know you are." He reached for my hand, but I pulled it away, refusing to be placated.

"Well, then, whatever it is you're doing, stop it. I mean it, Aidan. I can't . . . I won't hang out with you if you're going to do that."

"You're right," he said. "I'm sorry. It's just a . . . an old habit. I won't do it again."

"You promise?" I asked.

"I give you my word," he said, and I believed him. I *wanted* to believe him. "Let's just forget about it for now and enjoy what time we have left till curfew, okay?"

"Okay," I agreed. Relieved, I reclined back against the blankets.

After a second or two, he lay back down beside me. "It's

really beautiful tonight," he said. "I'm glad you came."

And just like that, everything was back to normal between us. Not because he was manipulating me, but because it *was*. I turned my head toward him; his profile was illuminated by the light of the moon. Just one glance, and my heart started to race. I was crushing on him big-time, I realized. Recognizing the train of my thoughts, I struggled to erect the wall protecting them, concentrating hard as I tried to remember everything Sandra had taught me.

"Hey," came Aidan's voice beside me, sounding surprised. "That's much better. I think you're starting to get the hang of it."

If not for his quiet chuckle, I might have believed him.

9 ~ The Day After

I slept right through breakfast the next morning and was forced to make do with a stale Danish and coffee from the vending machine in the dorm lounge. I ate quickly, figuring I didn't have much time till Cece and her posse showed up, ready to prod me for details about the night before.

When I got up to leave, my gaze drifted over to the mail cubbies beside the bookshelves. I hadn't checked my mail in days, I realized—not that I was expecting anything. Still, I brushed the pastry crumbs from my jeans and hurried over, surprised to see a small, square package there in my box. I smiled, recognizing Lupe's handwriting.

Lupe was more of a companion to Gran than a housekeeper these days, but try telling Lupe that. She took pride in doing whatever she could manage with her arthritic hands—drying dishes, ironing. It was impossible to think of Gran without picturing Lupe right there beside her. I tore off the paper, suddenly overwhelmed with homesickness.

Inside I found a lavender silk drawstring bag. Puzzled, I pulled it open and shook the contents out into my hand. I stared down in surprise at a delicate silver crucifix, hanging on a long silver chain. Clearly, the necklace was new. It still had the Neiman Marcus tag attached, which meant it wasn't cheap, either.

Why would Lupe send me this? She was Catholic, but I wasn't. Our family was Episcopalian, and not particularly religious.

Stranger still was the note she'd enclosed. All it said, in wobbly script, was, *Please indulge a silly old woman and promise me that you will wear this at all times. May the good Lord protect you*. And then she'd signed her name. Very, very odd.

I pulled off the tag with shaking fingers and clasped the chain around my neck, tucking the cross under my shirt. It wasn't exactly my style, but it made me feel closer to Gran and Lupe.

Suddenly there was a steady stream of kids coming through

the door, laughing and shouting as they headed for the couches by the TV or down the hall toward the rooms. Breakfast must be over, I realized. Time for me to go.

Unfortunately, I wasn't quick enough.

"Hey, Violet!" Cece called out. "There she is, the sleepy-head."

I looked up and saw her there by the door, Sophie, Kate, and Marissa trailing behind, looking almost predatory. Like lionesses on the scent of blood. In seconds they had me surrounded.

"Too bad you slept in," Marissa said with a sly smile. "Guess who we saw in the dining hall?"

"Really?" I asked, unable to hide the surprise in my voice. Somehow I wanted to imagine him lounging lazily in bed, relishing the memories like I had.

"No," Kate answered. "She's just kidding. But the look on your face was priceless. I take it someone had a good time last night."

"Hopefully not as good a time as you and Jack had," Marissa muttered half under her breath, and I saw Kate shoot her a deadly glare.

"C'mon, let's go," Cece said, tipping her head toward the door. "Give the girl some privacy, will you."

Everyone nodded, and soon I was following them back

down the hall toward our room. The door closed behind us, and they all turned toward me expectantly.

Kate was the first to speak. "Okay, spill it."

Marissa plopped down on Cece's bed. "We can't stand the suspense any longer."

But what to tell them? I took a deep breath, considering all my options. I finally decided to play it safe. Keep it simple. "Well, we mostly just sat and talked, but it . . . it was nice."

"Go on," Sophie prodded.

"Yeah, what did he want to show you?" Marissa asked.

"Just someplace on campus. A place he likes to hang out. It was quiet and private, and . . . well, we went there and talked."

Cece was nearly bouncing on the bed beside me. "And? Come on, dish."

"And he asked me to meet him tonight after dinner," I added, hoping that would be enough. What else could I say, really? That it had been the best date I'd ever had? That I was completely and utterly smitten? No, that was way too embarrassing to admit.

"Wow." Marissa looked impressed. "I still can't believe it—Aidan Gray, out on a date. With a girl," she added.

"Oh, give it a rest, Marissa," Kate said. "Just because he never asked *you* out doesn't mean he bats for the other team. Jack says he's incredibly smart, really intense. He spends way too much time in the lab, though. Pretty much all this free time, from what Jack says."

Just then my cell phone, still plugged into its charger on my desk, began to ring. I hadn't given him my number, but I knew by now that that didn't matter.

"Is that him?" Cece asked when I went over to the phone and looked at the caller ID screen. I didn't recognize the number, and hope swelled in my chest as I hit the answer button.

"Hello?" I squeaked, hating that I had an audience.

"Hi. Sleep well?"

Just the sound of his voice made my knees weak. "Yep. Right through breakfast, actually."

"Last night was great," he said. "Thank you."

"I had a great time too." I was facing the wall, but I could feel everyone's eyes on my back, watching me.

"About tonight, though . . ." He cleared his throat, and I could sense that he was uncomfortable. "I'm doing some work in the lab, and it's gotten really complicated. It's going to take me a lot longer than I thought, so I don't think I can—"

"That's okay," I interrupted, trying to sound cheerful. "I really should be studying, anyway. I've still got so much to catch up on." He was blowing me off, I realized. Already.

"Thanks for understanding, Violet. We'll talk later, then, okay?"

"Sure. Okay. Bye." I hit the end button and took a deep breath before I turned back to face my friends.

"Rat bastard," Marissa said. "I knew it."

"He says he's got some work to do in the lab," I offered lamely.

Sophie shook her head, her hazel eyes full of disbelief. "What kind of work? It's Sunday."

I just shrugged. I had no idea what kind of work he did in the lab. Kate had said it was some sort of medical research, but he'd never elaborated. Actually, now that I thought about it, there was an awful lot about Aidan that I still didn't know.

The next week passed mostly in a blur. I hadn't been lying when I'd said I had a lot of catching up to do. Winterhaven's academic expectations were high, even by prep school standards. Which was good, I guess—after all, the school's graduates had a ridiculously high rate of academic and professional success. PhDs, CEOs, industry leaders, and successful politicians . . . they all came from Winterhaven. The amount of notable grads listed in the admissions brochure was mind-bogglingly impressive.

Of course, now I realized why—because once students graduated and were free from the constraints of the COPA, they could use their gifts to their advantage. It was amazing, really, that no one had ever been exposed for what they were.

I couldn't help but wonder if there was some sort of safeguard in place for that, something I didn't yet understand. Regardless, a Winterhaven education was definitely a plus, and I spent pretty much all my free time trying to catch up.

I didn't hear from Aidan—no more tutoring sessions—although I did see him twice a day in the classes we shared. It was mostly awkward, me going out of my way to avoid him, and him studying me intently from across the room, then disappearing as soon as the bells rang. I didn't know what to think. I mean, we'd only had one date, so it's not like I had a claim on him. On the other hand, it had been a good date—or so I had thought. He'd said all that stuff about me being a part of his past and his future, and I had taken that as a pretty good sign. Like us coming together was fate or something.

What had changed? I had all kinds of theories, of course, most of them involving another girl. As I was pondering the possibilities for the millionth time that day, Cece popped her head into the room. "Hey, are you coming with us to the café?" she asked brightly.

"No, I thought I'd go to the gym. My shoulder's been hurting, and stretching really seems to help." *Liar.* I shut down my computer, my homework done.

"C'mon, Violet. All you've done is mope around all week. Is he really worth it?"

Yeah, he was. And that was the problem. That, and I was totally pathetic. But I couldn't say that. Instead I said, "I really do need to stretch."

"Okay, whatever." Clearly, she wasn't buying it. "You sure you won't come with us?"

"Yeah, I'm sure." I picked up my bag and hiked it up on my shoulder. "But I'll walk with you, okay?"

We made our way through the lounge in silence. Finally I spoke. "I don't think I've ever heard of a boarding school with a movie theater. Or a café. How come we can't just go into the village to hang out, at least on weekends?"

"I think they decided it's better if we don't mix too much with the townies. They worry we'd get careless or something. So they made sure we have everything we need right here at Winterhaven. I like it this way—it's more like a college campus or something."

"I guess," I said with a shrug. We passed the school store, which I now knew carried a wide assortment of clothes, shoes, and accessories in addition to school supplies and sweats with the school crest. There was a drugstore, too—rumor had it that they even carried condoms—but the bookstore was my favorite. It was as well-stocked as any major chain. Cece was right; there really wasn't any need to leave campus.

We parted ways at the atrium's exit, and I continued on

toward the gym. The sun was just beginning to set, the sky a deep purple with wide orange swaths. It was so pretty that I considered sitting down on a nearby bench to watch the sun melt into the horizon. Why not? The gym could wait.

So I sat.

"It's beautiful, isn't it?"

I whirled around to look over my right shoulder, and there was Aidan, leaning against a tree. I just swallowed, unable to speak. My heart was pounding, as it always did when he snuck up on me.

"This is my favorite time of day. The Scots call it 'the gloaming.' I like that."

"Sounds a lot better than 'dusk,' I guess," I finally said, turning my attention back toward the sky. I could just make out the first twinkling star, directly above my head. I stood up and reached for my bag. "I should go."

"Please don't." He was beside me now, reaching for my hand. "I want to apologize for ditching you like I did last weekend."

I shrugged, pulling my hand from his grasp. "Really, it's fine."

"No, it's not. I know it sounds like an excuse, but I had some important work to do, and it couldn't wait."

I finally gathered the courage to look up at him, and my

breath caught. His eyes were more darkly shadowed than before, as if he was in desperate need of sleep. He looked terrible, actually.

"You look exhausted," I said, my initial annoyance replaced with worry.

"I haven't had much time for sleep," he answered.

"What are you working on that's more important than sleep?"

He just shook his head. "I can't explain it."

I decided to press the issue. "You can't, or you won't?"

Surprisingly enough, that made him smile. "A little of both, actually."

I nodded, not quite sure what else to say.

"This is . . . it's hard for me, Violet." He shoved his hands into his pockets. "It's complicated, and I'm not sure what to do. I just didn't want you to think that I was blowing you off."

That was exactly what I thought he was doing. "I should be more focused on school, anyway," I said.

His eyes met mine, searching for something. "I don't want to hurt you," he murmured.

"Why would you hurt me?"

"Because that's what I do," he said, his voice suddenly sharp. "But not this time, not if I can help it."

What was he talking about?

"You've had the vision again, haven't you?" he asked, his voice softer now.

Yeah, I had. Twice in the past week.

"Well?" he prodded.

"Well, nothing. I don't want to talk about it, okay? Besides, you said I shouldn't worry. Stupid visions," I muttered. They were nothing but a curse.

"Your visions are a part of you, Violet. They're a gift."

"That's easy for you to say. You don't have to see awful things happen over and over again to people you—" I cut myself off, realizing what I was about to say. *People I care about*. Including Aidan? That was crazy, totally insane. We'd gone out *once*. He hadn't even kissed me.

"Trust me, Violet, I have my own demons to slay."

My hand went nervously to my throat, my fingers closing around something cold. The crucifix—Lupe's gift.

"What's that?" Aidan asked.

"What? This?" I fingered the cross, laying it against my shirt. "It's just a necklace."

"Are you Catholic?" he asked.

I shook my head. "No. Would it matter if I was?"

"I guess not," he finally said.

"Someone sent it to me as a gift," I said, clasping it protectively in my hand.

"Well, that someone is smarter than you think," he said with a low chuckle. "Not that it'll do much good, but it's a nice gesture, anyway." He reached for my hand, and I let him take it. "Do you want to go to the café and get some coffee or something?"

I *did* want to. But I'd just blown off my friends, insisting I needed to go to the gym and work out. How lame would it be to show up now with Aidan in tow, especially after the conversation I'd just had with Cece? Talk about humiliating.

An inner battle waged inside me—my pride versus my desire to spend time with Aidan. Ultimately, Aidan won out.

"Do you mind if we meet up with my friends there?" I asked, trying to see it as a compromise. "They were all headed over."

"Of course not," he said.

If they were surprised to see Aidan and me walk into the café together, my friends did a good job of hiding it. We joined them, pushing two tables together after buying some caramel mocha lattes and chocolate-chip cookies. Amazingly enough, it felt perfectly natural there, wedged between Cece and Aidan, holding his hand beneath the table.

A little more than an hour and two lattes later, everyone began to drift away. Sophie left to study, Jack and Kate went off together, and Cece and Marissa headed back toward the dorms. Aidan and I made our way back outside and plopped down beneath the drooping branches of an old oak, as far away from prying eyes as possible.

"It's nice out," he said, his legs stretched out toward me. A street lamp beside the sidewalk cast an oblong patch of light on the grass where we sat, making his hair look like gold.

"Yeah, it feels good out here," I said. The café had been hot and crowded. I still felt flushed all over.

He nodded. Above us, the light flickered, then went out, leaving us in total darkness.

I let out my breath in a rush. "Did you do that?"

"Do you want it on?" With a hiss, it popped back on.

I rubbed my eyes, seeing spots now. "No, it's okay."

Out it went again. You'd think I'd be used to such things by now, but it still gave me chills.

"So," I asked, figuring I might as well get it all out in the open. "What else can you do? I mean, besides read minds—"

"Not yours, not anymore," he interrupted, and I smiled in self-satisfaction. I'd gotten really good at blocking my thoughts. I did it automatically now, whenever I was with him.

"Let's see . . . you can speak telepathically," I continued, finally getting the lingo down, "and turn lights on and off. Does that make you telekinetic, too?"

"Yeah, I guess you could call it that."

"Oh, wait," I said, leaning toward him, trying to make out his face in the darkness. "I forgot the thing where you manipulate feelings."

"I promised not to do that anymore, remember?"

"And I'm supposed to trust you on that?" I asked, only half-kidding.

"You can trust me, Violet." His voice was silky smooth. Seductive.

"Then why won't you tell me what you were doing all week? Why the secrets?"

"Because I can't tell you." He took my hand and drew me closer.

"And that's all you're going to say about it?" I pressed, scooting a few inches closer, drawn to him like a bee to honey. I could feel his breath on my neck, and I shivered.

"I could tell you, but then I'd have to kill you," he teased, his lips moving toward my throat. I knew he was kidding, but there was an edge to his voice—something hard, almost angry.

"That's not funny," I said on a sigh, willing his mouth closer.

With a groan, his lips retreated. "Trust me, I know."

Disappointment washed over me. Suddenly cold, I pulled up my knees and wrapped my arms around them, studying Aidan's face—in focus, now that my eyes had finally adjusted to the darkness.

"What do you do when you're not in class?" I asked. "I never see you around campus."

"I told you, I work in the chem lab," he answered.

"Yeah, I know. But I meant, like, for fun."

"Well, to me, the work I do in the lab *is* fun. Challenging. I read a lot too."

"Yeah?" Well, that was one thing we had in common, then. "What do you read?"

"Classics, mostly. Some fantasy and science fiction." He reached for my hand. "Anything else you want to know?"

"What were you like as a kid?" I asked. It was hard to imagine Aidan as a kid. He seemed mature beyond his years, I guess you could say. I couldn't exactly put my finger on it, but there was none of that insecurity in Aidan, that awkward self-consciousness that most guys our age seemed to suffer from. He seemed pretty comfortable in his own skin.

I heard him laugh—a low, soft rumble. "Me, as a child? I can barely remember, it was so long ago."

"It wasn't *that* long ago. When's your birthday, by the way?"

"October ninth. You just missed it. When's yours?"

"March twenty-seventh," I answered. "I won't be seventeen till spring."

He nodded. "Anyway, to answer your question, I was arrogant and spoiled. Used to getting my own way. You wouldn't have liked me very much."

"And what about dreams, aspirations? I guess you want to be a scientist or something?" Considering he liked to work in the chem lab. *For fun*.

"I don't think about the future," he said, his voice sharp. He glanced off at the horizon, and then I saw him take a deep breath before he turned back to face me again, looking contrite. "I'm sorry, I didn't mean—"

"No, it's okay." I gave his hand a squeeze.

"It's not okay," he argued. "I . . . you must excuse me. I'm not used to . . . I mean, this isn't something I'm in the habit of doing."

"What, talking?" I asked with a laugh, trying to lighten the mood. Our eyes met, our gazes locked—literally. I couldn't look away, no matter what.

A tiny burst of light caught my peripheral vision, and I looked up, beyond the treetops. A shooting star. I scrambled to my feet, and he rose to stand beside me. "Did you see that?" I asked.

"Yeah," he said, but he didn't turn to look. Instead, he pulled me into his arms, his mouth moving toward mine.

For a moment time seemed to stand still. My breath came faster, my heart banging around in my chest, until his lips finally touched mine. An electric shock raced through my body, skittering across my skin as he kissed me—softly, gently, his hands against the small of my back. Rising up on tiptoe, I pressed myself fully against him, opening my mouth, inviting his tongue inside, moaning softly when I felt it skate across my teeth and touch my own tongue before retreating, teasing.

And then the bells began to ring—indicating midnight, curfew time. I tried to block out the sound, but it was no use. His lips left mine, and I stumbled backward a few steps, trying to regain my balance.

"How'd it get so late?" I murmured, glancing down at my watch, as if it might contradict the pealing bells. "Crap, I'm never going to make it in by curfew."

"Yes, you will," he answered, reaching for my hand and pulling me back toward him.

"It's a good ten-minute walk back to the dorm," I huffed. I could see the building in question, looming off in the distance. *Way* off in the distance.

"You'll make it. Come here."

"Oh, God, what're you going to do?" I took a step away from him, shaking my head wildly.

"Do you want to get busted? Or do you want to make curfew?"

Five, six times the bells had chimed. Six more to go, and

I'd get a demerit. "I don't want to get busted," I said in a rush.

"Okay, hold on tight. And close your eyes."

My fingernails were digging into his hand, but he didn't seem to notice. I swallowed hard and nodded. And then . . .

I don't know what happened. I felt myself being lifted from the ground. I could hear the whistling of wind, somehow melded with the bells—a strange, kind of blurred sound, like nothing I'd ever heard before. It seemed like only a second or two had passed, and then there was a pop. He pried my hand away from his, and I was suddenly aware of the grass beneath my feet again.

"Goodnight, Vi," he whispered in my ear, and then he was gone.

My eyes flew open, and there I was, right by the dorm. My hands shaking, I pushed the door open and stepped inside, just as the last chime sounded.

"Good heavens, Miss McKenna," Mrs. Girard said, startling me. "Whatever is the matter? You're as pale as a ghost."

I couldn't answer, couldn't take another step. All I could do was sway dizzily against the doorframe, wondering what the hell had just happened.

10 ~ Denial

I spent the next two days in the infirmary. I claimed a stomach bug, because what else could I say? That I was hiding out from my boyfriend? Too freaked out to go to class? I wanted some time alone to think, to get my head on straight, and the infirmary was the only answer. Over and over again I relived those seconds, trying to figure out how we'd moved so far so quickly. *It's impossible!* my mind screamed. There was no logical explanation, as far as I could tell, and that scared the crap out of me.

I mean, psychic stuff . . . sure. I was used to it all by now, pretty familiar with the range of seemingly impossible stuff that people could do. But this . . . this went far beyond anything else I'd experienced at Winterhaven.

Aidan was somehow *different*.

Still, I waited for him to come by—to send a message or something. I figured he would wonder why I wasn't in class, would ask around and learn where I was. But apparently he didn't. Or if he did, he didn't care enough to come by and check on me. Which hurt, despite the fact that he was the reason I'd fled to the infirmary in the first place.

By Monday night I'd convinced myself that I had imagined the whole thing, that we'd gotten back to the dorms by normal means—at least, normal as far as Winterhaven went. After all, he'd been so casual, so cavalier about it.

Once I finally made it back to class on Tuesday, Aidan wasn't there. He was gone—all week. Without a message, an e-mail, a text—*anything*. By Thursday I was starting to worry. After all, he *had* looked exhausted over the weekend. Maybe he'd gotten sick; maybe something was really wrong with him.

I could have called his cell, but I didn't want to seem desperate. I even thought about reaching out to him telepathically, but I wasn't sure if it worked from a distance. Even if it did, that just seemed too . . . intrusive. Even more desperate than calling him, really. Call me old-fashioned, but I wanted to be pursued, not the pursuer.

But by Friday morning the curiosity was killing me. "Hey, Cee," I called out as we were getting ready to go down to breakfast, "is there a student directory? You know, like with room numbers or something?"

"Sure, why?" She reached up to her bookshelf and pulled down a spiral-bound book. "Here."

My stomach in knots, I took it from her and sank to the bed, flipping through the pages. "Thanks. I just . . . well, Aidan's been absent from class all week, and I'm starting to worry."

"I thought everything was good between you two. I mean, after last Saturday . . ." She let the thought trail off with a shrug.

"I thought it was too." *Gray, Aidan*. There it was, along with his cell number and an address in Manhattan. *East Hall, Room 327*, it said. Not that knowing his room number was going to help me any. Girls weren't allowed on the boys' hall, and vice versa.

Cece sat down across from me, on her own bed. "Did you ask Kate if Jack's seen him?"

"Nah. I'm sure it's nothing. He's probably just sick or something."

"Yeah, maybe he got your stomach bug. You could call the infirmary and see if he's there," she volunteered.

"I guess I could." But I wouldn't. There wasn't really a stomach bug, and if Aidan wanted to talk to me, he would have called. Frustrated, I ran my fingers over the directory's cover, the word "Winterhaven" raised and bumpy beneath my fingertips.

And then my vision tunneled and the book slid from my lap, clattering to the floor beside the bed. *Oh, no.*

It was dusk, the sky a deep purplish gray. Leaves rustled in the wind, the breeze warm against my cheek. "Do it!" someone yelled. "Now!" I heard a scream, and realized it was my own. Closing my eyes, I took several deep, steadying breaths. I had to do it; I knew I was meant to. And then the picture sped up, fast-forwarded. Something smelled strange, salty, almost metallic, and I was suddenly filled with dread. Reluctantly I opened my eyes and saw blood everywhere. It darkened the grass around my feet, and somehow I knew it was Aidan's. There he was, just a few feet away, lying still. Aidan! I screamed the name over and over again, as I fell to my knees there in the grass.

And then I heard Cece calling my name, back in the dorm room. "Violet! Oh my God, what's wrong?"

I blinked hard, trying to look and sound normal before I spoke. "I'm . . . it's okay, I'm fine."

"Are you sure? You scared the shit out of me. You looked like you were having a seizure or something."

I rubbed my eyes with the heels of my hands, wishing I

could erase it, make it all go away. "It was a . . . you know, one of my visions. But I'm fine now."

Her brows drew together. "About Aidan? You yelled his name."

"Yeah." I didn't deny it. What was the point?

"Is he okay?"

"I . . . I don't know. I'm sure he is. Whatever I saw . . . it wasn't happening now. It was . . . I don't know, months from now. Spring or summer." There had been leaves on the trees, I remembered that. Everything had been green. That was all I was going to say, though; I wasn't getting into details. No *way* was I telling her about the blood. I shivered, feeling like a knife had pierced my heart. Had I just foreseen his death? Aidan's death? I squeezed my eyes shut, trying not to cry.

I forced myself to go down to breakfast, to go to class, to pretend that everything was fine. And maybe it was. I nearly wept with relief when Aidan walked into anthropology as if nothing was wrong, taking his seat across from mine. He gave me a little half wave, the faintest smile on his lips. Totally nonchalant. My relief at seeing him disappeared, and I suddenly wanted to strangle him. Time to put the telepathy to good use. *Where have you been?* I directed toward him with a scowl.

I saw him shrug. *Around*, came his voice in my head, along with the electrical buzz. It was so weird, this connection.

Are you okay? he asked.

Yeah, I'm fine. You're the one who's been MIA all week.

Just busy, came his reply.

I nodded, swallowing a lump in my throat. He was keeping things from me. I knew it shouldn't bother me, but it did. He was way too secretive, and it was driving me nuts. I was still freaked out by the vision, and I needed to see him. To talk to him. For real, not this crazy talking-in-the-head stuff. *Can I talk to you after class?*

I can't.

My cheeks burned. He was blowing me off again. Mercifully, Dr. Blackwell strode in just then, saving me from embarrassing myself any further.

"Hey," chirped Patsy's voice as I flipped open my cell phone. "Glad I caught you."

"Hey, Mom." She hated it when I called her Patsy. "Yeah, I'm just sitting here waiting on my psych—I mean, on Sandra. She's my, ummm . . . personal trainer." *I guess you could call her that.*

"Personal trainer?"

How to get out of this one? "I just figured, you know, with my shoulder and all . . ." I trailed off lamely, realizing I wasn't making a whole lot of sense. Now that I'd gotten the hang of blocking my thoughts, Sandra and I had begun to focus on my visions—trying to harness them, to gain a sense of awareness and look for clues while they were happening, for details that might help make them more useful. I'd hoped they could match me up with a precog for the rest of my training, but Sandra was what was called a generalist. For now it was Sandra or nothing. Anyway, I liked her.

"I hope they're not charging extra for that. God knows it's expensive enough—"

"No, it's included," I interrupted, rolling my eyes. "In the tuition, I mean."

"Well, that's a nice perk, I guess."

Cradling the phone between my ear and shoulder, I reached down and picked up the pajamas that Cece had left on the floor by her bed. "My shoulder's feeling better, by the way." *Not that she'd asked.* "Sometimes it gets a little sore after practice, that's all."

I heard her sigh loudly. "Maybe I was wrong to send you there. Spence is an excellent all-girls school here in the city, or there's Riverdale if you like coed and want to be—"

"I like it here at Winterhaven, Pats—Mom," I corrected. "Besides, it wouldn't make any difference to my shoulder."

"You're right." She sounded almost relieved, as if she'd been afraid that I might actually take her up on her offer. "I'm so busy that you'd be bored stiff here, anyway."

What else is new? "How's the new job?"

"Oh, it's great. Exhausting, overwhelming . . . but I love it. Have you talked to Gran?"

"I tried to call yesterday, but no one answered. Did you show her how to use the answering machine before we left?"

"I did, but you know your Gran. Try her again later. She says Lupe's been acting odd lately. I hope it's not the first stages of dementia, bless her heart. Anyway, she seems convinced your mortal soul is in some sort of danger, so I promised to call and check up on you. I told her that you sounded awfully happy in your e-mails, but apparently she was going on and on about battles between good and evil, and God knows what else."

I laughed uneasily. "Yeah, I think my mortal soul is pretty safe here."

"Well, that's reassuring. Poor Lupe, you know how fanciful her imagination is. She still swears that the blue bedroom is haunted. All these years, refusing to clean up in there."

I'd always thought that maybe there was more to Lupe's imaginings than my family knew, and now I wondered if maybe Lupe had "gifts" of her own. And if she did, well . . . it was going to be a little harder to brush aside her worries. "Tell her I'm fine, okay? Better yet, I'll tell her myself. I'll try them again later today."

"Great. Oh, wow, look at the time! I really need to run."

I could picture her glancing down at the diamond-encrusted Rolex my dad had bought her for their fifth anniversary. "No problem," I said.

"Take care, then. Bye, hon."

"Bye." I snapped the phone shut with a sigh. It was always the same with Patsy. Which, in this case, was probably a good thing. After all, there was so much I couldn't tell her, so much to hide. I knew with 100 percent certainty that if I told her about Winterhaven, about the "gifts" and "talents" that were fostered here, I'd end up just like Cece's old roommate.

No *way* was I going to let that happen. Not now, not when I was finally comfortable in my own skin for the first time in ages, when I finally felt like I didn't have to hide a vital piece of me.

All those years spent keeping secrets, even from my best friend. I glanced guiltily at my laptop, knowing that I owed Whitney an e-mail. She was so full of questions, and I wanted to tell her about my new friends, maybe even about Aidan, but something was holding me back.

A knock sounded at the door, making me jump. I banged my knee against the desk as I hastily shoved my cell phone back inside the top drawer. "Come in," I called out. I was actually looking forward to this session with Sandra. More than anything, I wanted to be in control of my visions, rather than have them controlling me.

Sandra bounced inside with her usual degree of perkiness. "Hey, good job," she said as I quickly imagined the thick, strong wall around my mind, guarding my innermost thoughts. She was still a mind reader, after all.

And I still had secrets.

11 ~ Unmasked

"Advil," I groaned. Sitting up in bed, I winced, feeling slightly queasy. My head was pounding, and for a moment I wondered if someone had slipped something into my drink the night before.

I shoved off the covers with a moan and stood, looking around for my bag. But when I looked over at the still-sleeping Cece, I stopped short. She was lying on her back, the covers bunched up around her waist. I'd never seen anyone lie so still. For a moment I just stood there staring at her, looking for that telltale rise and fall of her chest. But I saw nothing, no movement at all. She looked . . . *dead.*

Fear raced through my veins. Maybe I'd been right;

maybe someone had put something in our coffee. Maybe we'd been drugged.

"Cece!" I shrieked, bending over her. I called her name one more time, reaching for her hand and giving it a shake. She didn't move, didn't flinch. Nothing. I shook her again, harder this time.

At once her body jerked and she sat up, gasping for air. "Hey, why'd you do that?" she asked.

"Oh, thank God!" I breathed, stumbling back from her bed.

She glanced at the clock. "How long have I been gone? Oh my God, it's ten already?"

"G-gone? Where'd you go?" I sputtered.

"I was visiting Allison." Seeing my confusion, she added, "Astrally speaking. I meant to come back before you woke up. I didn't mean to scare you."

"Scare me? I was totally freaked!" My heart was still pounding, and my hands were shaking like crazy.

"Sorry about that. I should have warned you, I guess. You'd think we'd be used to each other's little gifts by now, wouldn't you?"

"So, how's Allison doing?" I asked, once I caught my breath.

"She seems okay. She's back home now, so that's good."

"So what did you do? When you were there, I mean."

Cece shrugged. "Not much. I mostly sat there watching

her. It was really weird—she was flipping through last year's yearbook and writing the same word over and over again on a notepad. *Julius.*" She shook her head. "I don't know anyone named Julius, not here at Winterhaven."

"Me either." I shook my head, and a wave of nausea washed over me. "I feel horrible," I said, shuffling toward my desk and reaching for my bag. "I swear I feel like I have a hangover or something." Not that I'd ever had a hangover, but I imagined this was what one felt like. I dug out the bottle of Advil and shook two caplets into my hand.

Cece swung her legs over the side of her bed and stretched. "It's probably just the Kahlúa."

"The Kahlúa?" I picked up the nearly empty bottle of tepid water that sat on my desk and unscrewed the cap with awkward fingers.

"Yeah, Jack had some Kahlúa in a flask. He put some in everyone's coffee, just a splash. Didn't you hear us talking about it? I thought you knew."

No, I hadn't known. I'd been way too distracted, I guess. I hadn't heard from Aidan, hadn't seen him since class on Friday. I had no idea where he was or what he was doing. So after my Saturday session with Sandra, I'd hung out with my friends instead—Jack and Kate, Cece and Marissa. Sophie had a date with one of Jack's friends from the football team, some guy named Ben who was telekinetic. The macro kind, like Kate. As it happens, that's the more common type. The things you learn.

So I really *did* have a hangover; imagine that. Patsy would kill me if she knew. I popped the two caplets into my mouth and washed them down with water, nearly gagging as the pills scraped down my throat.

Cece got up and went over to her desk, smiling at her reflection in the mirror above. She looked all bright-eyed and bushy-tailed, none the worse for wear.

"How come you look okay?" I asked. "You were drinking coffee last night too."

Cece just smiled. "Yeah, I had one cup. I think you had three."

Geez, three cups of spiked coffee, and I hadn't even noticed? I was worse off than I thought.

I sat down hard on my chair. "I need something to eat."

"Yeah, me too. I guess we'll have to hit the machines. We missed breakfast."

An hour later we had showered, dressed, and eaten stale bagels from the vending machine. The Advil had finally kicked in and my head felt a little better, so that was a start.

Once we'd returned to the room, I sat down at my desk and powered up my laptop, thinking I'd catch up on e-mails and maybe do some research for my anthropology class. I had a paper due in a few weeks—folklore in West African cultures—and I hadn't even picked a topic yet.

"I'm supposed to meet Marissa at the library to study for an English test," Cece said, grabbing her backpack. "And then I've got a student council meeting this afternoon. Want to meet up later for lunch?"

"Lunch?" I asked distractedly, waiting for my computer to log on to the school's network. "We just ate breakfast."

"Good point. Okay, I'll see you later, then."

I nodded. "Later," I called out.

She paused by the door, then turned back to face me. "Oh, and if Lover Boy calls, tell him you've got plans. Don't let him think you're sitting around here waiting for his sorry ass to call."

I started to protest. "I am not sitting here waiting—"

"Yeah, keep telling yourself that," Cece interrupted. "I know he's hot, but come on."

She didn't know the half of it.

Once she left, I opened my e-mail. Nothing. I guess Whitney had finally given up on me.

I dropped my hands to my lap, my frustration mounting. It wasn't that I didn't miss her—I did. It was just that I didn't know what to tell her. Anything I told her about my new friends would have to be edited. I'd have to keep the truth from her, just like always. And Aidan . . . what could I possibly tell her about him?

I couldn't tell her about being able to speak to him telepathically, or about the way he'd taken over my visions. So how could I explain the connection we had? The abridged version would sound so shallow, such a washed-out version of the truth. Anyway, what did it matter, since he was back to avoiding me?

Thank God I hadn't had a repeat of the last horrifying vision—all that blood soaking the grass. I must have misinterpreted what I saw; if anyone had lost that much blood, they'd be dead, and there was no way I'd seen Aidan's death.

No way.

My mind refused to accept it. Besides, it's not like my visions were usually so coy—I'd seen my father's death in full Technicolor glory, no detail spared. To this day, I was still haunted by those images. But this vision . . . it had somehow sped up, as if it had been edited. I had no idea what had happened between someone shouting "Now!" and the blood everywhere.

I stood, shutting my laptop. I needed to get out, to get some air. And then I'd go to the gym, to the fencing studio. It had become my refuge, my private retreat. As long as there was no class, no practice, I had the place to myself, and everything about it comforted me—the wall of mirrors reflecting my image; the smooth, shiny handle of my foil, heavy in my hand; the faintly rubber smell of the piste, lingering in the air.

There I could lose myself for a while, forget the sting of Aidan's rejection, forget the terrible images from my visions. I could focus on my parry instead—on the slash of the foil whistling through the air rather than the painful slash across my heart.

One wrist pressed firmly to the small of my back and the other holding the foil aloft, I silently called out the commands in my head: *advance, advance, retreat, lunge, recover, retreat, retreat, advance, lunge.* The rhythm was comfortable, like a familiar melody, soothing my nerves. Over and over I repeated the steps, randomly changing the order, till my legs and arms began to ache.

Exhausted, I collapsed to the piste, my foil clattering loudly to the ground beside me as I wiped the sweat from my brow. I knew without turning around that Aidan was there, in the doorway, watching me. He'd been watching me for the past fifteen minutes, silent and still as a statue.

"What do you want, Aidan?" I asked aloud, refusing to look in his direction.

"You're good," he said, taking several steps in my direction. "Really good."

"And that's a surprise because . . . ?" I looked up and saw his reflection in the mirror behind me.

He shrugged, his hands thrust into the pockets of his jeans. "Tell me more about it."

"Fencing? What do you want to know?"

He shrugged. "Everything."

"Let's see . . . two years ago I was the junior varsity state épée champion. All-around, not just girls. Then I injured my rotator cuff, and I had to give up the épée for the lighter foil. That's this," I said, hooking my thumb toward the weapon beside me. "Anything else you want to know?"

"I've hurt you," he said, sounding surprised.

"I'll survive."

"I had my reasons. This isn't easy for me, you know."

I scrambled to my feet, retrieving the foil and facing him across the empty studio on shaking legs. "No, I don't know, Aidan. All I know is that you're keeping things from me." Absently I waved the foil in the air with a flourish, emphasizing my point.

I could see the indecision playing across his features. The desire to tell me the truth battled against . . . something. Finally, he shook his head. "You wouldn't believe me if I told you my secrets, Vi."

"Gee, thanks for the vote of confidence. Why don't you just go, then, and—"

"And what? Continue to drive myself mad thinking about you? I try to stay away from you, but I just can't do it. I'm working night and day, trying to figure it out, trying to find a way to . . . to make it possible."

"To make what possible?" I shook my head in frustration. "Friday you came to class just to check up on me, didn't you?" I asked, the realization dawning on me all at once. "You knew I'd had a vision, and—"

"I heard you yelling. My name, over and over again. Do you want to tell me what you saw this time? And while you're at it, would you mind dropping your weapon?"

I glanced down, surprised to see that I still held the foil in one hand, pointed directly at his chest. "Sorry." I shook my head as it clattered to the ground by my feet. "But I can't talk about it, not right now."

"Can't, or won't?"

I let out my breath in a rush. "I don't know. Both."

"Were you—was someone hurt? You've got to tell me, Violet."

"Why?" I whimpered, my bravado fading.

"Because I need to know. It seems like they're escalating, and they always seem to involve me. I want to understand why, to know what I'm going to do to—"

He abruptly cut himself off, glancing down at the mat. I saw him swallow hard, a muscle in his jaw flexing. Finally his eyes met mine once more and the anguish I saw there nearly stole my breath away. "How else can we stop it?" he said, his voice soft now.

I didn't want to remember what I'd seen. I didn't want to give voice to it. But I had to. I had no choice. He was right—otherwise, how could I stop it from happening?

"I think it was . . . your death," I said, my voice a hoarse whisper.

"Is that all?" He actually laughed. "Don't worry, then. It won't happen."

I couldn't believe how sure he sounded. "My visions have never been wrong. Never," I added, hoping he understood the seriousness of the situation.

His gaze met mine, steady and penetrating. "Then tell me exactly what you saw."

So I did, trying to remember every tiny detail. The leaves, the grass, the voice, the blood—that was all I had. Not a lot to go on.

"Interesting," he said, once I'd finished telling him.

"That's it? I foresee your death, and that's all you have to say?" I asked, my voice rising in panic.

I heard him sigh. "It's . . . I can't explain it, but I don't think you should worry, okay? At least, not about me."

"That's easy for you to say, Aidan. You didn't have to see—"

I fought back tears, choking on the words. "There was blood everywhere." I took a deep breath then, fought to control my emotions, my pain. I allowed anger—a far more comfortable emotion—to take its place. "Why is it that I always have to tell you everything, but you get to keep your secrets?"

"Soon enough I'll tell you what you want to know—if you don't see it first, that is. And then I'll lose you, just like that." I saw pain flit across his face, and I felt it too—his pain.

"You won't lose me," I said, taking a tentative step toward him. Despite my anger, despite everything, I felt an overwhelming urge to comfort him. "No matter what your secrets are, no matter how terrible you think they are, you won't lose me."

He reached for my shoulders and drew me against his chest. "I'll make sure to remind you that you said that, okay? When you're running away from me as fast as you can."

"Not going to happen," I said, my voice muffled against his shirt.

He sighed loudly. "What makes you think you can forgive the unforgivable, Violet? Pardon the unpardonable?"

I breathed in his scent, unable to imagine what he meant by that.

"You didn't answer me," he prodded, his hand stroking my back, drawing gooseflesh on my skin. "Why? Why won't you run from me?"

I didn't know what to say; didn't know what he wanted to hear. All I knew was that I cared about him, way more than I should care about someone I barely knew. But I wouldn't say it—couldn't say it.

Several seconds passed in silence, and then his lips brushed my ear. "Well, until you *do* run, I'll just have to take what I can. Next weekend is the Halloween Fair. Will you go with me to the dance?"

My heart did a little flip-flop—he was asking me to a dance! An official school function, which meant going public.

"Do I have to wear a costume?" I asked, as *if* I would turn him down either way.

He released me then, taking a step back as his mouth curved into a smile. "Of course you have to wear a costume. That's half the fun of it."

"Well, then, how can I say no?" That meant I had to come up with a costume, and fast.

On most days I felt like the Violet I showed the world *was* a costume, a mask. No one knew the real me. But, as I looked up into Aidan's eyes and watched him smile that slow smile of his, I realized with a start that *he* did. He knew the real Violet McKenna, the essence beneath the mask.

And somehow that excited me and terrified me, all at once.

12 ~ The Night of the Living Dead

"A vampire, Aidan? That's the best you could do?" I shook my head with a smile as he stepped into the East Hall lounge with a flourish of his cape. "Totally cliché, you know. Besides, vampires are supposed to have black hair."

He looked more like an angel, my Aidan. Despite the black cape and plastic fangs.

I had managed something far more esoteric, if less easily identifiable—a fallen star. If nothing else, I figured it'd be a good conversation starter. Only problem was, I kept tripping on my dress—a long, crushed-velvet thing in silver with a big, sweeping train. I'd bought it online and paid a fortune to have it shipped overnight. Yellow glow-sticks around my ankles and wrists completed the look.

"C'mon, it's time to twinkle, little star." Aidan took my hand and led me out into the night, toward the gym. I could hear the music, feel the thump of the bass, from across the quad as I stumbled along next to him.

"Be honest," I said, careful with the hem of my dress. "Would you know what I was supposed to be if I hadn't told you?"

"Absolutely," he said, but his smile made me wonder. "I read Gaiman."

I reached down to adjust my shoes, a hot pair of strappy heels that I'd bought on a whim in Manhattan before I'd come to school. Patsy had insisted they were a ridiculous purchase, that they were way too much for boarding school. I was glad that I'd ignored her and listened to my instincts instead, because they looked perfect with the dress.

When I straightened, Aidan took a step back, his gaze traveling from the top of my head down to my toes, and back up again. I felt myself shiver in response; guys had *never* looked at me the way Aidan was looking at me now. It made my heart race, my knees wobble.

"You sure you can't read my mind?" I asked him.

He shook his head. "Nope. You've locked it good and tight."

"Good," I murmured, suddenly feeling naughty. "Because I'd hate for you to know what I'm thinking right now."

In a flash, he'd pulled me up against his chest, his fake teeth ripped from his mouth, his lips on mine. He'd moved so fast that he'd taken me entirely by surprise. His lips were soft, his kiss gentle, but I could hear the low growl in the back of his throat.

Guess he didn't need to read my mind after all.

It had been so long since he'd kissed me—*really* kissed me. Oh, he'd pressed his lips against my ear, against my hair, but nothing like this, like that first time, under the stars, his whole body pressed against mine. I'd been waiting, wanting . . .

"Hey, you two, get a room," someone called out from behind us.

He released me, and I stepped away. Barely able to catch my breath, I turned and saw Jenna Holley there, decked out in what I guessed was supposed to be a poodle costume. Floppy ears, pom-pom tail, a crystal-studded collar around her throat.

Aidan laughed, then reached for my hand. "Nice touch, Jenna," he called out.

"Yeah, I could say the same of you." She smiled sweetly at him, but I also detected hostility, maybe, mixed with something else, something I couldn't put my finger on. A wave of jealousy washed over me. There was something between Aidan and Jenna—something I didn't know about. Neither did my friends, or they definitely would have mentioned it.

"Don't you have somewhere to go?" Aidan asked her, breaking the uncomfortable silence.

"Yeah, I better go find my pack," she joked.

Speaking of packs, there came mine, and they were headed our way—Cece, Sophie, Kate, Jack, and Marissa.

For a second there I actually considered grabbing Aidan's hand and running off toward the woods where we could pick up where we'd left off when Jenna had so rudely interrupted us. Instead I allowed common sense to reign, and I raised my hand and waved.

As they approached, I reached for Aidan's hand and held it tightly in my own. This was our first public outing as a couple, and I really wanted it to go well.

"Hey, was that Jenna Holley?" Kate asked, once they'd caught up to us.

"Yeah," I answered, watching the poodle disappear into the gym, her tail swinging behind her. "The one and only."

Sophie readjusted her pointy hat. "Is she actually dressed up as a dog?"

"A *female* dog," Cece put in with a giggle. "How appropriate."

"Meow," said Marissa.

"Hey, are we going in, or what?" Jack seemed impatient.

We weren't inside for more than fifteen minutes, all of us clustered together around the refreshment table, when a man I'd never seen—obviously a teacher—made a beeline for us, his mouth drawn in a tight line.

"Mr. Gray," he said. "A moment, please."

"Wait for me," Aidan whispered against my ear, and he followed the teacher to a corner of the gym. They stood there talking, the man gesturing wildly with his hands. Aidan was very still and stiff, and I could sense that something was wrong. *Very* wrong.

A minute later he was back at my side, his face a complete and total blank. "I've got to go," he said, his voice tight. "I should be back soon. Stay with your friends; I'll find you." And then he was gone.

"Where'd Aidan go?" Cece yelled above the din of the music, reaching for a Diet Coke.

I watched as Jack led Kate out to the dance floor. "I don't know. Who was that guy he was talking to? Do you know?"

"I think his name is Dr. Hughes. A chemistry teacher. What'd he want?"

I shrugged. "I have no idea. Do you mind if I just hang with you till he gets back?"

"Course not." She nudged me in the ribs. "Don't look now,

but there's the shifters. Maybe one of them will ask you to dance."

"Hey, that's not funny." I still felt bad for them. They couldn't help what they were, any more than I could help having visions. It didn't seem fair that they were outcasts in a school like this, a school where kids should be more sensitive to people's differences—even if their "gift" *was* a little out there.

Kind of like carrying someone a quarter mile in the blink of an eye, I reminded myself, then shuddered.

Marissa and Sophie sidled up beside us, and I was glad for the interruption. "Hey, guys, I think Todd Moreland is checking out Cece," Marissa said, her little cat nose twitching.

I glanced over at Todd, a dark-haired guy I knew from a couple of classes, and yeah, he was definitely staring. A few minutes later, he elbowed his way through the crowd and asked Cece to dance.

Next went Sophie, off with the same guy she'd gone out with last weekend, Jack's football friend. I couldn't even remember his name, but he was pretty cute. That left Marissa and me. Of all my newfound friends, she was the one I felt the least comfortable with.

"I cannot freaking believe that Kate and Jack coordinated their costumes," she said, tipping her head toward where the couple in question—pirate and wench—stood swaying, their bodies plastered together on the dance floor. "I mean, how lame is that?"

"I don't know," I said with a shrug, wishing Aidan would hurry back. "I think it's kind of cute."

Marissa made a gagging sound.

"You don't like Jack very much, do you?"

She was still watching them, staring intently. "Eh, he's okay, I guess. Why?"

"I don't know." Did I really want to get into it with her? "It's just that you're always making these little digs about him and Kate."

"Don't tell anyone I said this, okay?" she demanded, and I nodded before she continued on. "But Kate's mom was only eighteen when she had her, and her dad was already long gone by then. I just . . ." She trailed off, shaking her head. "I worry that Kate's headed down that same path, that's all. She's convinced that she and Jack are going to be together forever. I mean, what are the chances of that happening?"

That was *not* the answer I had expected, and I wasn't even sure how to reply, so I just shrugged.

"Anyway, where'd Aidan go off to?" she asked, glancing around the crowded room.

"I don't know. Somewhere with a chemistry teacher, I

think. He said he'd be back," I added lamely, taking a sip of the now tepid Coke I held in one hand.

"I guess you two are getting pretty serious?"

I shrugged, scanning the dance floor, looking for Cece and Todd. "Maybe. I don't know, he's kind of hot and cold. Here one minute, gone the next." I have *no* idea what loosened my tongue like that, but it felt kind of good, saying it out loud.

"Yeah, well, he's never even given anyone else the time of day, so you must be doing something right. I hope you two can work it out," she said, and my gaze shot back to her. After what she'd just said about Jack and Kate, I really wasn't expecting *that*.

Marissa was full of surprises today. Truth was, she had always intimidated me—even when she was being nice. But . . . I don't know . . . I was starting to think that beneath her tough exterior, there was something soft, something vulnerable.

"You really like him, don't you?" she continued, still watching me closely. "And no, I didn't use any sixth sense to figure that one out. It's written all over your face. You can't take your eyes off the door."

"I'm just worried. It's been, what, almost a half hour now?" Maybe more. I wasn't wearing a watch, but it felt like forever.

"You didn't answer the question. Do you think you really like him, or is it just an extreme case of the Aidan effect?"

I had asked myself that same question more than once, and I always came up with the same answer. "Yeah, I do. Really like him, I mean." Way too much. Which was more frightening, really, than some freakish hormonal reaction.

"Well, then, I can't believe I'm saying this, but I think you should go find him." She wrapped her arms around herself, and I saw her shiver. "I think something's wrong. He's . . . angry or something. I don't know exactly. But I think he needs you."

"How can you . . ." I let it trail off. She *could*—that's all that mattered. "Do you know where he is?"

She nodded. "The chemistry lab."

"Thanks, Marissa." I hugged her fiercely. "If he does show up, will you tell him I went looking for him?"

"Sure. Now go." She stepped back, out of my grasp. "I think you should hurry. Corridor C. Third floor. Try room 329."

Soon I was sprinting back across the quad, holding up my skirt as I ran. I'd only gone a couple of yards when I felt the strap on my right shoe snap, and I almost fell flat on my face.

Bending down, I slipped off my shoes, wincing as my bare feet made contact with the cold grass. I hurried to the courtyard with the fountain, the lights illuminating the spray of water. Corridor C, Marissa had said, which was directly opposite the door I took to math class. In seconds I was through the stone archway and sprinting barefoot up the stairs, taking two at a time, my dress hiked up to my knees. Third floor, room 329.

There it was, at the end of the hallway. The door was closed, the lights out. Maybe I'd missed him; maybe he was already headed back to the gym. Just to be sure, I pushed the door open, my heart thumping, and stepped inside. Nothing but the emergency light glowed, but it was enough. I clamped my hand over my mouth.

Tables were overturned, chairs broken to bits. Glass was everywhere, and a weird, sulfurous smell made me gag. In the middle of the chaos stood Aidan, still wearing the silly vampire costume. As I watched, he picked up the one remaining table as if it weighed nothing and flung it against the wall, shattering glass, splintering wood. I must have screamed, because Aidan spun around, the cape billowing out behind him.

"Violet?" His eyes met mine, and I could have sworn they were glowing red. I took a step backward, reaching blindly for the door, and felt a piece of glass slice through the sole of my foot.

The lights flickered on at once. And then, impossibly, he was against the far wall, though I hadn't seen him move.

With a whimper, I dropped my shoes and reached down to pluck the glass from my foot, then tried to stanch the warm, sticky blood with my skirt.

"You have to leave, Violet. Now. *Now,*" he repeated, his voice so tight, so controlled, that it sent a shiver racing down my spine.

"What . . . what's wrong with you?" I stammered. He'd moved from the wall, but then stumbled back against it. He must be hurt, I realized. Terribly hurt. His face was pale, his eyes rimmed in red.

There was a path to my right, mostly clear of glass and debris. If I could just get to him—

"You've got to leave now. I mean it, so help me God." His hands were clenched into fists by his sides, and he looked like he was in physical pain. "I can't . . . I'm not this strong. Get out of here—*now*."

I staggered back toward the door, careful to avoid the glass. I couldn't quite process what I was seeing—the destruction, his reaction; none of it made any sense. "What . . . what happened?"

The muscles in his jaw tensed. He closed his eyes and took a deep breath before speaking. "Don't you see? This was two years' worth of work, destroyed. Damn it. You've got to do something about the blood."

"The blood?" I looked down at the floor, to the trail of bright red footprints I'd left on the linoleum, and shuddered.

"Listen to me, and listen closely," he said, leaning back

against the wall, his body tense and taut. "You wanted to know my secrets? Well, here they are, Violet McKenna. Right in front of you; just open your eyes."

"What are you saying?" I choked out, terror clutching at my heart.

He took a deep, rattling breath. "I'm trying to tell you that, in about thirty seconds, I'm going to be tempted beyond reason to sink these"—he grimaced, showing what looked like his fake fangs—"into your neck. Do you understand?"

Aidan was a . . . a . . . I could barely force myself to *think* the word, it was so crazy. *A vampire?* Or at least he thought he was. I shook my head wildly, my heart beating so fast that I thought I might faint, right then and there.

One of us was crazy, that was for sure, and I had no idea if it was him or me. I clamped my hand over my mouth, forcing myself to breathe—in and out, through my nose.

"Now turn around and leave, Violet. Run. And no matter what happens, promise me you won't come back here tonight."

I nodded mutely, unable to speak a single syllable. And then I turned and fled.

13 ~ Cue the Creepy Music . . .

I fidgeted in my seat as Dr. Blackwell sat down opposite me, steepling his hands beneath his chin as he watched me from across his desk.

I'd been summoned to the headmaster's office, probably for skipping my history and anthropology classes—the classes I shared with Aidan. Whatever punishment Dr. Blackwell handed down, it was worth it. I couldn't face Aidan, not yet. He was . . . crazy. Dangerous, maybe. But a . . . a *vampire*? I mean, c'mon. There's no such thing; it's all myth, legend—

Talk to me, Violet. Please? Aidan's voice in my head. He was somewhere, reaching out to me telepathically. Damn it.

Go away! I silently yelled. *Leave me alone.*

He'd been trying since Sunday morning—and I'd been ignoring him, over and over again, trying to shut out the weird electrical buzz in my head that accompanied the telepathy.

"Miss McKenna?" Dr. Blackwell asked, leaning forward in his chair. I'd almost forgotten he was there. "Are you unwell?"

"No, I'm . . . it's just a headache," I murmured, feeling like an idiot. "A migraine. Off and on, all day. I had to miss a couple of classes."

He nodded, mercifully accepting my explanation—just like that. "You've settled in well here at Winterhaven, haven't you?"

"Yes, sir," I said, my voice sounding strangely wobbly.

"Good, good. I'm always pleased to see a new student flourish in this nurturing environment. All your teachers are reporting that you are not only fully caught up but excelling at your studies." He smiled at me then, his silvery eyes crinkling slightly at the corners. "Have you considered what subject you might study in college?"

I shook my head, glad for the change of subject. "Not really. I'm only a junior."

"It's never too early to plan for your future. Have you considered any careers that might be aided by your special talents?"

"I can't really think of anything." I shook my head. "I mean, my visions are always about people that I know, that I"—I swallowed hard—"care about."

"Perhaps your visions could be better trained," Blackwell suggested. "You know, broadened to include larger segments of the population. Are you working with a trainer?"

"Yes, but she's just a general trainer. They're trying to find me a precog whose visions work similar to mine. But, I don't know . . ." I trailed off. "I guess mine are a little unusual."

"Perhaps." Dr. Blackwell nodded, reaching for a pad of paper and a pen. "I'll speak to Mrs. Girard about it, see what we can do." He scribbled something down, then laid aside the pen and removed his glasses. "Your anthropology essay was excellent, by the way. You'll receive it back in class tomorrow, but you should know you received one of the highest marks. Very impressive. Have you a particular interest in folklore?"

I wasn't quite sure how to answer that one. Truthfully, I'd never really thought much about it. "Maybe. Your class is interesting."

He leaned back in his chair with a smile. "Precisely what every instructor hopes to hear. You'll find I have a very extensive library on such topics, here in my office. Feel free to take anything that catches your fancy." He gestured toward the bookshelves to my right, row after row of books that nearly reached the ceiling.

"Thanks," I murmured, wondering if he had any books about vampires. Or crazy people who *thought* they were vampires.

"Very well, I suppose that's all for now, then. I do hope you'll find yourself well enough to attend your classes tomorrow, Miss McKenna. *All* of your classes," he added sternly.

"I hope so too," I answered. What I really needed was to get away for a while, to have some time to myself, away from Cece and the rest of them. Just to think, to get my head together.

Suddenly, I had an idea. "Can I ask you something?"

"Of course, Miss McKenna. Anything."

"I've been feeling a little homesick lately, and I was wondering if it was possible . . . I mean, I know it's kind of last-minute and all, but could I get a pass to go home for the weekend? After fencing practice on Friday night?"

"That's an excellent idea. I'll let Mrs. Girard know that I've given you permission, and you may go ahead and make the arrangements. You can take the seven forty-six train."

Relief washed over me. "Thanks. I . . . I really appreciate it."

"Now go on, before you miss dinner."

With a nod, I rose and made my way out of his office, moving slowly thanks to the cut on my foot, which hadn't yet had time to heal.

Just like my stupid heart.

* * *

Turns out I needn't have worried about avoiding Aidan the rest of the week. He wasn't in history or anthropology class, or anywhere else on campus, as far as I could tell. Even his voice in my head was silent. Which was fine by me.

On Friday afternoon, Cece and Sophie sat on the bed, watching me pack.

"I still can't believe Dr. B. gave you permission to go," Cece said. "He's usually pretty strict about weekend passes. Two-week notice, and all that."

Sophie frowned. "You look pale. Are you sure you're feeling okay?"

I tossed a pair of jeans into my bag. "Yeah, I'm fine. Still a bit of a headache, that's all."

"Would you mind if I . . . you know." Sophie shrugged. "Just let me check, okay? I'm worried that the cut on your foot might have gotten infected." She rose and moved to stand beside me, reaching for my hand.

I let her take it, a shiver working its way down my spine. My foot was fine. If I looked pale and haggard it was because I'd barely slept in days.

Sophie's brows drew together, her lips pursed as she held my cold hand in her warm one. "Your foot's okay," she said at last. "Everything seems fine, actually."

"Told you." I forced myself to smile. "I'm just tired, is all."

"Does Aidan know you're going into the city for the weekend?" Cece asked.

"No. Aidan and I—" I broke off, swallowing hard. How could I possibly explain it? "We're not, you know . . . it's none of his business. It's not like he'll even notice, besides."

Cece's dark brows drew together. "You're not going to tell us what really happened, are you?"

"I . . . I *did* tell you," I stuttered. I'd told them about finding him in the chem lab, everything smashed to bits. About cutting my foot. That was enough, as far as I was concerned. "I just . . . don't think it's going to work out between us. You know, too different and all that."

I could tell from their expressions that they weren't buying it, and who could blame them? Nothing had ever been that simple between Aidan and me. We'd always been too different; that was nothing new. But before now, I'd at least thought we were both *mortals*. I reached up and fingered the silver crucifix Lupe had given me.

Vampire. I forced myself to think the word, to at least consider the possibility, as whacked out as it seemed. No, I just couldn't buy it. It was too out there, too crazy to believe. Vampires were just make-believe; horror-movie stuff like demons and zombies. Aidan was either seriously deluded or seriously messing with my head. There had to be a more rational explanation, something psychic-related.

"Hey, earth to Violet."

I realized Sophie and Cece were staring at me, and I snapped my attention back to packing.

"God, you just mention his name and she's off in la-la land," Sophie said, shaking her head. "I don't care what you say, you've got it bad."

Cece nodded. "Yeah. Or maybe there's an Aidan effect by proxy. You know, where you don't have to see him, just think about him."

"Ha-ha, very funny." I tried to smile, but I don't think it worked. None of this was funny, not one bit. I zipped up my overnight bag and hefted it onto my shoulder. "I better go or I'll miss my train. Tell Kate and Marissa I said bye, will you?"

"Sure," Sophie answered.

For a moment I hesitated at the door. Then I hurried back, wrapping my arms around both Cece and Sophie at once.

"Hey, we'll miss you too," Cece said, her voice thick.

I knew I was being silly—it was only a weekend. Still, I had this feeling . . . I don't know. I couldn't put my finger on it, but something about this impromptu trip spelled "change" to me. Not that I'd had a vision or anything. Actually, now that I thought about it, I hadn't had a vision in a while. *That's a good thing,* I told myself. Before I'd come to Winterhaven, they'd been few and far between, and I liked it much better that way.

Only now . . . now I somehow felt blind. I glanced down at my watch and frowned. I was supposed to meet Mrs. Girard at the admin building in five minutes—she was calling a cab to drive me to the station.

A half hour later I was settled into a scabbed blue vinyl seat on the Metro-North train, headed south. Only then did I realize that I'd never even called Patsy to tell her I was coming. I had no idea if she was busy or, for that matter, even in town.

I pulled my cell phone out of my bag and started to dial, but something stopped me—a gut feeling. Deciding to trust it, I flipped the phone shut and shoved it back into my bag. I'd call her once I got into the city. If she was out, I had a key, and the doorman knew me.

With a sigh, I leaned back in the seat, closing my eyes. I was tired. Exhausted, really. All I needed was some rest and some time alone to figure everything out.

I must have dozed off, because the next thing I knew, the train was arriving at Grand Central station. I rubbed my eyes, my mouth all dry and cottony. Why hadn't I thought to bring along a bottle of water?

Beside me, a couple dressed up for a night on the town stood and joined the loud, raucous crowd of teenagers milling in the aisle as the train came to a stop. Outside the train's windows, the station had a dull amber-yellow glow.

Something inside me felt weird, slightly off. *Please, oh please, don't let me have a vision. Not now. Not in front of all these people.* My legs felt wobbly as I zipped up my coat and stepped out onto the platform, following the herd of people toward the exit.

For fifteen minutes I tried to catch a cab, with no luck. So I started walking instead. It was that gut instinct again, pulling me somewhere, toward . . . *something*. My heart began to race in anticipation while a nervous buzz in my ears reduced the city's noises to a faint hum. Ten minutes passed, then twenty. I realized I had walked south instead of north, and too far east. And yet I kept walking, on and on, as if I were in a trance. A light fog had rolled in, giving the night an almost surreal feel to it, and still I walked on, entirely in the wrong direction.

On purpose.

A quarter hour or so later, I blinked hard, as if waking up from a dream, and looked around. This was an unfamiliar part of the city—an area I'd never been to before. The Lower East Side, maybe? Or somewhere near Battery Park? I wasn't sure. Wherever I was, there wasn't much besides some run-down-looking storefronts, everything-for-a-dollar stores and stuff like that, mostly barred up for the night. Probably not safe, I told myself.

And then my vision began to tunnel, as if I were about to have one of my episodes. I swallowed hard, fully expecting the onslaught of the strange feelings that accompanied my visions. But they never came. Instead I simply began to walk, focused on a spot in the distance, maybe four or five blocks over.

My heart was pounding, keeping rhythm to the sound of my boots' heels against the sidewalk. Faster, faster . . .

I was entirely aware of the fact that I was being drawn somewhere, against my will, and yet I made no move to stop, to shake it off. I was supposed to go wherever I was headed—I was sure of it. I began to jog, my overnight bag jostling against my hip. I heard footsteps, saw the barest hint of a figure up ahead. I was following them, the footsteps. Keeping pace.

Looking around, I noticed a flyer taped to a post beside me: HOW TO WRITE A NOVEL IN A WEEK, it promised. So familiar. Everything seemed so familiar, as if I'd been here and done this before. And yet I was sure I'd never before been on this particular street in this particular part of the city.

Except in the vision, I realized. The one I'd had when I first came to Winterhaven. Of course—I was following Aidan. I stopped midway down a deserted block. To my right was an alley of some sort. He'd turned down the alley, and I was supposed to follow him.

Cupping my hands to my mouth, I called out his name.

"All alone, pretty girl?"

Startled, I spun toward the voice. There was a man standing beside the curb, leering at me in the moonlight, his clothing shabby and torn and reeking of smoke and beer and something sharp that I couldn't identify.

No, this is wrong. In the vision I'd been following Aidan, not some junkie.

"I got some good stuff, if you wanna share," he said, holding up a small Baggie. I saw the glint of steel in his hand—a knife, maybe.

I was breathing way too fast to respond—short puffs through parted lips making clouds of smoke in the cool night air.

"Nah? Maybe you just want to have some fun, then?"

I swallowed convulsively, terrified. I knew I should run—scream and run, as loud and as fast as I could. But I was frozen, unable to move a single muscle.

He reached toward me, dirty fingers clutching at my coat's sleeve. And that's when the world turned upside down.

Something—or someone—slammed into the junkie, dragging him farther into the alley and pressing him up against the graffiti-covered bricks.

I screamed, but nothing came out. My lungs were burning, my throat so tight I could barely breathe as I tried to run, but my legs buckled beneath me and I fell to the sidewalk. I heard a grunt and looked up to see the junkie's attacker dip his head toward the filthy man's neck.

Still pressed against the alley's wall, the junkie struggled, his feet dangling a foot off the ground while the attacker—my savior, I realized—held him by the throat. So help me God, the guy had his face buried in the junkie's neck, as if he were *biting* him. I could only watch in horror, unable to believe what I was seeing.

Seconds later, the junkie went limp and the attacker released him, stepping back as the man slid to the ground like a rag doll. My gaze was involuntarily drawn to the crumpled form on the ground, deep red blood trickling from a pair of puncture marks on the guy's neck.

The attacker took a step back, his hands clenched into fists by his sides. His shoulders rose and fell—once, twice. I was holding my breath, just waiting . . .

And then he turned, blond hair glinting in the dim light of the moon, familiar eyes reaching out to me through the hazy fog. Recognition washed over me like a dousing of ice-cold water, and I gasped.

Holy hell and God in heaven.

It was Aidan. Of course it was. Hadn't I known it all along?

As I sat there gaping in shock, he reached up and wiped a smear of ruby-red blood from his mouth with his sleeve. As he did so, I saw a flash of oddly long canine teeth. Long and sharp. Looking suspiciously like . . . like *fangs*.

That was the last thing I saw before I passed out cold, right there on the sidewalk.

14 ~ Fear of Flying

I awoke to the sensation of speed. Panicked, I began to flail around, but strong arms held me tight.

"I've got you," came Aidan's voice beside my ear.

"Oh, God," I moaned. "Where . . . what are you . . . how—" I swallowed hard, unable to form a coherent sentence.

"Shhh," he murmured.

Immediately I felt a calming sensation. I wanted to protest, to tell him not to manipulate my mind that way. But I couldn't speak, couldn't do anything but swallow, over and over again. I kept my eyes squeezed shut, praying for my stomach to settle, for the freaky sensations to go away.

There was a popping noise, followed by a rush of air, and

then . . . nothing. Scared out of my wits, I opened my eyes, half-expecting to see . . . I don't know what. But all I saw was a front door, painted a shiny black with a big, brass lion's-head knocker in the center and a mail slot down below. On either side of the door was a column of stained glass. I had no idea where he'd taken me, but we weren't downtown anymore, that was for sure.

I nearly jumped out of my skin when the door swung open. A well-dressed elderly man stood inside, gaping at us both. "Master Gray," he said with a nod, moving aside as Aidan carried me in. The old man's bushy gray brows knitted together as he peered down at me. "Is she injured?"

"Just scared, I think. Here, take her bag and draw her a bath."

"Of course. Right away."

I felt something slip over my head and realized it was my overnight bag. I shivered violently, and felt Aidan's arms tighten around me.

"Is he . . . did you . . . kill him?" I finally managed to ask.

"No. Though perhaps I should have."

"He was going to . . . to . . ."

"You're safe now, Violet. Let's get you upstairs and cleaned up. We can talk later."

"I can walk," I said, struggling against the confines of his arms.

"That's what you think," he answered with a chuckle. "C'mon, Trevors will have your bath ready soon." He carried me away from the front door, across a huge foyer lit by a glittering chandelier, and up a curved staircase. There was marble everywhere—marble and gilt and crystal.

"Where . . . where are we?"

"My home," Aidan said quietly. "Don't worry, we're still in Manhattan. Just off Fifth Avenue."

A door opened on its own, then another. Fear shot through me. Still, I clung to Aidan. I squeezed my eyes shut, but the image in my mind's eye was even worse. Aidan, fresh blood on his mouth, blood from the junkie's throat . . .

I won't hurt you, Violet. His voice, in my head.

I just nodded, exhaling slowly. In through my nose, out through my mouth. I had to concentrate on breathing, because if I thought about anything else, I might lose it.

"There you are, sir. Her bath is almost ready, and I've laid out fresh towels and a robe in the dressing room. Will you be needing anything else?"

"That's it for now, Trevors," Aidan said, and my eyes flew open, darting around, taking in my surroundings.

We were in a bathroom done in deep blue and gold. An enormous tub sat in the center, fragrant steam rising from the water. Beside the tub, thick towels the same blue as the walls were piled on a chair that looked like an antique, like something that belonged in Gran's living room. Gold velvet drapes were tied back from a large bay window with tasseled cords, fleur-de-lis-patterned shades covering the panes of glass.

Aidan gingerly lowered my feet to the plush patterned carpet, then reached across the tub to turn off the faucets. "Here, take all the time you need," he said, and I couldn't help but notice that his teeth were back to normal now. "There's a new toothbrush and some toothpaste in the closet over by the sink; help yourself to whatever you can find. Soak for a while, and then we'll talk, okay?"

I nodded mutely.

"When you're done, the dressing room is through there." He pointed to a curved door on the far side of the room. "Trevors left you a robe. I'll know when you're ready."

Aidan left me then, shutting the door softly behind him. A click sounded, and I realized that he'd locked the door from the inside, as if to reassure me that I had complete privacy, that I was safe. Of course, if he could lock it with his mind, then he could unlock it too. But he wouldn't. Call me crazy, but I truly believed that.

I swallowed hard, wincing at the nasty taste in my mouth. I found the toothbrush and toothpaste and turned on the faucet, glancing up at my reflection in the oval, gilt-framed mirror above it as I did so. I looked awful—pale and disheveled, with a terrified look in my eyes.

Yeah, what do you expect? You almost got yourself jumped by some junkie, then you watched your maybe-boyfriend bite the dude's neck and suck him dry before you passed out cold. Good times.

I finished brushing as fast as I could, desperate to get into the tub and scrub away the grime, the filth, the memories. In seconds I'd stripped down to nothing and climbed the marble steps that led to the tub, sighing with relief as I stepped into the hot water and sunk down to my chin. Spying a pair of buttons below the faucet, I punched one, firing up the jets. I closed my eyes as the water frothed, the steady hum of the motor soothing my jangled nerves. The water was the perfect temperature and scented with lavender, and I inhaled deeply as I laid my head back against the marble.

Still, I couldn't get my mind to relax. All I could think about was the fact that Aidan was a vampire—there was no denying it, not now. I'd seen the proof. He'd been transformed, his eyes glowing red, his canine teeth elongated. I didn't need one of Dr. Blackwell's books to spell it out for me. A vampire—creature with fangs, drinks blood, hides from the sun. Not a big fan of garlic or crucifixes.

How could I face him, knowing the truth? How could I sit

there, looking at him, knowing that he was a . . . a monster? Because that's what a vampire was—a monster. An undead *thing* that went around hurting people, sucking their blood. Killing them. Bile rose in my throat, and I forced it down, forced my hands to stop shaking.

Because that didn't describe Aidan. Or did it? I had no idea what he did when he disappeared, no idea where he went, even. I squeezed my eyes shut. One hot tear trickled down my cheek, and I wiped it away, wishing I could turn back time, that I could forget all this crazy vampire stuff and just be a normal kid with a normal boyfriend.

I reached for a bar of soap, brand-new, and began to scrub my skin with a lathered-up washcloth. I stopped only when my skin began to burn, nearly rubbed raw. Still, I didn't feel clean. Not entirely.

With a sigh of frustration I switched off the bubbles and flipped open the drain. I had to face him. I had to learn the truth, had to reconcile the Aidan that I knew—that I cared about, damn it—with the monster I'd seen. And then . . . then I could decide what to do. Taking a deep, calming breath, I stood and reached for a towel, trying to force my racing heart to slow. I had to give him a chance to explain. He deserved that, at least.

He said he wouldn't hurt me, after all, and I believed him.

Minutes later I was wrapped in a soft terry robe, sitting

on a velvet chaise by a crackling fire in what I supposed was Aidan's dressing room. A big armoire stood against one wall, a standing mirror beside it. Other than the chaise I was sitting on, there was no furniture in the room. Still, the room was as big as some of our bedrooms back home.

A knock sounded softly on the door, and I sucked in my breath.

"Violet? Can I come in?"

"Yeah, I . . . it's fine." I cleared my throat and clasped my hands together in my lap. They'd have to stop shaking at some point.

Without making a sound, Aidan stepped in and closed the door, leaning back against it and watching me from across the room. It was as if he wanted to stay as far away from me as possible. Whether this was for his benefit or mine, I had no idea.

"So now you believe me," he said softly. His blue-gray eyes looked so sad, so haunted. He looked exhausted, vulnerable—nothing like the killing machine I'd just seen in action. "My God, Violet. I could feel your fear, your revulsion."

"Just . . . just tell me everything," I said, trying to make my voice steady and sure. "Who are you, really?"

"I'm Aidan Gray, just as I said. The fourth Viscount Brompton, or at least I would have been. Instead, I am this." He spread his arms wide. "A monster."

Gooseflesh rose on my skin, and I wrapped my arms around myself. Hadn't I thought exactly that, just moments ago? I pushed aside the prickle of guilt, willing him to continue.

"I was born into privilege in 1875," he said, his voice hard. "The son of a peer. I was schooled at Eton, and set to take a grand tour of the Continent before continuing my studies at Cambridge." He paused, watching me, as if he were gauging my reaction.

"I was seventeen then, arrogant and rebellious," he continued on. "Just days before I was to leave on my travels, I accompanied my parents to the opera. Though I didn't enjoy the music, I found I very much enjoyed watching one of the opera dancers, a beautiful girl with eyes the color of emeralds. Just like yours, Violet. Isabel intrigued me. I went backstage to meet her that very night.

"After that, I spent every spare moment with her, abandoning my travels. I even set her up in a small town house in Soho Square, where I spent most of my nights."

"But . . . but you were just seventeen," I muttered. His *nights*, he said. Which meant in bed, with her. The jealousy I felt surprised me, caught me off guard.

He shook his head. "Those were different times. I was considered a man at seventeen, and as a viscount's heir, I possessed a sizable income and a great deal of independence. Still, my father was not pleased. One night I went to the opera house as I always did, to accompany Isabel home. I waited outside the theater door, as was our custom, but she never appeared. I hurried to Soho Square, but all her things were gone. She left no note, nothing. For weeks I searched for her, my heart broken as only a young, besotted boy's can be. I hired a Bow Street Runner, and for several weeks heard nothing. Finally, I received word that she'd been seen in Whitechapel, working in some seedy public house.

"I went looking for her, and ended up in an alley somewhere, my valuables stripped away and my throat slit. It would seem a vampire stumbled upon me in that state, had a little snack, and then turned me, though I've no idea why. I was simply left there, unconscious, with no memory of what had happened to me. I went back to the town house, to recover from what I thought to be my injuries. Yet suddenly I had these unexplained . . . abilities. After that, I was quickly able to track down Isabel.

"Turns out my father demanded her dismissal from the opera, and threatened her if she continued our association. Still, I needed her, and she agreed to shelter me. Not wanting to return to the town house where my father would no doubt find us, we holed up in Whitechapel instead. Isabel said I would often disappear at night and come home in the morning disoriented, sometimes covered in blood. Though we could barely credit the notion, we both suspected what I had become.

"Soon after, there was unrest in the streets. A mob formed, claiming there was a monster in Whitechapel, out hunting at night. They had tracked me down, and they surrounded us, carrying torches and calling for my head. We tried to flee, to evade them. But"—his voice broke—"they got Isabel. I tried to save her; tried everything I could think of, but it was too late. Isabel was dead, and it was entirely my fault."

"It wasn't," I argued, but he ignored me, continuing on as if I hadn't spoken.

"Dr. Blackwell was in London then, the leading authority on preternatural folklore. It's a brilliant cover—cloaking it all in myth and legend. Anyway"—he waved one hand—"I went to him, told him my symptoms, and he confirmed what I'd already come to believe. I spent many years in seclusion after that, trying to come to terms with the impossible. Still, I inherited everything upon my father's death, thanks to the unbendable laws of primogeniture. They had no idea what I'd become, of course. God only knows I wished I was dead instead."

Again he paused, watching me intently.

"Go on," I urged, feeling oddly detached, as if we were sitting around a campfire, telling scary stories. It was all just so surreal.

"Those were my darkest years by far. Then, just before the Great War, I decided to fight this curse, to try and cure it. I traveled extensively throughout the Continent, learning everything I could about vampirism, trying to sort out the myths from the truth. I met others like myself. Now and then we would form loose alliances, stay together for a few years, but eventually we'd part ways. Most did not share my optimism that a cure could be found. I refused to give up.

"But things have become more complicated in the modern world. It's not always easy to get access to the kinds of biological agents and chemicals I need. When I heard about Winterhaven, learned that Blackwell was here, I set sail for New York on an ocean liner where several passengers fell inexplicably ill with anemia." He paused, smiling at his own joke.

"You didn't . . . kill them?"

He looked taken aback. "No, of course not. Is that what you thought—that a vampire's bite meant certain death?"

"Well, yeah, I guess." I shrugged. "Either that, or it turns them into a vampire."

Apparently that amused him, because he laughed. "No, it takes much more than that to make a vampire. And there's no reason for a vampire to kill his victim, unless he wants to. One can simply drink enough to slake the thirst. A little here, a little there."

All I could do was nod, willing him to continue.

"Anyway, I spend four years at Winterhaven every decade or so. Blackwell makes sure the faculty forgets me between my stints there. Occasionally I change my name."

"Because it . . . it wouldn't be okay to have a vampire there?" I stuttered.

"No, it wouldn't." He shook his head. "Vampires must remain entirely secret from the rest of the world, even the psychic world. It's part of our rules, our laws. So in between my time at Winterhaven, I travel, or stay in Manhattan. My work is ongoing, even now."

"And have you managed to develop a cure?" I asked. "I mean, is it really possible?"

His entire face lit up with hope, his features animated. "It's entirely possible, and I've come very close. Vampirism is nothing more than a sort of . . . parasitical infection, you might say. For now I can extend the period between feedings, subdue the cravings, lessen the symptoms. But it's not quite enough, not yet. It's only a temporary sort of cure, and not systemic."

Wait—something he'd said earlier finally registered in my brain. "You said Dr. Blackwell was in London, back when you were . . . you know, made what you are." God, I couldn't even say it. "How can that be?"

His eyes met mine, steady and direct. "Think about it, Violet."

"Oh my God!" The truth hit me. "He's . . . he's one too?"

"Yes. I hadn't meant to tell you, though I suppose there's no getting around it."

"But . . . but I've seen you—both of you—out in the daylight. How can that be if, you know . . ." I trailed off miserably.

"The elixir. With it I can withstand the sun without any negative effects. Once it begins to wear off, I'm forced to utilize Winterhaven's underground passageways during daylight hours. And I doubt you've seen Blackwell in the sunlight."

Actually, now that I thought about it, I hadn't.

"Anyway," he continued, "I need the elixir. Which is why I was so . . . discomposed . . . when you found me in my lab, all my work destroyed, all the vials I'd stored there gone."

"But you have some stored somewhere else, right?"

"Of course. I keep some here, and all my notes are backed up. Still, whoever destroyed the lab, their intention is clear. They want to stop me."

"But who would do such a thing?" I asked, almost afraid of the answer.

He raked a hand through his hair. "One of my kind, I suppose. There are those who wish to see my work stopped, who fear that, were a cure developed, it would be used against them. These are the most dangerous of our kind, the ones who feed from innocents, who enjoy taking lives. What I can't figure out is how they gained access to Winterhaven without me sensing their presence."

"So, what do you do now?"

"I go on with my work. I won't be cowed into submission. Blackwell will find out who did this, and they will be punished."

It all seemed so crazily rational, and yet it didn't change the fact that Aidan was a vampire. Fear still niggled at my mind. "So, where do you, you know . . . drink?"

"I feed here in the city, for the most part, though occasionally I venture farther afield. I only hunt those who hunt humans—criminals, murderers, rapists. Evil for evil. I like to think I'm personally responsible for the city's low violent-crime rate," he said wryly, but his eyes wouldn't meet mine. I said nothing, just waiting for him to continue.

"It's where the mind reading comes in handy—I go out seeking people who are looking for trouble. I can see into their souls when I'm feeding from them, you know. If I sense some good in them and their mind is malleable, I plant a warning—a threat—and let them live. But those whose souls are entirely black, I kill." His gaze finally met mine, as if he wanted to impress the point on me. "Let's just be clear on that point, Violet—I *am* a killer, a monster."

I took a deep breath, tapping my intuition, prodding it for

all it was worth. Was he a monster, or just a more complicated version of the guy I'd come to care about *way* too much?

I watched him closely, allowing my instincts to guide me as they always had. I could sense his indecision, his own struggle between self-loathing and acceptance. But try as I might, I couldn't quite see the monster he wanted me to see. All I saw was . . . Aidan.

I let out my breath in a rush, relieved at the strength of my certainty. Even though I'd seen him in action tonight, seen things that scared me senseless, I knew that, at his core, Aidan was *good*. He was the same Aidan he'd always been, and my feelings for him remained intact.

Gathering my courage, I rose from the chaise and slowly made my way across the room, drawn to him. "You're not a monster, Aidan."

"You saw me that night in the lab," he said, taking a step away from me. "I have no idea what I might have done had you not run from me. I haven't been that out of control in . . . well, in a very long time. I was upset, and you were bleeding profusely. Still, I can't excuse it—"

"Stop," I said, reaching for his hand. *Cold.* It was cold as ice, and that same frisson of electricity passed between us, as always. "We *do* have some sort of connection, don't we?"

"Probably one best ignored," he said, brushing my burning

cheek with the back of his hand. I knew I should be frightened, but I wasn't. I trusted him, maybe more than he trusted himself.

"Why?" I asked. "Why do you always draw me in and then push me away?"

His eyes widened slightly, as if he was surprised by the idea that he was doing that. Or maybe he was just surprised that I noticed. Either way, his grip tightened on my hand before he spoke, his words careful. "You've got to understand that whenever I'm with you, there's this battle raging in my mind. The selfish part of me wants you, wants you to accept me, to care about me. But the other part . . ." I saw him shudder, and he took a deep, rattling breath before continuing on. "The logical part of me wants to protect you from me, because how can I ever be sure I won't hurt you? Or that someone else won't? The last woman I truly cared about was killed. Because of *me*," he added, his voice catching. "I want to protect you, but I don't want to treat you like some fragile flower, because you're not. You're smart, Violet, and strong. I know that. Still, I have to remember that you're not like me. You're mortal, and that makes you vulnerable to things that I . . . I don't really want to consider." He closed his eyes, as if trying to block out unpleasant images.

I rose up on tiptoe and kissed his eyelids—one, then the

other. They were slightly damp, salty. "You've got all that going on in your head, *every* time you're with me?" I asked in amazement.

"Every time," he answered, his eyes fluttering open to meet mine. The fear I saw there, the terror, nearly took my breath away.

I swallowed the lump in my throat, wanting more than anything to take that fear away, but knowing I was helpless to do so. "Wow, that's taking teenage angst to a whole other level, isn't it, Aidan?" I teased, trying to lighten the mood. Because otherwise, I was going to cry.

"Your stepmother isn't expecting you," Aidan said. A statement, not a question. But he was right, she wasn't. "Stay here tonight. With me."

Any sane person would have said no, would have gotten the hell out of there as quickly as possible.

I said yes.

15 ~ Falling Stars

An hour later, I lay snuggled beneath a blanket, staring up at the night sky. Aidan had an entire garden up on his roof—potted trees, chaise longues covered with plush cushions. It was perfect. The night's horrors were forgotten as I lay there drowsily, struggling to keep my eyes open as I traced the constellation Orion with one finger.

"I don't want this night to end," I murmured, turning my head toward where he stood a few feet away, leaning against the door, watching me.

"We should go in," he said. "You're exhausted, and it's getting cold."

"Not yet. Hey, do you sleep at night?"

"Most of the time," he said, folding his arms across his chest. "In a bed, in case you're curious. Not a coffin or anything like that. I have no idea whose bright idea it was to propagate *that* particular myth."

"And other times? When you don't sleep?"

"I work on my research. Sometimes I feed."

I shuddered at the word "feed." It just sounded so . . . animalistic. Like he was some sort of beast, put out to pasture.

He must have noticed my reaction. "It's what I am, Violet. To accept me, you must accept that I'm a predator. A killer. I want you going into this with your eyes wide open. It's the only way I can justify it."

"What about that first night you took me to the chapel? You had a cut on your head, and you wouldn't tell me how you got it. Were you . . . you know?" I still couldn't say it.

"Yes, I had gone to feed. Things didn't go quite as planned."

Huh. I didn't dare ask what he meant by that. Instead, I sat forward on the chaise, taking in the view beyond the rooftops surrounding us. I could just make out the Metropolitan Museum of Art, off in the distance. "I still can't believe I almost got jumped," I said, shaking my head. "I mean, what are the chances of that? Statistically speaking, the city's pretty safe."

"Unless you go looking for it," he replied.

My gaze snapped over to his. "You think I went looking for it?"

He nodded. "You needed to see it—to see what I am—to truly believe it. Your intuition just helped you along, told you where to find me."

He was probably right, but I didn't really want to think about it too much, to examine it further. Not right now, at least. Right now, I just wanted to enjoy being there with him, sharing his secrets—even if those secrets did include some woman named Isabel.

"Was she very beautiful?" I asked, unable to curb my curiosity.

"Who?"

"What do you mean, who?" I asked. "You know exactly who I'm talking about."

For a while he said nothing. His face was in profile, turned toward the sky, and I could see pinpoints of light reflected in his eyes—stars, streetlights. I held my breath, waiting.

"I suppose she was," he said at last.

Of course she was. I just nodded, wishing I hadn't asked. What did it matter, anyway? She'd been dead for more than a century. Still, I was jealous. So jealous that I could taste it—a bitter, ugly taste in my mouth.

"Look, a falling star," he said, pointing to the inky canvas above. "Quick, make a wish."

So I did. *Please let Aidan find his cure.* I repeated it over and over silently in my mind. He had to figure it out. Otherwise, there was no hope for him, for us.

"It's late, Violet," he said, pushing off the door and moving to stand beside me. "You really should go to bed."

"Are you"—I swallowed hard—"are you going to bed too?" No one had mentioned the sleeping arrangements.

He nodded, reaching for my hand. "Trevors has made up the rose room for you. I'll just be next door."

Inexplicably disappointed, I pushed aside the blanket and rose from the chaise.

"Does that frighten you?" he asked, his brows drawn. "Having me next door?"

"I'm not afraid, Aidan." Well, maybe I was . . . a little. But not of him. No, I was more afraid of this unfamiliar, overwhelming desire I felt—this crazy rush of emotions, the way my skin flushed hotly when he looked at me. I wanted to wrap my arms around him and press my body tightly against his. I wanted to tempt him, to make him want me as badly as I wanted him, vampire or not. But apparently he was putting me in the "rose room," so my virtue was safe. Unlike Isabel's, all those years ago. Try as I might, I couldn't stop thinking about it, couldn't stop picturing him in some opera dancer's bed. What *was* an opera dancer, anyway?

Wordlessly I followed him back downstairs to the second floor and into a pretty, feminine room decorated with pale pink rosebuds and cream-colored lace. "Your bag's right over there," Aidan said, motioning toward my suddenly ratty-looking overnight bag. "And Trevors has filled a water pitcher for you there on the commode."

Commode? He was pointing to what looked like a nightstand to me.

"Thanks, Your Highness," I teased, trying to lighten the mood. He suddenly seemed so serious, so uncomfortable. "Or would it be Sir Aidan? What do they call viscounts in merry old England, anyway?"

His eyes met mine, the connection so strong that for a second there, I could barely breathe. "Lord Brompton, at your service," he said with a mock bow. And then he looked away, that troubled expression back again. "You've your own bathroom, right over there." He indicated a door behind me, half ajar. "And my room's just through here," he said, pointing to a door on the opposite side of the room. "If you should need me."

I *did* need him, and not on the other side of the door. I wanted him there, next to me. It's not like I wanted to . . . well, you know. I wasn't even sure that he could, being what he was. But still, I wanted him close by. Touching me. Holding me.

Summoning all the courage I could muster, I spoke the words in my head that I was too embarrassed to say aloud. *Please stay with me tonight.*

"Probably not such a good idea, Vi," he said aloud, his voice a hoarse whisper.

I tried to hide my disappointment, but it was no use. My cheeks were burning, and I couldn't meet his eyes.

"It's . . . I have my reasons. Trust me."

I shook my head, annoyed. I mean, he'd already told me the worst of it. Why keep things from me now?

"It's just . . . my God, Violet, I've been alive, what? A hundred and thirty years now? Trapped forever inside this boy's body, with a boy's raging hormones and a vampire's desires. I can't . . ."

He trailed off, and I saw him swallow hard. When he spoke again, his voice was more controlled. "It's so much easier at school, where I can send you off to your dorm room. But here in my house, alone . . . I had no idea it would be so difficult. I thought I would be more . . . mature."

I almost laughed at that, but somehow managed to squelch it. It was just so . . . *crazy*. "So you're saying, what? That you might be tempted to ravish me? Or bite me?"

He sighed, looking defeated. "I'm just saying that it's late, and that you're swaying on your feet you're so tired."

He was right—I could barely keep my eyes open. Still, I'd never felt so rejected in all my life.

"Sleep tight, Vi," he said, reaching for the door that led to his room.

"Yeah, you too," I muttered.

Fifteen minutes later my teeth were brushed, and I'd changed into my pajamas and collapsed onto the huge four-poster bed. The goose-down pillows were fluffed, the satiny sheets pulled up to my chin. The house was quiet, and I could hear Aidan pacing back and forth in his own room. Guess he couldn't sleep either. I sighed, snuggling lower beneath the covers, trying not to think about Isabel, trying not to picture him kissing her, touching her.

And then my vision began to tunnel. My stomach pitched; bile rose in my throat. Everything went dark.

There was a bed, one I had never seen before. It looked old-fashioned, like an antique. I couldn't place the room, didn't recognize my surroundings. My gaze shifted back to the bed, and I saw two people there, their bodies pressed close together. I heard a moan; could have sworn it was my own. And then I recognized myself on the bed, lying beneath someone, my skin pale as moonlight washed over me. "So beautiful," someone murmured, the voice familiar. Aidan's voice. And then it was as if I were seeing him from the vantage point of the bed, looking up into his face, his eyes red-rimmed and his jaw clenched as he stared down at me with pure, raw lust in his eyes.

I gasped loudly as the vision swam and disappeared. Blinking hard, I sat up, trying to catch my breath. *Whoa.* One minute I'd been trying to picture him in bed with his little opera dancer, and the next I was seeing something that looked like *us* in bed together instead. Doing . . . well, it was pretty obvious what we were doing. Or what we were *about* to do.

Thank God he couldn't see my visions—and since I hadn't felt any fear or called out his name while experiencing this one, he wouldn't even know I'd had it. I decided to test it, just to make sure.

Aidan? I called out telepathically.

There was the familiar tickling sensation in my brain. *Yeah, Vi?*

Nothing. Just . . . just seeing if you were asleep yet.

Not yet. You still mad at me?

Who said I was mad? Just because you didn't make Isabel sleep alone—

Goodnight, Violet, came his exasperated reply, cutting me off, and the connection was closed.

I had only been teasing him, especially now that I was armed with the knowledge that at some point in time I'd get my way. Problem was, my visions were usually warnings. Only this one hadn't seemed like a warning—in fact, it had seemed awfully pleasant.

I prodded my memory, trying to remember every detail. The bed. The moonlight. His eyes rimmed in red. A shiver raced down my spine. Just like they'd been in the chem lab on Halloween, when he'd been out of control and freaking out about the blood.

Uh-oh. Maybe I'd been mistaken; maybe the lust I'd seen in his eyes hadn't been desire, but bloodlust. Well, that certainly changed things, I realized. At least it should.

Only problem was, I was pretty sure it didn't. With a groan, I fell back onto the pillows and pulled the covers up over my head.

It was going to be a long night.

"Did you get any sleep last night?" I asked, perched beside Aidan on the sofa. A fire crackled in the hearth, and I turned my face toward its warmth.

"Yeah," Aidan answered absently, trailing his cold fingers down my shoulder. "A little. I heard you in there, tossing and turning."

"I just don't get it," I said, trying not to think about the vision that had kept me awake half the night. "Legend has it that vampires sleep during the day."

He nodded. "Vampires *are* essentially nocturnal creatures. Our senses are stronger, sharper at night. Staying up during daylight hours and sleeping at night is against our nature, but it's not impossible. Probably why I look so tired most of the time."

"What about eating? You know, food," I clarified, trying not to shudder as I thought about the alternative.

"Sure, I eat. Blood is our primary source of sustenance, but food is just"—he shrugged—"extra. Kind of like dessert is for you. You don't need to eat cake or pie to stay alive, but you eat it anyway, because you like it. I'm told the more ancient ones usually lose their taste for food and drink, but I'm still young, as far as vampires go."

"Hmmm, interesting. What about stuff like garlic and crucifixes?" As soon as I said it, I remembered Lupe's gift. The crucifix necklace. I'd been wearing it when I'd left school, and now—I reached up and felt my neck. It was gone.

"It's in your bag, Vi. It broke and fell off in the alley. Just needs a new clasp. Anyway, I'm fine with crosses and garlic. The chapel, remember?"

A log in the fire spit, sending up a spray of red-hot ash. I shivered and realized I was cold despite the fire.

"Want me to move over?" Aidan asked. "I can't help it; my body temperature's a little lower than yours."

"No," I said, scooting closer to him, wanting to prove to him that it didn't bother me. It didn't—not really. Kind of reminded me of Gran, who was always cold and complaining about poor circulation. "Now, let's see, what else? You said the elixir makes you able to withstand the sun. What if you found yourself without the elixir? At school, I mean? Then what?"

"I have special quarters at school, in the underground tunnels. It's really just a study with a daybed. My lair," he said, raising his brows menacingly. "Just in case. But the sunlight won't kill me—it won't burn me to a crisp or anything like that. At least, not for a while. Just makes me weak and vulnerable, that's all, especially if I haven't fed in a while."

"So why don't you take the elixir every day? To make sure the effects don't ever wear off?"

"The most I can take is a dose every two weeks," he answered, shaking his head. "I have to allow the effects to completely wear off before I can take more. Trust me, I've tried to take it more frequently, and let's just say it wasn't pretty."

I digested that in silence. "So what about the vampire who . . . you know, did this to you? Do you think it was Dr. Blackwell?"

Aidan shook his head. "No, he didn't turn me. That's impossible."

"How so? I mean, how many vampires are running around at any given time?"

"Far more than you realize," he said. "But only a female vampire can make a male, and vice versa."

"Really? I've never heard that one before. How . . . weird." And sort of unsettling, too, though I didn't quite know why. "So a female turned you, but you have no idea who, or why?"

"Pretty much," he muttered.

"So, how do they do it, then? I mean, I don't quite understand the mechanics of it."

"Do I really have to tell you every unpleasant detail?" he asked with a groan. "It's all so . . . ugly."

I wasn't buying that. Not entirely. I mean, I'd already seen his fangs, seen him nearly rip out someone's throat. What could be uglier than that? And yet I still found him beautiful, my Aidan.

"Is it somehow . . . sexual?" I pressed, swallowing hard. "You know, since a man can only do it to a woman and, like you said, vice versa?"

"Well, that would imply that all vampires are heterosexual, wouldn't it?" he said, and I was relieved to see a hint of a smile back on his lips. "I guess you could say it's somehow sexual, more so from the vampire's perspective. Though I'm told that some mortals find it enjoyable too."

Now my curiosity was piqued. "Okay, it's not fair to tease

me with something like that. Can't you elaborate just a tiny bit?"

For a moment he said nothing. I figured he was going to refuse to answer. The look on his face reminded me of Patsy's when she was forced to give me the sex talk years ago—that deer-in-the-headlights look.

"One of the more unpleasant side effects is that a vampire can't achieve . . . er . . . sexual release without simultaneous penetration of the fangs," he said at last, obviously choosing his words carefully.

Simultaneous penetration? It took a moment for that to sink in. "On . . . on the neck?" I stammered.

"It can be on the neck. Or . . . anywhere, really."

I could only stare wide-eyed at him, unable to believe what he was saying. Finally I found my voice. "So you have to be *biting* someone while you're . . ." I trailed off, unable to complete the bizarre thought, much less say it.

"Yeah, that pretty much sums it up."

"You have *got* to be kidding me" was all I could manage in reply.

He shook his head. "I wish I was."

"That's . . . I mean, in all the legends, I don't think I've ever heard that one. It's just so weird." Still, I was overcome with the desire to know more. "You wouldn't even be able to—"

"No," he interrupted. "I just wouldn't be able to fully . . .

enjoy it." He was blushing, I realized. Which didn't make a whole lot of sense, considering *he* was the experienced one, not me.

"Anyway," he continued, averting his eyes, "you can see how that complicates things with mortals."

"Yeah, I guess so." I nodded, feeling a little dazed by this revelation. Especially in light of the vision I'd just had. Time to change the subject. "Okay, you said it was sort of like an infection. Like a sexually transmitted disease, then?"

"No, it's much more complicated than that. It's an actual exchange of mitochondria, and then the infected mitochondria attack the host's cells. Almost like a parasite. The change occurs at the cellular level, though. Have you ever heard of adenosine triphosphate, ATP? Cellular energy?"

I shook my head, noticing that the science talk seemed to perk him right back up.

"Well," he continued, "in the case of vampirism, infected proteins synthesized in the cytoplasm are targeted to the mitochondrial surface by an N-terminal signal sequence. Then they're transported into the organelle by a large enzyme complex embedded in the mitochondrial membrane, and—"

"Hold on, science boy." I held up one hand. "You might as well be speaking Swahili."

He shook his head. "Just consider it a blood-borne disease

very much like malaria. And, like malaria, ultimately treatable and possibly curable."

"You're sure of that?"

"Pretty sure. Like I said, with the elixir I can temporarily suppress some of the effects. It's only a matter of time before I figure out how to reverse the process entirely."

"Say you do reverse it," I said, my brain spinning. "What then? Do you just become mortal again? I mean, would you just go back to being a healthy seventeen-year-old?"

He shrugged. "I don't know. It's possible that the mitochondria will be fully repaired to their original state. Beyond that, I can't say."

"So it's possible that, in curing yourself, you might"—I swallowed hard, barely able to say the words—"you might kill yourself?"

"Possible, yes. But I think the body will simply pick up where it left off. That's my hope, at least. Either way, it's better than *this.*"

I squeezed my eyes shut, blocking out the look of despair I saw in his eyes. "Please don't say that."

"I'm sorry, Violet, but I won't lie to you. Given the choice of an eternity damned to this fate of mine, or death—well, I'll take a mortal's death any day. Have you *any* idea just how long an eternity is?"

I buried my face in his neck. A shiver ran down my spine as he kissed the top of my head. "I'm sorry that you've suffered," I said, my voice muffled against his skin. I couldn't help but open my mouth ever so slightly, pressing the inside of my lower lip against the spot where his pulse leapt. "But I'm not sorry that it happened to you. Otherwise you'd have died a long time ago, and I never would have met you."

"Agreed on that point," he answered, his voice strangely tight.

"Do we really have to go back to school tomorrow?"

"We do. I've work to do in the lab, re-creating everything that was destroyed. I'm afraid you won't see much of me in the days to come. At least now you'll know why."

"I wish we could stay here forever. By the fire." Despite the faint chill in my bones, I'd never been more comfortable. In fact, the entire day had been pretty much perfect, even though we'd done nothing but lounge around and talk.

"Do you want to go out tonight? After dinner, I mean. I think Trevors is probably outdoing himself in the kitchen right now."

"He cooks, too?" I sat up quickly, wondering if he was joking.

"Oh, he cooks, all right. Loves the opportunity to show off. I asked him to prepare a meal fit for a queen, and I just bet he will."

"Is Trevors . . . you know," I said with a shrug. "Like you?"

"Yeah, he is. But you've got nothing to fear from him. He owes me a life debt, and he would never lay a hand on someone under my protection."

"So he's your servant for . . . for life? For eternity?" I wondered what Aidan had done for Trevors to earn that kind of loyalty. Must have been something big.

"Our arrangement works well for us both" was all he said in explanation. "Anyway, we could go out after dinner, if you'd like."

"Out where?"

"I don't know. A club. Webster Hall, maybe? Roseland?"

"Nah, if you don't mind, I'd rather stay in." I had to share him at school, but not here. Not now. I wanted to spend every possible moment with him—alone but for Trevors, who was so discreet that it was easy to forget his very existence.

Aidan nodded. "Whatever you want. Which train did you plan to take tomorrow? We'll need to make sure you're at the station on time."

"We're not going to go back together?" Disappointment shot through me.

"I don't think we should. You're supposed to be visiting your stepmother right now, remember?"

"Yeah. It's a good thing I never called her to tell her I was coming. But Dr. Blackwell will know the truth, won't he?"

"Yes, because I'll tell him."

"Why would you do that?" I asked.

He sighed. "Because he needs to know that you've learned the truth. I can't keep something like this from him, not after all he's done for me."

"The two of you are pretty tight, I guess?"

"I suppose you could say that. We've known each other a very long time, and he's given me the opportunity to pursue my research without interference."

"Can the two of you speak telepathically? Like we do?"

He nodded. "All vampires can communicate with one another telepathically, if they want to. But it's not really true telepathy, psychically speaking. It's more like . . . a vampire channel. Which is why it's so strange that it works between you and me. Have you ever tried it with anyone else?"

"Yeah, Suzanne Smith. She's on the fencing team with me, and she's a telepath, so we gave it a try once. Oh, and her friend, the tall redhead—I tried with her, too. Nothing," I said, shaking my head. "I don't get it."

He reached for my hand and turned it over, tracing the lines on my palm with one finger. "Me either. There's a lot about you and me I don't get."

"But you can read anyone's mind, right? Not just mine."

"Sure, anyone who doesn't block it. Any mortal, that is," he clarified.

"So, you just walk around all day, hearing everyone's thoughts?"

He lifted my hand to his mouth and kissed my knuckles. "No, it takes effort. It's almost like there's an on-off switch in my head. Otherwise, it would be sensory overload, all that noise. It's something I use sparingly."

"But what about other vampires? Can you read one another's thoughts?"

"No, a vampire can't breach another vampire's mind. It's kind of hard to explain, but mind reading and telepathy are two very different skills." The clock on the wall chimed the hour, and we both looked toward it. The day was slipping by far too quickly. "Anyway," he said, releasing my hand, "not to change the subject, but I've got to go out later, after you go to bed. I might be gone till dawn. I just . . . I thought you should know."

"Out to . . . you know . . . drink or whatever?" I mumbled.

He smiled sympathetically. "Yes, Violet. To feed. Before I go back to Winterhaven."

"But didn't you just . . . you know, with that junkie last night?" Would I ever be able to say the words? *Feed. Drink blood.*

"Yeah, but I have to get what I can, while I can. It's easier here. The more I feed, the longer I can go, and the less elixir I need. It's as simple as that. Anyway, I didn't want you to come looking for me and find me gone without an explanation. You'll be safe here with Trevors."

Great. So I would lie awake all night, imagining him out hunting murderers and rapists instead. Yeah, that was comforting.

Something else was bothering me too. I hated to give voice to it, but after what I'd seen in my vision the night before, it seemed kind of necessary to bring it up. "You've been alive more than a century, right?"

"I'm not sure I'd call it 'alive,' exactly, but yeah," he muttered. "Why?"

"Well, you know . . . isn't it kind of weird, being in school, surrounded by kids all the time? I mean, the age difference between us . . ." I trailed off, shrugging.

"No, that's another one of vampirism's cruel tricks," he said with a grimace. "You'd think that with immortality would come maturity, wisdom. Instead, you're basically stuck with whatever level of maturity you managed to reach as a mortal. More than a century of life experience, and I'm stuck forever with youth's impetuousness, with the mind of a boy." He shook his head. "Trust me, there's a marked difference between a vampire who was turned at seventeen and one who was turned at seventy. We don't just even out eventually, no matter how long we go on living. Seventeen—that's all I'll ever be. I guess I should consider myself lucky that I wasn't turned at ten instead."

I tried to imagine what it must be like to live all those years and not mature. It didn't make sense—I just couldn't wrap my mind around it. "It's good in *one* way," I offered teasingly. "I mean, I don't think I'd be all that into you if you acted a hundred and thirty."

"Sure, it's fine for now," he said, shaking his head. "But what happens in a few years when you've matured into an adult, and I'm still stuck in this damned eternal boyhood? Like Peter Pan."

He was right, and I was an idiot for being so flip about it. The impossibility of our situation—of any relationship between him and a mortal—became crystal clear. I would mature; he wouldn't. He would live forever; I would die one day. There was no reconciling it. God, no wonder he didn't have a lot of friends.

"Wendy grew up," he said, his voice hard. "And so will you."

16 ~ Truth and Consequence

"Hey, earth to Violet!" Sophie tapped on my desk and I looked up, startled. "That was the bell. Wow, you look like your mind's a million miles away. I hope you took notes for the quiz tomorrow."

"Quiz?" I asked a little dazedly. My mind kept drifting back to the weekend, trying to remember every little detail, every—

"Duh. Were you completely zoned out?" Sophie peered down at me with drawn brows. "Hey, are you okay?" She reached for my hand.

"Yeah, I'm fine." I snatched my hand away, then instantly regretted it. "I'm sorry, Soph. Here"—I reached out a hand to her—"go ahead and do your thing."

Sophie clasped my hand in hers and closed her eyes, her mouth pursed. "Hmmm. Well, your lymph nodes are a little enlarged, but that's about it." Dropping my hand, she opened her eyes and smiled at me. "I'd take it easy for the next couple of days, just to be sure."

"Believe me, I'd like to. But there's a big fencing tournament coming up, and I've got to practice." Already I was the varsity girls' top-ranked fencer, and I'd go into any tournament as the top seed.

"Well, you'll be happy to know that your shoulder felt fine. It hasn't been bothering you lately, has it?"

"Nope," I agreed. "You know, you really are amazing."

"Yeah, aren't we all?" Sophie sighed as she gathered up her backpack and slung it over one shoulder. "Too bad I can't actually heal, though. C'mon, or we'll be late for our next class."

After lunch I was called to Dr. Blackwell's office. I figured it had something to do with my weekend, and I was scared to death. I was about to get busted—and by a vampire, no less. I knew I was safe with Aidan, but Dr. Blackwell? Aidan trusted him, I reminded myself. He'd been the headmaster for years, and as far as I knew, he'd never hurt anyone.

Just as I arrived outside the headmaster's office, I saw Jack leave, a scowl on his face. He grunted a greeting to me as he passed me in the hall. I just waved, feeling terrible for him. According to Kate, he'd been caught using his telekinesis to manipulate a physics experiment—a pretty serious COPA violation.

Kate said he was probably going to get benched at this weekend's football game, and with playoffs coming up everyone was going to be pissed. Poor Jack. I imagined it must be difficult to possess the power to make things do what you wanted them to do, and not be able to use it when and how you wanted to. Unlike my useless so-called talent, which basically served no real purpose.

"Come in, Miss McKenna," Dr. Blackwell called out, and I hurried inside.

"Please have a seat," he said, his voice full of kindness as he gestured toward the chair across from his desk.

I shut the door and did as I was told, erecting the solid wall around my thoughts. I had to, now that I knew what he was capable of.

"I'm sure you know why I've summoned you," he began, leaning back in his chair with his hands folded in his lap. "A weekend pass is a privilege, and not one to be abused. I believe the purpose of your pass was to visit your stepmother, was it not?"

I swallowed hard before replying. "It was, sir. And I meant to visit her. I had every intention to, and then—"

"Mr. Gray told me what happened when you left the train station," he interrupted, his voice gentle. "I know you received quite a shock that night, and if you wish to discuss it, do not hesitate to do so."

"No, I . . . uh, I'm okay."

"Mr. Gray is certain of your discretion on the matter, and therefore I don't need to remind you . . . well, never mind. His assurance is all I require. Anyway, where were we? Oh, yes. The weekend pass. I'm afraid I'll have to give you a demerit, as using the pass for purposes other than those for which it was issued is strictly against the rules. I'm sure you understand."

"Yes, sir," I said miserably. I couldn't help but study his incisors. They looked pretty normal to me.

"Rule breaking aside, I must say how pleased I am to see you and Mr. Gray getting on so well. He works too hard, pushes himself . . . well, far more than is necessary. I'm happy he's found a friend at last."

Dr. Blackwell stared at me expectantly, obviously waiting for me to say something.

"I'm happy to be his friend," I said, wincing at just how lame it sounded.

"I'm glad to hear you say that. I realize there are certain complications with . . . well, with the situation as it stands. As it was, he was robbed of his youth, and in all these years he's never once recovered it. I guess what I'm trying to say, Miss McKenna, is that I hope you'll help him find that youth again. After all, despite a lengthy existence, he's still a teenager at heart—that's the way our condition works, you see. He spends far too many hours in the lab working on . . . well, I'm certain he's told you of his work. I'd like to see him out more, enjoying himself instead."

"But his work is really important to him," I mumbled, not quite sure what to say.

He waved one hand dismissively. "Yes, yes, of course. Still, he has all the time in the world for that, doesn't he?"

He doesn't think Aidan will ever find a cure. All I could do was nod mutely.

"Good, good. Well, I believe our business is concluded, then. I'll inform Mrs. Girard of your demerit. I'm sure it won't happen again, now, will it?"

"Definitely not," I said, relief washing over me as I stood and reached for my bag. I wanted to get out of this office, and fast.

"Excellent." Dr. Blackwell rose, smiling warmly at me. "I'll see you fifth period, then."

It was odd that the first vision I had after spending the weekend with Aidan didn't involve him or anyone at Winterhaven, but

Lupe. It happened just before I walked into fifth period, and luckily Aidan was able to catch me as I stumbled, helping me, to lean back against the wall until it passed.

It lasted only a few seconds—it was a quick one, as far as my visions went. I did everything Sandra had taught me too. Studied clues, looked for specifics. I was armed with everything I needed to prevent this one from coming true. Which was good, because I hadn't yet mastered summoning a particular vision, no matter how hard I tried.

As soon as sixth period let out, I hurried back to my room and quickly changed out of my sweaty fencing clothes. I had to do this—had to at least try. My cell phone clutched in one clammy hand, I sat on my bed and stared at the clock. 3:14. I'd wait one more minute, just to be safe. Gran played bridge at the club every Monday at 3:00 p.m. That meant Lupe would be home, and I needed to talk to her—alone.

Taking a deep breath, I hit the speed-dial button and connected the call. It rang three times before Lupe picked up.

"Hey, Lupe, it's Violet," I said, trying to keep my tone light.

"Violet! Is everything okay?"

I should have figured that my call would alarm her. After all, I always called on Sundays, right after dinner. I looked forward to that call every week, to that connection with home. But I never called during the week.

"Sure, everything's fine. I, uh, I just wanted to talk to you about something, that's all. Do you have a minute?"

"For you, *m'ija*? Of course."

"Well, it's just that I heard on the news that you're going to get some bad weather on Saturday," I improvised. "And . . . you know, the paper boy might miss the porch. And if you're not careful, you could . . . um . . . slip going down the stairs trying to get it. You could break your hip."

I'd seen it happen, exactly like that. And I was sure about the timing, because I'd managed to see the date on the paper.

"*M'ija,* are you saying that if I go out to get the paper on Saturday, I'm going to slip and break my hip?"

I let out my breath in a rush. How was I going to explain it? "I know it sounds crazy, Lupe, but just trust me on this. Forget the paper on Saturday. Just leave it, okay? Stay inside where it's dry and safe, that's all."

There was a moment of silence, though I could hear Lupe breathing, so I knew she was still there.

"I understand," she said at last.

But did she? "And I'd really rather you didn't tell Gran about this. It would just upset her."

"*Sí,* Violet," she said on a sigh. "Your mama, she was just like you, you know."

"Wha—what do you mean?" I stuttered. Was she . . . was she saying what I thought she was saying?

I could hear Lupe drumming her nails against the table, like she always did when she was thinking something over. "She had . . . intuition. Good instincts," she said at last. "Like you."

Tears burned behind my eyelids. I tried to picture my mother in my mind's eye, but the image was fuzzy, indistinct. I glanced over at the photograph I kept on my bedside table—my mom, my dad, and me. I couldn't have been more than two. That image of her—sitting beside my dad, smiling happily, me on her lap and her hair blowing behind her—was the only one I could see, no matter how hard I tried. I'd forgotten her, I realized. I had no solid, concrete memories of my mother, none whatsoever.

"Thank you, Lupe," I murmured, suddenly overwhelmed with emotion. "For telling me that about my mom. It . . . it really means a lot."

"Of course, *m'ija*," she replied. "Can I ask you one thing, though? One favor?"

I cleared my throat. "Of course. Anything."

"The necklace—the cross I sent you. Promise me that you'll wear it every day."

The clasp was still broken. I had to get it fixed, right away. "Of course. But . . . but why?"

"I had a dream," she answered, her voice nearly a whisper now; I had to press the phone against my ear to hear her. "A nightmare. Evil things, there at your school."

I shook my head. "I'm safe here, Lupe." The key rattled in the lock—Cece was home. "I've got to go. Just remember . . . Saturday."

"*Sí,* Violet. I'll remember. And *gracias*."

"'Bye," I murmured, then snapped the phone shut.

Mission accomplished.

17 ~ Down the Rabbit Hole

"Hey," Cece called out as I walked in and plopped down on my bed. "You look exhausted."

"You have *no* idea," I said with a groan. Fencing practice had lasted two full hours, and I hurt all over. "And I've still got to study for a trig test. I think this is going to be an all-nighter."

"That sucks. Want me to go get you some coffee?"

I sat up and smiled at my roommate. "Would you?"

"Sure! I'm too lazy to walk to the café, though, so the coffee from the lounge will have to do."

"Trust me, *any* coffee will do." I reached across to rub my sore shoulder—a dull, throbbing ache was radiating from the joint, all the way down to my elbow. "Man, it's killing me today."

She pursed her lips, her brow furrowed with worry. "You go take a hot shower, and I'll be right back."

"Thanks, Cee. I owe you big-time."

As soon as the door shut behind her, I stripped off my clothes and reached for my robe.

When I returned from the shower, Cece was back, two steaming Styrofoam cups beside her on the desk. "Here you go," she said, handing me one. "Hey, your cell phone was ringing when I came in."

"Thanks." I'd check it in a second; right now I needed my caffeine fix. Still wearing my robe, my hair wrapped up in a towel, I sat down on my bed with the cup clutched in one hand. Opening the lid, I blew on the dark liquid, then took a sip.

"Blech, this stuff is awful," Cece said, setting down her cup. "I thought I got hazelnut."

"I think it *is* hazelnut." I took another sip, trying not to grimace. "Or at least it's supposed to be. Anyway, how was your day? Better than mine, I hope."

"Okay, I guess. I'm thinking about joining the debate team."

"Debate team? Why?" She'd never mentioned any interest in debating before.

She bit her lip, eyeing me sharply. "Promise you won't laugh?"

"C'mon, give me some credit here," I said with a scowl. "You *did* just buy me a cup of this craptastic coffee, you know."

She smiled at that. "Because Todd's on the debate team, that's why. I don't know, I thought it might be fun for us to do something together."

"Todd?" I asked, trying to remember when I'd heard his name before. "As in Todd from the Halloween dance?"

She nodded. "That's the one."

"He's cute. But debate team? I mean, you've already got tennis, drama, student council." I ticked them off on my fingers. As it was, Cece barely had a minute to spare—she was always running from one extracurricular activity to the next.

"I guess." She shrugged, then took another sip of her coffee. "But I *am* getting sick of tennis. The coach is working us way too hard. You'd think this was the Olympic trials or something."

"Okay, you must *really* like him," I teased. "I mean, if you're considering quitting tennis for debate."

Her dark eyes twinkled with mischief. "Hey, he's smart, he's cute. He's even really sweet. It almost seems to good to be true, you know?"

"Yeah, I know exactly what you mean," I said with a nod. Boy, did I ever.

"I bet you do." She raised her eyebrows suggestively. "Considering the hot pocket that you run around with."

"Hot pocket?" I repeated with a laugh. "Where'd you get *that* one?"

"I don't know. Around," she said with a grin. "Hey, I almost forgot to ask, are you and Jenna Holley getting chummy or something?"

"Are you kidding?" I shook my head. "I don't even know her. What's her gift, anyway? I don't think anyone ever told me."

"She's got something unusual—I can't remember what it's called, but it's some sort of extrasensory thing. You know, like her sense of smell and hearing are heightened or something? Anyway, the weirdest thing happened while you were away this weekend. After you left Friday, we were all hanging out at the café. When I came back for curfew, Jenna was standing outside the door, and she was acting really weird. She asked where you were, and I told her you went into the city, so then she asked where Aidan was. As if *I* would know! Anyway, she was asking all these bizarre questions and, I swear, she seemed worried about you. I finally made her go away, but she told me to tell you to watch your back. At first I thought she said 'neck,' but that wouldn't make sense."

I choked on my coffee. *Watch my neck?* Did Jenna know Aidan's secret? No, she couldn't. Cece must have misheard her. "That's totally freaky," I finally managed, wiping my mouth with the back of one hand. "I don't think I've ever spoken to her. We don't have any classes together or anything."

Cece set her cup on the desk and stood up, smoothing down her sweatshirt. "Well, I always figured she was jealous of you, anyway. You know, about Aidan. Not that they've ever . . . you know. I mean, he's always ignored her like he ignores everyone else. But, I don't know . . . something about the way she looks at him. Hey, don't forget your phone. I think whoever it was left a message. It made that little chirping sound."

"Oh, yeah. Thanks." *Please, let it have been Aidan.* I flipped open my phone and held my breath as I dialed voice mail and punched in my code.

"Hey, Vi," came Aidan's voice, soothing my jangled nerves. "I just wanted to tell you that I've got to go away for a few days. I'll be thinking about you, okay? Sleep tight, love." And then a click.

"Aidan, huh?" Cece asked with a grin.

I just nodded as I flipped shut the phone, my skin warming all over. He'd called me "love." I liked that. *A lot.*

Five days later, I had another vision. It happened right by the fountain in the courtyard, while I was on my way to trig class. I'd run into Kate and we were walking together, talking about Jack and his suspension from the football team, when my vision started to tunnel and the dull humming began in my ears. I was barely aware of Kate calling out my name as I stumbled to my knees.

It was daytime, in Manhattan. I saw Patsy, dressed in a gray pin-striped suit and black wool coat, standing on the sidewalk under a burgundy canopy. Cars were rushing by, and Patsy held up one hand, as if she was hailing a cab. She pulled out her BlackBerry and slipped her headset over one ear. I forced myself to concentrate, to look for clues that might help me figure out when this was going to happen. There, in the corner of the BlackBerry's screen, I saw a date. Today's date.

A yellow cab pulled up. She shoved the BlackBerry back into her purse as she opened the door and got into the cab. She called out an address, but I couldn't make it out—Madison Avenue, maybe, but I couldn't be sure. The radio was on, some sort of smooth jazz playing as the car slid away from the curb and into traffic.

Patsy pulled out a file from her briefcase and started flipping through it, and I noticed a chip in her brownish-pink nail polish. It was just a small chip, barely noticeable, but— a car horn sounded, and then another. A screech of tires, and then the impact—hard, and I heard someone scream.

"Violet!" Kate cried, her voice pushing through the fog in my brain. "Violet, hey, come on!"

I opened my eyes, my breath coming in fast puffs as I

clawed at the stones behind me. "It's my stepmom," I said, my voice sounding far-off.

Kate reached for my arm, steadying me. "What happened? What did you see?"

"She was getting into a cab, and then . . . then there was a crash," I stuttered, barely able to catch my breath.

"Was she hurt?"

"I . . . I don't know. It ended right there, right with the crash. But it was today; I saw the date on her phone. Oh, God, I've got to warn her!"

"Come on, let's go."

Next thing I knew, I was running beside Kate, her blond hair fanning out behind her. We were headed back toward the dorms, and as we approached the building, the door swung open. We made our way up the stairs and down the corridors toward my room. Thank God that Kate was with me, because I'd dropped my bag back by the fountain and didn't even have my room key with me.

But as long as I was with Kate, that didn't matter. The door to my room burst open just as we reached it, and before I'd taken even one step toward my desk, my cell phone flew right across the room, into my shaking hands.

With fumbling fingers, I dialed Patsy's cell. Seconds later, it began to ring.

"Hello? Violet?"

She was outside; I could hear the sounds of cars whizzing by, of car horns and jumbled voices as people walked by. Thank God, there was still time!

"Pats—Mom?" I corrected myself. "Mom, listen, I know this sounds nuts, but don't get into the cab, okay?"

"What? I can barely hear you; I hate this headset."

"Listen to me!" I yelled. "Don't get in the cab. Take the subway or something."

"There's a cab. I'm sorry; I'm running late to a meeting. I'll call you tonight, okay?"

"No, don't get in the cab! Do you hear me?"

"You're breaking up, Violet. I'll call you later." *Click.*

"No!" I screamed, sinking down on my bed.

Kate's face paled. "What should we do?"

"There's nothing we *can* do." I threw the phone across the room, watching helplessly as it skittered across the floor and banged against the desk.

"I'm going to go tell Mrs. Girard what happened, okay? She can send word to your teachers." Kate rushed out, and I closed my eyes, hoping for another vision. I had to know what happened, damn it. Sandra had tried to teach me to summon a vision, to replay it so that I could look for details I'd missed the first time.

I closed my eyes, trying to concentrate, trying every trick that Sandra had taught me. *Nothing.*

I wanted Aidan. He was back at school; he'd come back the day before. I reached out to him telepathically, calling out his name in my mind.

Are you okay? Aidan's voice, inside my head.

It's Patsy!

Meet me at the chapel.

I snatched my cell phone off the floor, shoved it into my back pocket, and ran out without even closing the door behind me. I knew I was breaking a rule, taking my cell with me, but I didn't care. I ran the entire way to the chapel, my heart pounding.

As soon as I stepped inside, Aidan's arms were around me. "What happened?" he asked, his lips against my ear.

I started to cry again. "A vision. I saw Patsy get in a cab—today—and then there was a crash. I tried to warn her, but she couldn't hear, she wouldn't listen," I sobbed, my face pressed against his chest.

"And you're sure this is going to happen today?"

"Yes! Yes, it was exactly like I saw it happen. I even saw her take a call. It was me! Calling to warn her, but she wouldn't—"

"Shhh, calm down. Okay, how long ago did it happen?"

"I don't know. Maybe ten minutes?"

"Have you tried calling her back?"

I swallowed hard. "No. Do . . . do you think I should try?"

"Do you have your phone?"

"Yeah, right here." I pulled it from my back pocket, but my hands were shaking so badly that I dropped it. No way was I going to be able to dial.

As if he understood, Aidan picked up the phone and hit the redial button, then handed it back to me.

I held my breath as it began to ring. Once, twice, three times. On the fourth ring, she picked up. "Hello?"

"Mom!" I nearly screamed it, I was so relieved to hear her voice. "What happened? Are you okay?"

"Hey, can you hear me?"

"Yeah, I can hear you just fine."

"I was just in an accident, nothing major."

"I told you not to get into the cab. I had a vision; I knew something was going to happen, and—"

"Please, Violet," she said, then sighed loudly. "Don't start this again. Anyway, I'm fine. They're taking me to the hospital, just to check everything out. The driver . . . well, he's in pretty bad shape. Thank God I was wearing my seat belt."

"What hospital? Where are they taking you?"

"What? Oh, I don't even know, maybe Mount Sinai? Wait, no, the EMT is saying Lenox Hill. But listen, Violet, you do *not* need to leave school and come down here, okay? I'll call you after I leave the hospital. I have to go now. They're putting me in the ambulance, and I can't use the cell—"

I heard a click and she was gone. I let out my breath in a rush, and Aidan's arms went back around me, steadying me. "You okay?" he asked.

"Yeah," I lied. "Sounds like she's fine. She told me to stay here."

"Good. I imagine she's a tough lady."

"She's pretty tough," I agreed. "But what about next time? Why won't she listen to me?"

"Like I said before, some people don't want to believe in things they can't understand."

"I hate this stupid gift of mine. Hate it! What good is it?"

"I think time will tell, Violet."

"Yeah, right," I muttered, wiping my eyes. "Oh, great. I forgot all about Kate."

"What about her?"

"She went to tell Mrs. Girard what happened."

"You've got your phone. Call her and leave a message."

"Okay," I said, my hands still shaking. "I don't think I can go back to class, though. You think they'll understand if I skip?"

"Definitely," Aidan said. "I'll skip the rest of my classes, too. Blackwell will understand."

I called Kate and left a message while Aidan went to the café to get us something to drink. Fifteen minutes later, we sat side by side up in the chapel's dusty loft. Patsy had already called to tell me she'd been released from the hospital and was resting up at home, no worse for wear.

"I ran into Jack at the café," Aidan said, handing me my coffee. "I told him to tell Kate what happened. You know, if he sees her before she gets your message."

"Thanks." I wrapped my hands around the cup, warming them. "Actually, speaking of Jack, what does he think you're working on? You know, in the lab?"

"A blood-borne, parasitical disease, similar to malaria—which is pretty much the truth. He's probably managed to put two and two together by now, though he's never come right out and asked. He's got a brilliant scientific mind, though. The work he's doing, studying his brother's medical condition, is graduate-school-level work. He's a good guy. I trust him."

I nodded. Jack seemed like a good guy. Still, I hoped Aidan was right to trust him. "Speaking of his brother, what's the deal with the only-child thing here at Winterhaven?"

"Oh, I've got a theory about that," he said with a smile.

"Somehow I knew you would, Einstein," I murmured.

"I think it's an evolutionary mechanism of some sort. Similar to the Rh factor, some protein left behind that affects the mother's subsequent pregnancies. The only kids at Winterhaven who have brothers or sisters have half siblings through their father. In fact, in all the years I've been here, Jack is the first person I've ever known with a full-blood sibling. I have to think that's somehow related to his brother's condition. Maybe his seizures are caused by a circuit overload of psychic abilities. It kind of makes sense, and that's where Jack is focusing his research."

"Huh. Interesting. Okay, so tell me more about *your* research. You said your . . . condition . . . was sort of like malaria," I prompted. "How?"

"Well, I compare it to malaria because malaria is probably the best known parasitic disease, and certainly the most studied one," he said, suddenly sounding much more like a professor than a student. "Anyway, the more I learn about parasites and their crafty ways, the more I realize that genetic variation and natural selection can yield behaviors in single-celled organisms that look like pure malevolent genius.

"For instance, the malaria protozoan *Plasmodium falciparum* infects humans, causing the malarial symptoms that everyone knows about, but it affects the mosquitoes, too. For years people thought that the mosquitoes suffered no ill effects from infection by *Plasmodium falciparum*. They thought they just served as a handy way for the parasites to get from person to person. But it turns out the infected female mosquitoes *do* display one unusual behavior—they bite more often, seeking more blood than they need to nourish their developing eggs. This increased biting leads to a higher death rate for infected mosquitoes. You know why?"

"Why?" I played along.

"Because what happens when a mosquito bites you?"

I just shrugged.

"You smack it," he answered with a smile. "It's not a big stretch to say that this parasitic infection turns the mosquitoes into vampires of a sort. Just like malaria, vampirism is transmitted by a bite, and just like malaria, the vampirism parasite multiplies in the red blood cells, causing behavioral changes as well as physical symptoms. And this is pretty interesting too: You know how I said that it's the female mosquito that transmits malaria to humans? So in essence, it's the female becoming the 'monster'?"

He paused expectantly.

"Yeah?" I prodded, having no idea where he was going with this.

"Remember how I also said that only a female vampire can make a male? Well, from what I can tell, there's probably, oh, a hundred male vampires in the world for every one female. Maybe more. Fascinating, isn't it?"

"Really?" That *was* surprising, actually. "But still, there *are* some female vampires, right? So some male vampires must be able to . . . you know, transmit the parasite or whatever you call it."

"Any male can. It's just that they don't have the primal urge to do so, like the females do."

"Okay, that's just weird."

He laughed. "Trust me, you don't want to meet a female vampire."

"I don't want to meet *any* vampire," I shot back, before I realized what I was saying. After all, it was so easy to forget what Aidan was.

"I'm sorry," I said, reaching for his hand. Aidan remained silent, but I could see the hurt in his eyes.

"Don't be," he finally said, giving my hand a squeeze.

"But hey," I said, trying to lighten the mood, "I guess this means that I don't have to worry about you infecting me, right?"

"It takes more than a bite to infect a person. Much more."

"Like . . . what?" I prodded.

He shrugged. "It starts with the bite, but then the vampire must drink until the exact moment that the victim's heart stops beating. Then you begin replacing their blood with your own—your infected blood. You start off forcing it, but eventually they'll begin to drink."

"From . . . from the vampire?" I stuttered, my stomach roiling at the very thought.

"From the vampire," he conceded. "The vampire's infected blood reanimates the victim's body, so to speak. Like I said before, it occurs on the cellular level, and the body is kept in a state of suspended animation. Your body temperature drops, you don't age, your hair and nails don't grow. You become, in essence, immortal. Broken bones heal, damaged tissue regenerates."

"And the special powers?" I asked, morbidly fascinated.

He nodded "Yes, superhuman strength and agility, heightened senses, telekinetic powers. Actually, the vampire's powers are derived from the cellular energy that's created when fresh blood is converted to infected blood. That's why a vampire is stronger when he's just fed, and weaker the longer he goes without feeding."

"But what would happen if you just . . . you know, stopped feeding? Would that eventually kill you?"

He exhaled sharply. "No. Trust me, I've tried. At first you start to weaken, but then it's like some self-preservation autopilot kicks in. The thirst becomes unbearable, unstoppable. A vampire starving himself is dangerous and unpredictable, an indiscriminate killer."

I shook my head, trying to clear it of that image. "But back to the whole making-a-vampire thing. Anyone can do it?"

"Yes, but it's not easy. It takes a great deal of focus and control to ensure that you stop feeding at precisely the moment the heart stops beating. Otherwise, it's too late."

I *had* to ask. "Have you ever turned someone?"

"No, Violet," he said with a sigh. "I've never even had the urge to infect someone. The whole male/female thing, remember? Still, being a male doesn't diminish the bloodlust, so let's not get complacent about it, okay? I'm still a monster. If it weren't for the elixir—"

"I don't believe that," I said, shaking my head. "You're not a monster, Aidan."

"Are you so sure, Violet? Because, honestly, you have no idea what's going through my head at any given moment. I can hear the blood rushing through your veins, you know. My hearing is *that* good. And right now, it's rushing faster, which means your heart is beating faster. And you know why?"

All I could do was shake my head. He was right; my heart was racing like a rabbit's.

"Because you're frightened of me," he said, leaning in toward me. "Because that's nature's way of protecting you—making you fear me, telling you to get away, and fast. Because nature knows how much I would love a taste of your blood."

"You . . . you really want to drink my blood?" I stammered.

"More than you'll ever know." Those words were whispered against my neck, his breath warm against my skin. A shiver worked its way down my spine. I felt his lips, just below my ear, pressing lightly against my flushed skin.

I was supposed to be frightened. But there was no denying that I was totally turned on. I desperately wanted—no, needed—something that I couldn't even explain. My head fell back, and I'm pretty sure a moan escaped my lips.

More. I wanted more; didn't want him to stop.

Then I felt it—a hard pressure on my neck, the scrape of teeth. Instantly, my focus snapped back to attention and my entire body froze.

18 ~ Testing, Testing . . .

"Aidan!" I managed to yell, scrabbling to my feet in a panic. I knocked over my coffee in the process, the caramel-colored liquid splashing all over the place.

He didn't stand, didn't move but for clenching his hands into fists by his sides. His eyes looked cold, hard, and for a moment I considered getting the hell out of there, as fast as I could.

He took a deep breath, and I could see the struggle on his face, could see the vein in his temple throb, the muscle in his jaw flicker. Finally, he spoke. "I think I just proved my point."

"Your . . . your point?" I stuttered, barely able to breathe. "You almost bit me!"

His eyes met mine. "I wasn't going to bite you, Violet. But you sure as hell thought I was, didn't you?" His voice was suddenly cold, clipped.

"What, are you saying that you were . . . you were *testing* me?"

"Something like that." He nodded, his expression softening. "It's okay, Violet. You *should* be scared; I can't hold it against you. Anyway, I should go." He got to his feet and brushed off the coffee I'd spilled on his jeans.

I shook my head. "No, not like this."

He smiled then, a sad smile that almost made my heart break into a million little pieces. "Look, I shouldn't have scared you like that. You'd already had a bad day, and now this—"

"Don't go," I pleaded, hating myself for it. But I didn't want him to leave, didn't want him to think I was afraid of him.

But you were, my mind reasoned. *You were scared shitless for a second there.*

"I've got to prove . . . that, you know . . ." I trailed off miserably. The words just weren't coming.

"You don't have to prove anything to me. Honestly, I'd think you were a fool if you weren't frightened. My point is that we should be careful, that's all." He glanced down at his watch. "Anyway, you should probably go to dinner. Don't you have practice later?"

"Yeah, " I said with a sigh.

"Hey, come here." He pulled me into his embrace, and I went there gladly. "I'll meet you after practice and walk you back to the dorm, okay?"

I just nodded. My mind was going in a million directions, but somehow it kept coming back to the feel of his lips against my neck, to the fleeting sensation of his teeth against my skin. Sure, I'd been terrified, but I'd been excited, too. It was almost as if . . . as if I *wanted* him to bite me. It had felt like a craving—a physical craving—like lust, only stronger, more potent.

And the revelation that he'd only been testing me? That should have made me feel better. Instead, I felt disappointment, as if he'd somehow *rejected* me.

I zipped up my coat to my chin, shivering in the cold night air as I stepped out of the gym and looked around for Aidan. For weeks now, he'd met me each night after practice and walked me back to the dorm. Sometimes we'd linger outside, talking in the moonlight till curfew; other times, he was in a rush to get back to his work. I wondered which it would be tonight.

Glancing up at the crescent moon, I shoved my hands into my pockets. My fingers were turning into icicles, and my muscles, so limber after practice, were beginning to bunch up. The wind picked up, howling between the buildings, bending the branches of the bare trees that lined the walkway. Technically, there was still a week or so of autumn left, but it sure felt like winter to me. Other than the sound of the wind, the night was quiet. I imagined everyone else, tucked inside the cozy café or sitting beside the crackling fire in the East Hall lounge.

I'd give Aidan another couple of minutes, and then I'd start walking back alone. I knew he was working like a madman these last few days before winter break, trying to catch up on his work as best he could before he left for two weeks in Manhattan—two weeks that I'd insisted he spend at home, like everyone else.

I could barely wait—fourteen days in Manhattan, not twenty blocks away from Aidan, no classes, no chemistry labs, and no curfews. Well, that wasn't entirely true, I realized. I was sure Patsy would enforce some sort of curfew, but I'd have far more freedom there than I did here at school.

More than anything, I didn't want a replay of Thanksgiving break. Aidan had stayed at Winterhaven, and my friends had all gone off with their families. So I'd mostly sat around the apartment wishing I'd gone to Gran's instead. The days dragged by—when Patsy hadn't been *at* work, she'd be talking about work, and I'd been bored stiff. And that had only been a long weekend, not a two-week vacation. Thank God, Aidan had finally agreed to take the time off and keep me company.

But he wasn't meeting me tonight, I decided. I briefly considered calling out to him telepathically to make sure, but I didn't want to interrupt him if he was busy working. After all, his cure was as important to me as it was to him. It was important to *us*. Because, let's face it, without it, there *was* no "us."

I started off down the lighted walk, then decided to cut through the buildings instead. It was quicker, and anyway, if Aidan came looking for me, he'd find me, path or not. With a shrug, I ducked between the gym and the field house, a route much more direct than the meandering sidewalk.

"C'mon, you freak," I heard someone say, and I stopped dead in my tracks. Up ahead, just under a flickering light, I saw some guy—a football jock, no doubt—holding a much smaller guy in a headlock.

"If you want me to let you go, all you have to do is shift," the bully said. "You know you can do it, you little freak. Do it, and I won't kick the shit out of you."

"Asshole!" the smaller guy spat out.

Without even thinking about what I doing, I took off at a run toward the two. "Let him go!" I called out.

The jock turned toward me, his eyes glittering in the lamplight. Football team, all right. He was still wearing his practice jersey under his coat. "You talkin' to me?" he slurred.

"Yeah, I'm talking to you." I took two steps toward him, refusing to back down, even though my heart was pounding. "All those steroids messing with your head or something? You know what they say about 'roids? They shrink your equipment, if you know what I mean."

The guy in the headlock actually had the nerve to laugh—which, of course, only made his tormenter angrier. "Do I know you, bitch?" he asked, tightening his hold on his prey.

I saw what looked like a blur, and next thing I knew Aidan had appeared out of nowhere and was on the guy, pinning him to the ground.

I sucked in my breath. "Aidan, don't!"

As if in slow motion, he turned toward me. Holy crap, but his eyes were glowing red. Our eyes met and held, and after a second or two, the red glow drained away, replaced by the familiar blue-gray.

"Apologize to her!" Aidan demanded, still pinning the jock to the ground. "To them both."

The poor guy who had been the jock's plaything only moments ago now stood a few feet away, watching us. He'd seen those red eyes too. I was sure of it.

"I'm sorry," came the choked reply. At least the stupid jock had the good sense to sound terrified.

"Thanks for the saving, you two," the other guy said, "but I'm outta here." He turned and jogged away.

Aidan finally stood up, towering over the jock's trembling body. I wrinkled my nose, suddenly smelling something weird, something like . . . pee. Oh my God, the guy had pissed himself. The front of his jeans was dark and wet.

"You leave them alone, all of them," Aidan said, and I assumed he meant the shape-shifters. "And you even get *near* her, and I'll—"

"I won't, I swear," he blubbered.

"Get out of here." Aidan tipped his head toward the gym, and the jock stumbled to his feet and took off in that direction without a backward glance.

Aidan took my hand, cold as ice now, and we continued on. "Don't you have gloves?" he asked, rubbing my hand between his palms.

"I forgot them," I said with a shrug.

Neither of us said another word till the dorm came into sight.

"I'm sorry," he said at last, stopping and taking both my hands in his. "I'm usually in such control, but this . . ." He trailed off, shaking his head. "It's because of you." He looked down at me with darkly shadowed eyes. "I would have ripped open his neck."

"But you didn't," I said, my voice a little shaky.

He dropped my hands and raked his fingers through his hair. "This is getting dangerous, Violet. These . . . protective instincts, I've never had to deal with something like this. I don't even understand it."

"Maybe you should talk to Dr. Blackwell."

"Maybe," he agreed. "You should go in; you're freezing."

"Yeah, I guess. Hey, you're coming to the tournament Friday night, aren't you? This is the big one, the All-Ivy tournament."

His lips curved into a smile. "Of course. I wouldn't miss it for the world."

"You know Patsy's going to be there, right? She's going to want to meet you." I wasn't quite sure how I felt about that, but I figured I might as well get it over with.

"Of course," he said softly. "I'll try and leave the beast at home that night."

"That's not funny." My voice was sharp.

I'm sorry. As usual, when he spoke in my mind it felt more intimate, his voice a secret caress. *Forgive me?*

I wasn't sure if he meant for the self-deprecating comment, or for what had happened earlier. Either way, it didn't matter.

"Always," I said, rising up on tiptoe and pressing my lips against his.

His arms went around me, holding me tight, his kiss stealing away my breath. Finally, he pulled away, pressing his forehead against mine. Our breath mingled, and gooseflesh rose on my skin—but not from the cold.

"Good night, Violet," he said at last, stepping away from me.

"Good night," I replied with a sigh, closing my eyes. When I opened them, he was gone.

Twenty minutes later I had showered and changed into my pajamas and was just climbing into bed when my vision began to tunnel. I squeezed my eyes shut, but it was no use. The images came anyway.

It was the same as I'd seen before—dusk, the sky almost purple. This time I forced myself to glance around, looking for clues. Daffodils. I saw yellow daffodils in the fading light. We were somewhere on Winterhaven's grounds—I could see the administration building off in the distance. "Julius, now!" someone called out. A woman's voice, and I didn't recognize it. Everything was fuzzy, going in and out of focus, but I realized that my friends were there—some of them, at least. Marissa and Kate. But someone had them, was holding them. "Now, Sâbbat,*" someone said. A man, and he was speaking to me. Calling me by some other name. "Now, or your friends die."*

I shook my head, my vision blinded by tears. Aidan was there. I called out his name. They wanted me to hurt him, to kill him. I had something in my hand, something smooth, something sharp. "Do it, now!" someone screamed. Marissa. It was Marissa, urging me on. No!

Suddenly I was back in my dorm room, sitting half on the edge of the bed, clutching the sheets. "No!" I screamed it over and over again, and Cece came rushing into the room wearing nothing but a towel wrapped around herself. Her hair was dripping wet as she leaned over me, calling my name.

"Violet! Oh my God, what happened? Violet, talk to me!"

I looked around wildly, my vision slowly coming back into focus.

"No!" I whispered, my throat aching.

"Another vision?" Cece turned and reached for her robe, putting it on over her towel.

I just nodded, my breath coming so fast that I thought I might start to hyperventilate.

"Was it your mom again?"

"No. Aidan," was all I could say, my voice strangled.

"Does he . . . did you see him get hurt?"

"There were . . . I saw daffodils."

"Springtime," Cece said. "Do you want to call him?"

"He's at the lab, he won't have his cell."

"Do you want me to . . . you know. Go find him?" she offered. "I mean, project to him? I'm kind of tired, but I think I could do it."

She had no idea that I could talk to him anytime I wanted to, telepathically. I shook my head. "N-no. I can . . . it's okay. I'll . . . later." God, I was so messed up, I couldn't even string together a sentence. My hands were shaking and a bead of cold sweat dripped between my breasts.

Later. In New York. I'd talk to him when we were home, when I'd had time to think about it. Any minute, he'd speak to me; he'd know something happened, he always did when my visions terrified me like that. But I wouldn't talk it about now—I couldn't. Not till—

He was there. Outside my window. I had to get rid of Cece, and fast. I took a deep, steadying breath. "I'm fine now, Cee. Really. I just want to go to sleep."

"You sure? Do you want me to get Mrs. G.?"

"Definitely not. I'm sorry I dragged you out of the shower. Go on, you've still got conditioner in your hair. I swear I won't start screaming again." I tried to laugh, but it came out as more of a squeak.

For a second she stood there watching me, clutching her towel around herself. Then she nodded. "Okay, if you're sure. Oops, I'm dripping all over the floor."

"It's my fault; I'll wipe it up. Go, before you catch pneumonia."

She nodded and scurried out, and as soon as her footsteps disappeared down the hall, I turned the lock on the door. Hurrying to the window, I pulled aside the curtains and lifted it open, trying to be quiet, trying not to draw any attention to my room.

In a flash, Aidan was beside me. I'd known he was there, but still, the shock made me suck in my breath. My room was on the fifth floor. "What happened?" he asked, putting his arms around me. "I sensed your fear; you seemed terrified."

"Nothing. A vision. This is crazy, you're going to get caught." Still, I was so glad to see him.

"I'll be gone before Cece gets back, and no one will see me. Don't worry." I felt his lips on my hair, and my heart slowed to a near-normal rate.

"Do you know someone named Julius?" I asked.

"Julius?"

"Yeah. And there were two others with him, maybe more, because someone had Marissa and Kate. And this Julius guy, he called me by another name. Shabbit or Sabbit or something like that. It was definitely springtime; there were daffodils."

"Sâbbat?" he said, shaking his head.

"What does it mean?"

"I can't stay. Cece's on her way back." He was halfway out the window already. "But don't worry, Vi. You've got nothing to worry about. I'll explain it all later, over the holidays, okay?"

"Okay," I mumbled.

"Close the window. I'm unlocking the door for Cece."

Just as I pushed the window down, the door opened and Cece stepped inside. "Hey, whatcha doing?"

"I had to get some fresh air," I lied.

Later, I promise. I heard his voice in my head, and then it was gone.

"It's pretty cold out there." Cece shivered.

"I know, sorry. But I feel much better now."

"Good. You look better, actually. Less pale."

"Do I really get pale when I have a vision?"

"You have *no* idea. Scares the crap out of me every time."

"Oh, yeah?" I countered. "Well, you should see yourself when you're off traveling. You look like a corpse."

Cece laughed. "Hey, just be glad you don't have to room with a shifter!"

"Or Jenna Holley," I said, not wanting to talk about the shifters.

"Now *that* would be a nightmare." Cece started getting ready for bed, and I climbed into my own bed and pulled up the covers.

Later, he'd said. Over the holidays. Three more days of school, and then the tournament on Friday night—that was it. The weekend couldn't come fast enough. And in the meantime, I wasn't supposed to worry?

Yeah, right.

19 ~ Have a Holly, Jolly Christmas

"That was *so* embarrassing," I said, plopping down on the sofa in Aidan's living room with a sigh. It was Christmas Eve, and we'd just had dinner at a swanky French restaurant on East 65th with Patsy.

Aidan just shrugged. "I had a nice time. I like your stepmother."

"Yeah, she obviously likes you, too," I muttered. Considering how much more time she was spending with me now than she did over Thanksgiving, when Aidan *hadn't* been around. She still got all flustered and weird around him, though; she dropped her fork three times at dinner tonight. I'm pretty sure the waiter thought she was wasted.

"Hey, can I help it if I'm irresistible?" Aidan joked, and I just shook my head.

"Oh, pul-eeze," I said, rolling my eyes. "It's just the Aidan effect."

"The what?"

I kicked off my shoes with a sigh, tucking my feet beneath myself. "Never mind. We're all alone now. Are you going to tell me who this Julius dude is, or not?"

"Can't it wait?" he asked, sitting down beside me and drawing me close.

"Why are you putting it off? C'mon, you promised you'd explain it to me. So explain."

"I'm putting it off because it's Christmastime, Vi, and I'd like you to enjoy your holiday. That's why."

I shook my head. "Not a good enough reason. Try again."

"And because I'd like to do a bit more research first."

"Research? About what?"

"*Sâbbat,* that's what. What Julius called you."

"So what does it mean?"

"Let's start with Julius first. I guess you could call him an enemy, though I've no idea how he tracked me here. I haven't seen him in, oh, forty or fifty years? Maybe more. My sources place him in Paris these days. We were turned about the same time, and for a while we were on friendly terms. I later found that I didn't agree with his philosophies, and we parted ways."

"So, you're not friends. That doesn't make you enemies."

"Let me finish. I soon became known throughout our world for my work, my research. I made no secret of my goal—to cure vampirism. Julius, on the other hand, is what is known as a Propagator. From what I understand, he leads a sect of Propagators, now based in Paris. This makes us enemies, I suppose."

I wrinkled my brow, totally lost. "Propagator?"

"Julius's mission is to spread vampirism as far and wide as possible. He's one of the odd males with a desire to do so, and his sect is mostly made up of females. Very aggressive females."

I shuddered at the thought. "Why hasn't anyone tried to stop him?"

"Like I said, he surrounds himself with very powerful female vampires, for one. And his sect moves around, never settling in one place for long."

"Well, what difference does it make to him if you want to cure yourself? Why should he care if there's one less vampire in the world?"

"I can only assume that Julius fears that, were I to succeed and develop a cure, it could be used against him and his kind without their consent. Like a weapon, you might say."

"Great. So you're saying there's a dangerous vampire

coming after you, and he's probably bringing a bunch of even more dangerous vampire chicks with him?"

He shook his head and reached for my hand. "Your vision aside, there's no evidence to support that. Dr. Blackwell has extensive contacts among our kind, and he's heard nothing about Julius—"

"That's because it isn't springtime yet," I reminded him.

"I suppose it's possible," he said, looking skeptical. "Anyway, he won't get far without Blackwell knowing."

"I hope you're right." He had a lot more faith in Dr. Blackwell than I did. Then again, he'd known him longer than I had—a lot longer. "But my visions have never been wrong before. What makes you think that this time—"

"Because we know. We can be prepared, right?"

"I guess," I conceded.

"Hey, are you cold? I can have Trevors light the fire."

"Nah, I have to leave soon, anyway. So, go on, let's hear the rest of it."

"Okay. First, a question. Were you, by chance, born on a Saturday?"

"Yeah," I answered with a shrug, "I think. So what?"

"Most of it fits, then. You're *their* weapon." He said these last words so quietly that I was sure I must have heard him wrong.

My heart accelerated, and my palms started to sweat despite the cold. "What are you talking about?"

"A *Sâbbat*. Born on a Saturday. Comes from the word 'Sabbatarian.' It's an old legend, and fairly obscure. But, according to my sources, there are never more than three *Sâbbats* in the world at any given time, all females, all born on a Saturday. They're vampire hunters—slayers. Their weapon is a stake, usually made from the wood of the hawthorn tree."

I felt the hair on the nape of my neck rise. A *stake*? That sounded way too much like traditional vampire lore—garlic, crucifixes, stuff like that. Stuff that I'd since learned was completely made-up. "So the thing about a stake, that's true? Not just legend?"

"Oh, it's true to a degree, especially in the hands of a *Sâbbat*. You see, a *Sâbbat*'s powers are, in many ways, equal to a vampire's. They can breach a vampire's mind, read his thoughts. Some say one can even communicate with a vampire via telepathy."

He paused, watching me closely.

"And . . . no other mortals can?" I asked, even though I already knew the answer.

He squeezed my hand. "No, love. No other mortals can. "

For a minute there my vision began to swim as I digested the meaning of his words. It was crazy. *Crazy.* "So you're saying . . . what are you saying? That I'm one of these *Sâbbats*? That I'm supposed to be some kind of vampire killer?"

"Something like that. Possibly," he amended. "I'm not yet entirely convinced."

"But . . . but I can't read your mind," I stammered. "Or Dr. Blackwell's."

"Are you sure about that? Have you ever tried?"

I shook my head. "No. Why would I? I don't even know how."

"Well, I can teach you."

"You're not supposed to just go around reading other people's minds. It's against the COPA."

"Not if I teach you to read mine; I'd give you permission, which makes it okay. It's not any different from working with Sandra."

"I guess," I said, not completely convinced.

"I doubt you'd be able to read Blackwell's, regardless. Even amongst our kind, his mind skills are unparalleled. I'm sure he's figured out a way to protect his mind from any possible threat, *Sâbbat* included. But you should probably give it a try, to be sure. Just . . . don't tell him, okay?"

"Don't worry, I wasn't planning to." I wasn't going to take a chance like that, not with the headmaster. What if he could somehow sense it?

"Anyway, if it's true, if you are a *Sâbbat,* then you and I . . . well, we have a very unusual connection. Something never before encountered."

I shuddered, completely unnerved by the whole idea.

"Hey, you're not scared, are you?" He drew me closer, cradling me against his chest. "Because if it's true, then I'm the one who should be afraid. You know, of *you,*" he added, his tone teasing and light.

I pressed my face against his shirt, breathing in his scent. "That's not funny."

"Sorry," he said with a chuckle. "Still, you must at least appreciate the irony of the situation."

I sat up, shaking my head. "I don't buy it. I mean, what are the chances? Three girls at any given time—just three—and you think I'm one?"

"Clearly Julius thinks you are, though I've no idea how he would know such a thing. It would seem that he wants to use you to kill me."

"Well, why would he need me? Can't a vampire kill another vampire?"

"They can, but there are consequences for such an action. For all he knows, that would start a war against the Propagators. No, he'd much rather *you* do it. It's your purpose, after all."

"What does that mean?" I asked, my voice rising. "My purpose? Like, my purpose in life?'

"Something like that, I guess. It's hard to explain, but you know how I said that female vampires have this biological urge to spread the infection? Well, I think it's something like that for *Sâbbats*. An irresistible urge, coupled with the ability to take a vampire by surprise, catch them off guard. The stake, put precisely through the vampire's heart, temporarily immobilizes him, making him vulnerable. Giving the *Sâbbat* time to, well"—he winced—"permanently destroy him. Or her, of course."

Horror coiled in my belly, just imagining myself doing such a thing. My purpose was to kill vampires? *No way.* I couldn't even kill a spider, as much as I hated them. "I should go," I said, struggling to stand.

Aidan held me firmly. "Don't, Violet. Not yet. Not like this."

I sensed something in his voice, something vulnerable, and I relaxed against him, dropping my head onto his shoulder. "This is just too crazy. I mean, it's *all* crazy. Everything, since I came to Winterhaven. It's just been, like, one crazier thing after another. But this . . . this really takes the cake."

I felt his fingers stroking my hair. "Now you see why I wasn't anxious to tell you?"

"But how is it possible? You're saying we're, like, mortal enemies or something. Wouldn't we have . . . oh, I don't know, hated each other from the moment we met?"

"I don't know, Violet. Honestly, none of it makes much sense to me, either. But what I *do* know is that we should probably discover the full extent of your skills, and then hone them."

"Hone what?" I asked, my voice rising. "My vampire-hunting skills? Do you realize how totally insane that sounds?"

"To me it doesn't. You should know exactly what you're capable of. If nothing else, for your own protection. If what you've seen . . . well, if Julius comes for me—"

"Don't even say it. You told me not to worry about that. Besides, there's not a chance in hell that I would ever hurt you, so whatever I saw—"

"It's not just me that you're capable of hurting. Remember that. If you're capable of slaying me, then you're also capable of slaying them. And I'm willing to bet that Julius is counting on the fact that you have no idea what you're capable of."

"Why would he think that?"

"Because you're not of age. A *Sâbbat* doesn't reach maturity until eighteen; only then do they become aware of their purpose, their mission."

My head was beginning to pound. "But I'm *not* eighteen.

Are you saying I won't have any of these . . . slaying powers, or whatever you want to call them, yet?"

"No, just that under normal circumstances, you wouldn't become aware of them until your eighteenth birthday. But since you somehow got inside Julius's thoughts, because you heard him call you a *Sâbbat,* and because now you understand what that means . . . well, Julius tipped his hand. You weren't supposed to know, not until he forced you to slay *me.*"

It still didn't make sense. "Okay, but if I didn't know ahead of time that I was a *Sâbbat,* how did he expect me to be able to kill you?"

Aidan shrugged. "On-the-job training, I guess. It's not all that difficult, and I doubt he cares too much if you botch it a little. It's not like he expects me to be able to fight back. Wasn't he holding me captive in your vision?"

I just nodded, wishing I didn't have to remember.

"I may be smarter, but he's a lot bigger than me, and stronger, too. If it came down to brute strength between us, he'd win. But what's the saying? Forewarned is forearmed?"

"Yeah, that's great. Just great." I folded my arms across my chest, suddenly wishing I hadn't pushed him to tell me this stuff tonight.

"I'm sorry, Vi. But you wanted to know."

I let out my breath in a huff. "Did you ask Dr. Blackwell about any of this?"

"No, I . . ." he trailed off, shaking his head. "I decided to keep this just between us. For now, at least. Because . . . well, I've never told him that we can speak telepathically."

That took me entirely by surprise. "Really? Why not?"

"I don't know," he said with a shrug. "Except that I wanted to figure it out myself, this connection we share. And then once I got to know you . . . well, it just seemed like something personal, something between you and me."

I nodded, glad for his discretion.

"Anyway, there are still some things I don't understand. For one thing, I don't know how Julius knows you're a *Sâbbat*. And two . . ." He rubbed his chin, looking suddenly uncertain. "Two, I've found no recorded cases in our history of a vampire and a *Sâbbat*, well, being in any way friendly toward each other, much less—" he cut himself off abruptly, shaking his head.

What had he meant to say? Dating? Hanging out? Hooking up? What exactly *were* we doing together? We'd never put a label on it.

"Much less what?" I prodded.

His gaze met mine. "I was going to say 'in love.'"

I smiled, my pulse racing. *This is it—the declaration that I've hoped for.*

"I love you, Violet McKenna. God help me, but I do."

My heart triumphed, despite the torment in his voice. "I love you, too," I said, marveling at the pleasure I got from saying it out loud—and meaning it with every inch of my being.

"Then God help us both," he said quietly.

Not really the response I wanted, but I'd take it.

For a moment we both sat there in silence. The ticktock of the clock on the wall mirrored the sound of my heart. Knowing that he loved me made all of this *Sâbbat* stuff better—and yet somehow worse.

Finally he broke the silence. "Anyway, now that you know the truth, it's possible that your feelings toward me might begin to change. There's no precedent for it, but—"

"C'mon, Aidan, you don't really believe that, do you?"

He spoke slowly, deliberately. "I think it's important that we're both aware of the possibility."

An unpleasant thought flitted across my mind. "You think it's possible that your feelings for me might change too," I said, my voice barely above a whisper.

"No, Violet, I don't," he said, shaking his head.

I just nodded, my throat suddenly dry. Aidan bent his head toward me and pressed his lips against mine—a firm but gentle kiss, more reassuring even than his words.

Before I knew exactly what had happened, I was flipped

over onto my back, Aidan holding himself above me. A split second later his lips crushed mine, his mouth opening against my own. I heard him groan, a low, animal sound, as my tongue touched his.

My head was spinning, my heart pounding as I pulled him closer, wanting to feel his body against mine. I arched against him as he kissed me harder, deeper. His lips moved to my chin, my ear, my throat, his mouth hot and demanding. More than anything, I wanted to feel the firm pressure of his teeth against my skin, right where my pulse leapt. I craved it, a physical hunger that made no sense to me, that terrified me beyond belief.

I felt a rush of cool air and he was gone, on the other side of the room in the blink of an eye. I sat up, struggling to breathe.

"I can't," he said in a strangled voice, the faint red glow in his eyes fading away as I watched, stunned.

I rose on unsteady legs, wanting to go to him, wanting to wrap my arms around him and tell him that everything would be all right.

"Don't," he rasped. "Please. Just give me a minute."

I sank back to the sofa, my knees practically buckling beneath me.

"I'm so sorry, Aidan," I said, wishing I could erase the pain that was etched all over his face.

"You have nothing to be sorry for." His voice was tight, clipped.

What was going through his mind?

Remembering the powers I was supposed to have, I gathered my thoughts—focused them, directed them. And then it happened, like a dam opening and water rushing over me.

I would have killed her; I would have drained her entirely before I'd even known what I'd done. I'm a monster, a fucking monster—

A hot tear fell from my eye and rolled down my cheek. *Stop it, Aidan!* my mind cried out. *It isn't true.*

His gaze snapped to mine, his eyes round with surprise. "What did you just do, Violet?"

I licked my lips before I spoke, carefully choosing my words. "I . . . I think I just read your mind. I'm sorry," I said, my voice thick. I had no idea why I was apologizing, except that it had seemed like such an invasion of his privacy.

"No, I . . . it's okay. So you *can* do it, then. I guess that means it's true."

Some weird, triumphant feeling rushed through my veins. For the first time, Aidan and I were on equal ground. As much as I'd resisted the whole idea of being a *Sâbbat,* this felt somehow, I don't know . . . *empowering.*

I guess my breaching his mind had cured the vampire

version of a hard-on he'd been suffering from, because he suddenly looked like himself again. Raking a hand through his hair, he took a couple of steps toward me. "I should probably walk you home."

"Yeah, I guess it's about that time." I glanced at my watch. Twenty till twelve. Almost Christmas. "Hey, you're coming over tomorrow, aren't you? Patsy's expecting you for dinner." I'd explained Aidan's parents' deaths to her in a series of lies that filled me with guilt. But what choice did I have? She would have had me institutionalized if I'd told her the truth. So I made up a fatal car accident instead.

"Of course I am. But before you go, I have something for you." He went over to the big, carved writing desk against the wall and opened a drawer. I watched as he retrieved a flat, rectangular box wrapped in gold paper.

"I have another present for you, for tomorrow, but I'd like you to open this one now." He handed me the box, and I took it with trembling hands.

My nervous fingers fumbled with the wrapping paper. It finally slipped away, revealing a cream-colored jewelry box. My heart pounding, I opened the lid and peered inside.

Lying against the satin was the most beautiful necklace I'd ever seen—a series of teardrop-shaped diamonds and aquamarines set in what looked like platinum. It was clearly an antique, probably priceless, and I'd never seen anything like it in all my life.

"It's . . . it's beautiful," I murmured.

He smiled as he lifted it from the silk and undid the clasp. "It was my mother's," he said. "Aquamarines were her favorite. Here, turn around."

He put the necklace around my throat, and I lifted my hair as he clasped it.

"I can barely picture my mother without remembering this around her neck," he said, his voice heavy with emotion. "I had the clasp replaced, so it should be pretty sturdy now."

My eyes were suddenly damp. "But it was your mother's, Aidan. You can't just give it to me."

"Of course I can. There, turn around."

I did, raising my chin, trying to make my neck as long as a swan's.

"Perfect," he said. The look in his eyes took my breath away.

"Thank you," I said, knowing it wasn't enough, would never be enough. "Just seeing that around your neck makes this the best Christmas I've had in . . . oh, more than a century, I'd say."

"And they say we're mortal enemies," I joked.

"Funny, isn't it?"

But it wasn't funny, not really.

"Merry Christmas, Violet," he said, kissing me softly on the lips.

"Merry Christmas," I replied, feeling somehow sad and elated, all at once.

20 ~ Blindsided

"I don't want to do this," I said, shaking my head. "Enough, okay?"

Aidan scowled at me. "No, Violet. It's not okay. This is important."

I nervously ran my fingers down the smooth piece of wood I held in one hand—a makeshift stake, blunt on both ends. For practice. "We don't even know for sure if I'm a . . . you know, whatever it's called."

"Yes, we do," he insisted. "And it's *Sâbbat*. Get used to the word. Now, c'mon, concentrate. Right here." With a fist, he tapped his left pec. Which I couldn't help but notice looked nice and sculpted beneath the T-shirt he wore.

"Yeah, I got it," I said, rolling my eyes. "The stake, through the heart. You're out of your mind if you think I can do it."

"You *can* do it, Vi. It's not that different from fencing. Just think of the stake as a slightly thicker foil. You're already well-trained; this should be easy for you. You *did* win the All-Ivy title last month, after all."

I glared at him, my hand tightening on the wooden stick. This was *nothing* like that, and he knew it. "Yeah, just call me Buffy."

"Just tell me you're paying attention."

"I am. Is that all?"

His eyes were hard. "No, that's not all. Once that's done, you've got to separate the body from the head, and—"

"What?" I screeched. "You're kidding, right? Because there's no way in hell—"

"Listen to me, Vi. If I'm around, I can take care of it, but you need to be prepared to do it yourself. Separate the head and body, and then burn them both. It's the only way you can be sure—"

"What, that they're not going to . . . to come back to life? This is crazy, Aidan. Totally nuts."

"Maybe so, but I need assurances that you understand what I'm telling you."

I just stood there staring at him like he'd gone mad. Because he must have, if he thought I was going to "separate" someone's head from his body, vampire or not!

Aidan just glared at me from across the chapel's wide aisle, our so-called training ground. Christmas seemed so long ago, as if it had been months since we'd sat opening presents together in Patsy's living room. An antique copy of *Pride and Prejudice* for me—and by antique, I mean it probably came from his personal library back in England—and an iPod for him, since I'd never seen him with one. By unspoken agreement, we'd decided to keep the necklace he'd given me a secret.

In reality, it had only been two weeks since we'd returned to Winterhaven—two *very* long weeks in which Aidan had spent every spare moment trying to convince me to learn to use the stake. He'd finally won the battle, and here we were.

"Anyway," I muttered, "don't you think it's a little weird, *you* teaching someone how to kill a vampire? I mean, is this normal?"

He shrugged, and once again my attention was drawn to his pecs. Somehow I'd never realized how cut his chest was. *And if his chest is that sculpted, what about his stomach? Ripped abs, maybe?* I was suddenly overwhelmed with the desire to see him without that shirt.

"I have no idea what's normal," Aidan said, interrupting

my lustful thoughts. "I've never met a *Sâbbat* before, so I don't know how they usually get their training."

"Maybe you should take your shirt off," I offered. "It'll be easier for me to see where the stake goes." Yeah, that was a good excuse.

His scowl deepened. "My shirt stays on."

Amazing how he knew exactly what I was thinking without even reading my mind. When had I become so needy, anyway—so aggressive and clingy?

Since this morning. Cece had pulled me aside right after breakfast, just before first period. "I have to tell you something," she'd said with a frown, ducking into a little alcove. "I don't think it means anything, but I feel guilty keeping it from you."

I followed her into the quiet, windowed space. "What is it?"

"Last night, I was having trouble sleeping, so . . . I went for a little walk around campus. Astrally speaking," she added.

She glanced around furtively, then lowered her voice even though we were alone. "I saw Aidan. Right at the edge of the woods, over toward the river. *Way* after curfew. He was . . . with Jenna Holley. They were just talking," she put in quickly, seeing my eyes widen. "Actually, I think they might have been arguing. I thought about eavesdropping, but it's against the COPA. But if you want me to . . ." She'd trailed off.

I'd told her no, but the curiosity had been eating away at me all day.

"What's the deal with you and Jenna Holley?" I asked Aidan before I had the chance to think better of it.

I caught a flash of surprise in his eyes. "What do you mean, me and Jenna? There *is* no deal with us."

"Hey, I'm a *Sâbbat,* remember?" I threatened. "I can get inside your head if I want to." For a second there, I actually thought about doing it—without his permission. But it seemed so wrong, so sneaky. Like reading your boyfriend's e-mails or texts when he wasn't looking. I didn't want to be *that* kind of girlfriend, no matter how curious I was.

"If you're asking if I've ever hooked up with Jenna Holley, the answer is no. But go on, feel free to read my thoughts if you don't believe me."

"That's okay," I said, deciding to trust him. "But I'd watch out if I were you, because I think she wants you." It was the only other explanation I could come up with.

But he laughed at that. "I don't think so. Jenna and I . . . well, let's just say there's an uneasy truce between us. An understanding of sorts, end of discussion."

I folded my arms across my chest. "That's all you're going to tell me?"

"Jenna's secrets are not mine to tell," he said quietly.

"Great," I muttered. "Keep her secrets, then."

"Are you jealous?" he asked, sounding surprised.

Yeah, I was, and I hated it—I felt like a total bitch. "Maybe," I said, hedging. "Just a little. I mean, c'mon, have you looked at her? Who could compete with that?"

"You've no competition, Violet. Not ever," he added, with such assurance that I felt small and petty for doubting him.

I nodded, swallowing a lump in my throat.

"Let's get back to work," he said, tapping his chest again.

Which only drew my attention back to his pecs. There went my thoughts, right back into the gutter. "You know, there are much more interesting things we could be doing right now," I said.

He just stood his ground, completely unaffected. "Not today."

Immediately I thought of Isabel. There it was again, that ugly green-eyed monster. "I bet you never refused your little opera dancer."

"And she ended up dead for her pleasure," he reminded me. "Remember that."

"What, now you're going to get all protective of me? Ten minutes ago you were showing me how to *kill* you. Or do you prefer the word 'slay'?"

"Call it what you like, so long as you learn how to do it properly."

I took a deep breath, then exhaled slowly. "This sucks, you know that? Big-time."

"Yeah, I know. Now, come on, let's try it one more time. You've got to get the angle right, or you'll miss the heart." His voice softened. "How about this? A compromise—I'll reward you with a kiss if you get it right."

"Fine, then," I conceded. "Let's up the ante. Say I get it right *three* times. Then what do I get?"

"You sure like to live dangerously, don't you?" he asked, obviously following my train of thought. "I'm not sure whether I should applaud your bravery—"

I perked up at that.

"—or chastise you for your stupidity," he finished with a shake of his head. "You really are your father's daughter, aren't you?"

I advanced toward him, clutching the stake so tightly that my knuckles were white. "What is *that* supposed to mean?"

"If he'd listened to your warning, he'd still be alive, wouldn't he?"

The stake clattered to the ground, and I slapped him. *Hard.* "Fuck you!"

He didn't even flinch; he just continued to stare at me, his eyes shifting from blue to a stormy gray.

Tears flooded my own eyes, but I wouldn't give him the

satisfaction of seeing them fall. I retrieved my bag and headed for the door. "We're done. I'm going back to my room now."

As I pushed open the heavy double door, I heard him mutter, "Well, at least I get to keep my shirt on."

I fumed the whole way back to the dorm. Only when I stepped into my room—empty, thank God—and slammed the door shut did it occur to me that maybe he'd made me mad on purpose. Ever since Christmas Eve, when he'd almost bitten me, he'd been careful to keep his distance. His kisses had been brief, almost chaste, as if he feared what might happen if we lost our heads and started making out.

And while I respected that—the rational part of me really didn't want to get bitten—it was frustrating as hell. Maybe he was frustrated too. I hoped he was; it was only fair. Maybe that would explain the sniping, the short tempers.

Or, even worse, maybe it was just our natural instincts finally developing. We were supposed to be enemies, after all. Mortal enemies. "I'm supposed to rid the earth of your kind" enemies. I didn't want to believe it; it broke my heart to even consider it. But what he'd just said to me . . . he'd called me stupid, called my dad—

No. Oh, no. My vision started to tunnel, and I felt like I was falling into the abyss as I sank to my bed.

"Now, Sâbbat." *It was Julius. I recognized his voice from*

before. "Now, or your friends die." I looked behind me—a woman with long, dark hair held Kate in front of her. Beside her, a second woman held Marissa. Both of my friends looked terrified. I turned back toward the voice, saw Julius, saw Aidan beside him. Aidan's gaze locked with mine, and he nodded, a faint smile on his lips. "Do it, now!" Marissa screamed, her voice full of terror. Aidan spoke in my mind, his voice calm and soothing, "Do it, Violet. There's no other way. Go on, I taught you how . . ."

"No!" I screamed, burying my face in the quilt. I beat the bed with my fists, fighting against hysteria, my throat so tight I thought I might pass out. And then the tears came.

I must have lain there, sobbing on my bed, for nearly an hour. And the worst part? I kept waiting to hear Aidan's voice in my mind, comforting me; to feel his presence outside my window; to hear my cell phone ring . . . something, anything.

Instead there was nothing.

21 ~ Smoke and Mirrors

Kate came in and flopped down on Cece's bed. "Hey, why so glum?"

Sitting beside me, Sophie winced. "She and Aidan had a fight. Where's Cece?"

"She and Marissa have a study group for English," I answered, my voice dull. "And it wasn't a fight, not really."

"Yeah? So dish," Kate said.

"I'd rather not. It's kind of personal, you know?"

"Let me guess." Kate smiled knowingly. "He tried to get in your pants, and you weren't quite as easy as he hoped?"

I almost laughed, she was so far off the mark. As *if* things were as simple as that. "No," I said, choosing my words carefully. "He just . . . he said something about my dad that pissed me off, that's all."

"Your dad? But I thought . . . you know." She cleared her throat uncomfortably. "I thought your dad was dead."

"He is. And I really don't like talking about it, not even with Aidan."

"I get it," Kate said, nodding. But she didn't get it, not really.

Everything was so damn complicated, and I had so many secrets to keep, besides. Aidan's *and* my own. Everything my friends saw, everything they believed . . . it was all just smoke and mirrors. I felt the weight of the world on my shoulders, an unyielding pressure to make sure they saw only what they were supposed to see; believed only what they were supposed to believe.

Aidan was just a regular teenager with psychic powers, like the rest of them, and I was just his precog girlfriend. That was it, the whole truth, as far as they knew.

Forget parasitic infections; forget rogue sects of vampires and slayers born on a Saturday. Forget the fact that I'd foreseen my friends in the clutches of vampires who would kill them as sure as look at them, who expected me to shove a stake through Aidan's heart.

No, instead I had to fake normal teenage angst—or, at least, normal by Winterhaven standards. I had to pretend that Aidan and I were fighting over stupid stuff like him trying to get some ass, and me playing hard to get.

I took a deep, steadying breath. In through my nose, out through my mouth. "It wasn't much of a fight," I said at last. "I'll get over it."

"So, what do you guys do?" Sophie asked. "You and Aidan, I mean. You're always off somewhere together, but no one really knows what you're up to."

I shrugged. "I don't know, we just hang out and talk, mostly."

Kate lay back on the bed, propping herself up on one elbow. "Yeah, but about what? I mean, I don't mean this to sound bitchy, but do you even have anything in common?"

"What do you mean?" I asked, hedging. I mean, it's not like I could say, *Well, he's a vampire, and I'm a vampire slayer—there you have it.* "Like, our taste in music and movies and stuff like that?"

"Just . . . anything," Kate said with a shrug. "You two seem so . . . different."

"I guess we *are* pretty different, but you know what they say—opposites attract, and all that." I laughed uneasily. "It's not like you and Jack have all that much in common either, do you? I mean, he spends almost as much time in the lab as Aidan does."

"Touché," Kate said with a scowl. "Actually, I'm pretty sure that's where he is right now."

"But the two of you must do something other than sit around talking all the time," Sophie pressed. "You've been disappearing with him every single night lately."

I couldn't tell them about the training, so I needed to think up a lie, and fast. "He's been tutoring me again. I'm still a little behind in some of my classes, and—"

"Oh, give me a break!" Sophie waved one hand in dismissal. "I've seen your grades; you're doing great. If you don't want to tell us, fine, but at least you could come up with a better lie than that."

"We're not the virtue police, you know," Kate said, a wicked gleam in her eyes. "Apparently, that's Marissa's job. If the two of you are busy hooking up, it's not like we'd blame you."

I feigned an embarrassed smile and shrugged. "Maybe we are, and maybe we aren't," I said coyly. Let them think whatever they wanted; it was better than them knowing the truth. "Hey, you want to go to the café?"

"Sure," Kate said.

"Yeah, I guess," Sophie agreed, but I could hear the reluctance in her voice.

She's worried about me, I realized, feeling like a total jerk.

She knows there's more to the story, stuff I'm keeping from her.

But really, what choice did I have?

"Okay, try again," Aidan said, and I closed my eyes while he studied the photograph he held in his hand. We'd been doing this for nearly an hour now—he would look at the picture, and I was supposed to describe exactly what he saw. Apparently this was different from simply reading his mind—more visual. Whatever it was, I couldn't seem to get the hang of it.

I took a deep breath and attempted to focus, to see the picture through Aidan's eyes. But all I saw was a blur, muted colors swimming in and out of focus in my mind's eye. I concentrated harder. *Something green. Like a solid blanket of color, dotted with colorful little splotches.* But what was it?

"I don't know," I finally said, shaking my head. "A field of wildflowers, maybe?"

He sighed loudly, and I could hear his frustration. *Wrong again.*

"You're not focusing, Violet. C'mon, keep trying."

"I can't." I let out my breath in a rush. "Enough for today, okay?" Exhausted, I collapsed back against the blanket spread on the loft's dusty floor. The sun was just beginning to set, and candles lit the space, throwing flickering golden light about us. I'd just handed in a big research paper in English class that morning, one I'd been working on for weeks, and I was totally brain-dead.

"You're a slave driver," I said, glaring up at him. "How do you find time to work in the lab anymore?"

He sounded slightly annoyed when he answered. "I make time."

Which meant he didn't sleep.

Two days after our big "fight," we'd made up. Correction—Aidan had made up. He'd apologized profusely, nearly to the point of groveling—and I'd accepted. How could I not? He was so contrite, and let's face it, the guy hadn't had a real relationship in more than a century. I had to cut him a little slack. Besides, two days of total telepathic silence from him was about as much as I could take.

Ever since then, we'd spent every evening in the loft, training. He must have been working in the lab late into the night. The shadows under his eyes were the worst I'd ever seen them, and he seemed constantly irritated with me, as if I weren't trying hard enough.

"When are you going to admit that I'm not ready for this yet?" I snapped, knowing that as far as *Sâbbat* legend went, I hadn't come of age. I wasn't supposed to be able to do this stuff yet. Still, he insisted on trying to teach me, which only made me feel like a failure when I couldn't get it right. "Ten tries, and I got, what? Two right? I just can't do it."

"You *can* do it," he countered. "You can breach my mind and hear my thoughts. This isn't all that different. Which reminds me, did you ever try with Dr. Blackwell?"

"Yeah, in class the other day. Nothing." *More* failure.

He nodded. "I didn't really expect you to be able to. Like I said, he's a special case. It's too bad there aren't any other vampires around for you try it out on."

"Are you kidding me?" I asked, my voice rising. "Anyway, I should be in the gym right now, practicing. For the upcoming tournament. We're in the regional finals, you know." I had a title to defend.

His steely gaze softened. "I know, and I'm sorry, Vi. Maybe I *have* been pushing you too hard."

"You think?" I said acidly.

"It's just that spring's almost here, and we need to be prepared. Just in case. I can't take any chances with your life, not when—"

"According to my visions, it's *your* life we should be worried about," I snapped. "Yet you refuse to even talk to Dr. Blackwell about it—"

"I'm taking every precaution necessary, Violet." He reached up to pinch the bridge of his nose, and immediately I felt bad.

He looked exhausted. Paler than usual, his eyes the only bright spot of color in his face.

"I'm sorry, Aidan," I said, my voice breaking. "I'm tired, and I miss just hanging out with you. You know, staring at the stars, talking about whatever. All this training is killing me."

He reached for my hand, and I shivered when he laced his cold fingers with mine. An electric jolt went through my body at his touch—our connection. So it wasn't totally gone, not yet.

"You're right, it's too much. It's easy to forget that you're not . . . well, that you're a mortal, with a mortal's limitations."

He looked so sad, so lonely. I gave his hand a squeeze and scooted closer to him. "So, is it happening yet? You know, your feelings for me, changing?"

He smiled—a slow, bittersweet smile that made my breath hitch in my chest. "Do you want to check for yourself? Go on, read my thoughts," he offered.

"I'd rather you just told me."

A dark look flashed across his face, and then it was gone. He bent his head toward me, his lips just inches away from mine. "No, Violet. My feelings haven't changed. Do you wish they had?"

"Of course not," I whispered, my heart hammering against

my ribs. We stayed just like that—staring into each other's eyes, his mouth inches from mine—for several moments.

And then his mouth came down on mine—hard. I felt myself shudder, a ribbon of cold running down my spine. A fierce heat soon replaced the cold as he pressed me back against the blanket, his body held rigid above me while his lips crushed mine. I couldn't help myself—my hands were under his shirt before I thought better of it, exploring the taut muscles of his stomach, his chest. My fingers tingled as they skimmed over his cold skin, as if electric currents flowed between us.

Somehow I was pushing up the soft material of his shirt, wanting it off, wanting to remove the barriers between us. I felt him shudder, heard him say my name against my lips.

Next thing I knew, my wrists were manacled in his grip as he dragged me to a sitting position beside him. "You've got to stop that," he groaned, his face buried in my neck. "My God, I can barely control . . . I can hardly rein it in anymore."

Every reasonable part of my brain told me that I should shove him away; that his teeth were way too close to my neck. And yet . . . I didn't. I couldn't. My mind was spinning, trying to find a solution, something that would satisfy us both.

"What if I pricked my finger or something?" *Oh my God,*

what was I saying? I couldn't stop the crazy words from spilling from my mouth. "Would it help if you had just a taste, or—"

"I would suck you dry in a matter of minutes," he said, thrusting me aside. "Don't ever suggest something like that again, do you hear me? Just . . . just give me a second."

He was fighting against it, the bloodlust. By now I recognized the signs. The cords on his neck stood out, a vein in his temple throbbed. His jaw was clenched, his hands fisted by his sides.

Sadness filled me as I watched his struggle, knowing there was nothing I could do to help him; there would never be anything I could do to help him.

"Aidan, look at me," I said miserably. "Please, just look at me."

He did, and I sucked in my breath at the sight of his eyes glowing faintly red, his canine teeth just a little longer than usual. Would I ever get used to it, seeing him like this?

"I don't understand what's happening . . . this change," he said, sounding almost strangled. "The hunger . . . it's never before been associated with physical desire, not for me. And now, with you, the two are somehow intertwined. I don't want to hurt you. I swore I wouldn't."

"You won't hurt me, Aidan," I said, feeling less sure of it

than I sounded. It was a stupid thing to say, anyway, with the evidence to the contrary right before my eyes. I scrabbled away from him, wanting to make it easier on him.

He dropped his head into his hands. "I want to be rid of this," he said, his voice breaking. "A few more years and . . ." He trailed off, raising his gaze back to mine. I could have sworn his eyes were damp. I'd never seen him like this—weak and vulnerable. It nearly cleaved my heart in two.

"It gets worse as a vampire ages, you know," he continued. "More and more, they disconnect from the mortal self they used to be. You can tell by looking at their eyes. The paler, more washed-out they are, the older, more dangerous a vampire is. It will happen to me, sooner or later."

"But not for a while, right?" I ventured. After all, he was already pretty old, and I couldn't see any of what he described in his eyes. Time moved slowly in vampire years.

"Yes, but don't you see? The stakes are higher now. You've given me hope, when I had none. I cannot fail, not now."

I just swallowed hard, unsure of what to say, how to comfort him. It seemed best to keep my distance, and yet I wanted to hold him, to wrap him in my arms and tell him that everything would be okay. But it wouldn't—how could it? How could I make such a promise, knowing full well that if he didn't find his cure, he was doomed to this existence forever?

"What's going to happen to us?" I asked, my voice nearly a whisper. "I mean, how is this going to end? I don't want to lose you. I can't lose you."

He took a deep, ragged breath before he spoke, his eyes full of despair. "There are only two ways it can end, Violet. Either I find a cure, or you fulfill your destiny and destroy me. There's no other way."

"Then find a cure, Aidan," I said, my voice shaky. "And find it fast."

Practice was canceled. Three of my teammates were down with a stomach bug, and in the interest of keeping everyone else healthy, the coach decided it was probably better if we took the rest of the week off.

I glanced at my watch, wondering where Aidan was and what he was doing. He'd been pretty scarce the past couple of weeks, throwing himself back into his research, more determined than ever to find his cure.

I'll go to the lab and see how it's going. Once or twice I'd joined him there, but I mostly felt in the way. It wasn't like I was any help.

Still, I wanted to see him. Needed to. I knew what he was

doing was important, that he felt the time slipping away more keenly than I did. But it didn't change the fact that I missed him. I would stop by and say hi, that was all—I wouldn't disturb him if he was busy working.

I jogged to the lab, figuring I could use the exercise. A few minutes later, I pushed open the door and stepped inside, slightly breathless from taking the stairs two at a time. Aidan was there alone, slumped in a chair, a hypodermic needle lying on the black-topped table in front of him.

"What are you doing?" Wincing at the stitch in my side, I hurried over to where he sat, looking almost lifeless.

He shook his head, barely acknowledging my presence. "Nothing. Damn it, nothing."

I noticed then that one of his sleeves was rolled up to his shoulder, exposing one pale bicep. Reaching down, I ran the pads of my fingers over his smooth skin and across what was clearly a needle-puncture mark. "Is that what you do? Inject yourself with whatever you're working on? I thought the elixir was something you drank?"

"It is," he answered distractedly, "but the cure has to be injected intravenously. I really thought I had it this time. There don't seem to be any ill effects. Just . . . nothing."

My stomach knotted with fear. "Ill effects? What, you mean like a reaction or something?"

He finally swiveled his head around to look at me. "There's no other way to test the cure but to inject it in myself."

"But . . . but is that safe?" I stuttered, horrified by the idea of him using himself as a guinea pig. "There must be some other way to test it out."

He shook his head. "There's no other way. Anyway, what's the worst that could happen? Turn myself into some *other* kind of monster?"

"I wish you wouldn't say things like that," I snapped.

"Sorry, Vi." He reached for my hand and held it tightly in his. "Anyway, I'm usually pretty careful, and if there was any other way . . ." He trailed off, shaking his head. "But there isn't, and occasionally I have to pay the price."

"Is that why you disappear sometimes?" He'd been gone for two full days last week. Gone, with no word, no message. I'd assumed he'd been caught up in his work.

He nodded, releasing my hand to rub the reddened spot on his arm. "Some reactions are worse than others. Normally I wait till I'm in my room to inject it. But this time I was so sure . . ." He sighed, his shoulders sagging. "Anyway, I thought you had practice."

"I did. Canceled. How can you be sure it isn't working?" I glanced back down at the needle. "I mean, would you notice right away?"

"I take a blood sample." He tipped his head toward a microscope on the table beside us. There was a glass slide still sitting beneath the lens, a bright splotch of red on it. "I already checked."

"Oh," I said, feeling stupid. "Oh, well."

He said nothing in reply, just continued sitting there staring at the table. I'd never seen him look so down, so defeated.

"You'll get it right someday, Aidan. Soon," I added.

He rose from his seat. "You should go. I'm going to work on this a little more tonight, see if I can make a few changes in the formula and try again."

"I've got some homework to do, anyway," I said, even though I'd pretty much finished it all during study hour. He was clearly in no mood for company. "Promise me you'll get some sleep. Don't stay in here all night, okay?"

He shook his head. "I'm not making any promises. It's not like the lack of sleep is going to *kill* me."

I rolled my eyes in frustration. "You're impossible."

His gaze met mine, steady and insistent now. "Maybe, but now I've got more reason than ever to get this right."

Tears burned behind my eyelids. "I know. I want this as much as you do, Aidan."

"I'll see you tomorrow in class." He leaned toward me and kissed me on the forehead.

"Yeah, I guess so," I mumbled, hoping I could make it out the door before the tears began to fall.

22 ~ Cupid's Prank

It was Valentine's Day. In case you somehow managed to forget, there were red streamers and little cupid cutouts all over the dining hall—you know, subtle reminders. I shook my head in amazement. The holiday committee had really gone above and beyond the call of duty.

"What is that?" Kate asked, glancing down at my plate.

"Chicken salad," I said, pushing aside the half-eaten sandwich. "I think they put red food coloring in it." Instead of looking festive, it just looked gross. I'd taken two bites, but couldn't stomach the rest.

"That's disgusting," Kate said. "I think I'm going to hit the salad bar today."

"Yeah, me too." Cece traipsed off after her, leaving me, Sophie, and Marissa alone at the table.

"So, are you and Aidan going to the dance tonight?" Sophie asked.

"Yep." I opened a bag of chips. "For a little while, at least. Are you going with Jack's friend? What's his name, Ben?"

Sophie sighed. "Yeah, why not? It's not like anyone else asked me."

"You could have asked someone else," Marissa offered. "If there's someone you'd rather go with, that is."

"Does this mean you asked Dean to go with you?" Sophie launched back. Everyone knew that Marissa was crushing on Dean Wilson, a senior who was an empath, like her.

"Course not." Marissa reached for my bag of chips and helped herself. "I like to play hard to get."

"I'm going to get another Coke," I said, pushing back from the table.

"Hey, get me a Diet Coke, will you?" Marissa asked.

Nodding, I stood and headed toward the fountain drinks. I had to pass the table of so-called shifters, and I couldn't help but steal a peek at them, trying to see if I could recognize the guy who had been terrorized by the obnoxious jock back before Christmas break.

There he was, at the end of the table. Kind of small, with

a shock of blond hair that fell across his forehead. Our eyes met briefly before I looked away, my cheeks suddenly burning. He'd seen Aidan's eyes; he knew too much. I continued on toward the drinks, trying not to think about it.

"Hey, Violet, isn't it?"

I spun around, and the shifter guy was right there beside me. "Yeah, um, hi," I said, feeling like an idiot.

"I never got to thank you," he said, his brown eyes earnest. "You know, for that night."

"Hey, don't worry about it." I waved one hand dismissively. "It was no big deal."

"Yeah, it was, actually. No one here ever stands up for my kind. Besides, Scott was wasted and who knows what he might have done to both of us if your boyfriend hadn't shown up when he did. Anyway," he went on, "I'm Joshua. And if I can ever do anything for you—you know, return the favor somehow . . . well, I owe you one. You and Aidan."

"Thanks." I cleared my throat, wondering how much he'd seen that night. Just the eyes, or the fangs, too? "I mean, I really appreciate the offer, and I, uh, I'll tell Aidan."

"Cool. Later, then," he said with a nod. Again, our eyes met and held for a fraction of a second. There was something honest about his gaze—something reassuring. No matter what he'd seen, he wouldn't betray us. I don't know how I knew it, but I did. Joshua was a friend, an ally. I had come to his aid when no one else would, and now he would come to mine, if need be.

I took a deep breath before continuing on, feeling my friends' eyes on me the whole time. They were going to want to know what we'd talked about, and I'd have to come up with something plausible. I just hoped they weren't going to make any snide remarks about the shifters, because frankly I wasn't in the mood to listen to it. Maybe it was time to tell them how I really felt about their prejudices where the shifters were concerned.

Feeling emboldened, I got the drinks and headed back toward the table. Cece and Kate had returned and taken their seats, and everyone looked up at me expectantly as I settled back into my chair.

"So," Marissa drawled. I knew she'd be first. "What was that shifter freak saying to you?"

I felt myself flush as I handed Marissa her Diet Coke. "First of all, his name is Joshua," I bit out. "Second of all, I'd appreciate it if you didn't call him a freak. Or any of them, for that matter."

"Whoa, what's gotten into you?" Kate asked as she speared a cucumber slice.

"Nothing." I sighed heavily. "It's just that I don't really like the way y'all talk about them. The shifters, I mean. It's not like they did anything to you. Can't you just leave them be?"

"You have to admit, it's a little freaky," Sophie said. "I mean, c'mon, they're shape-shifters!"

"How is that any more freaky than what the rest of us can do? Where's your compassion?"

Marissa stared at me like I'd grown two heads or something, her catlike eyes narrowed to slits. "Is there something going on with you and this Joshua dude?"

"No, of course not. He's just a . . . a friend," I sputtered. "I barely even know him."

"Maybe he'd like to get to know *you*," Kate said, raising her brows suggestively. "Give Aidan some competition."

"Actually, that's not such a bad idea," Marissa said. "Keep Aidan on his toes, and all that. I just think you could do better than a shifter—"

"I'll see y'all later," I said, standing up abruptly and reaching for my tray.

Cece rose too. "Hey, I'll come with you."

I couldn't even meet her eyes. "No, that's okay. I've got . . . I'm meeting Aidan before fourth period."

I wasn't really meeting Aidan, but I had to get away from them—all of them. I'd spend some time in my room before my next class, banging things around till I felt better.

They were all staring at me as I stomped off, but I didn't care. It was Valentine's Day, my first Valentine's Day with a serious boyfriend—or any kind of boyfriend, for that matter. I wanted to enjoy it, to savor it, no matter how weird things were between Aidan and me at the moment.

For today, at least, we were going to act like normal teenagers, doing normal teenage stuff. Exchanging cards. Going to a dance. I'd bought a cute little lavender baby-doll dress over the holidays—one that looked great with black leggings and boots. After dinner I planned to take a long, hot shower, paint my nails, take my time with my makeup—all normal "getting ready for a date" stuff.

Hours later I was doing exactly as I'd planned, primping in front of the mirror. Cece was doing the same.

"Hey, I'm really sorry about what happened at lunch," she said, turning toward me with an eyelash curler clamped on one eye. "I don't really like it when they talk that way either. I've just never had the guts to say anything about it."

"It's okay," I said with a shrug, trying to decide between plum or brown eye shadow.

"I didn't even realize you knew any of them."

"Only Joshua, and just barely," I said, deciding to go with plum. "But I don't understand why everyone has to pick on them all the time. It's not like they can help it."

"No more than I can help the projecting. I don't get it either, not really. I guess . . . I don't know. There's always some group that gets picked on, though, isn't there? Geeks, dorks, Goths, whatever."

She was right, but that didn't make it okay. I'd never pick on a Goth, so why would I pick on a shape-shifter?

Fifteen minutes later everyone was gathered in our room, exclaiming over outfits and hairstyles, pretending like the scene at lunch had never happened. I was zipping up my boots when someone knocked on the door.

"Come in," Cece called out, and Kate helped her by opening up the door—from across the room, of course.

The room went entirely silent as we all looked up and saw Jenna Holley standing there, looking gorgeous, as usual. She must have been six feet tall, thin but not too skinny, with high cheekbones and bright blue eyes. Her hair was a mix of brown and gold—expensive highlights. Everything about Jenna looked expensive, even her clingy black halter dress.

"Hey, can I talk to you for a sec, Violet?" she said, as if we were friends or something.

As if perfectly synchronized, everyone's head swung around toward me, waiting for my reply.

"Uh, yeah, I guess." I finished zipping up my boot, and made my way over to the door.

I felt her gaze sweep from the top of my head down to my toes, as if she was appraising me. "Never mind. I just . . . here," she said, holding something out to me. "I'm supposed to give you this. From Aidan."

I let her drop whatever it was into my hand, and then she turned and walked away.

"Well, that was weird," someone said behind me, and then the door slammed shut on its own.

I don't know why, but I felt a little queasy, my heart beating too fast for comfort as I turned around to face them.

"Well, what is it?" Cece asked, coming to stand next to me.

Completely bewildered, I opened my fingers and stared down at what lay in my palm.

All the air left my lungs in a rush. It was a painting, a little miniature painting set in filigreed gold. An antique, I was sure of it. And the woman in the painting . . .

Oh. My. God.

It was me. At least, it looked just like me. Same light brown hair, same green eyes, same smile. Only she was wearing clothes like nothing I'd ever seen, not in this century, or the one before.

My heart skipped a beat as I turned it over, somehow knowing exactly what I'd find on the back. One word: *Isabel.* Written in old-fashioned black script. It was Isabel, Aidan's Isabel, and she looked just like *me*.

"What is it?" Cece asked again, taking it from me as I sank to the bed, too stunned to say a word.

"That's weird. It's like a painting of you, in costume or something." She turned it over, just as I had. "I wonder why it says 'Isabel'? Maybe she's the artist or something?"

Everyone else had gathered around her—Marissa, Kate, Sophie. They were all examining it, passing it around, almost as if they'd forgotten my presence there.

"But why would Aidan give it to Jenna to give to Violet?" Marissa asked, her voice loud above the din. "Why not give it to her himself?"

Finally Cece turned toward me. "Hey, are you okay? You look like you're going to puke or something!"

Bile rose in my mouth, and I swallowed it down, gagging as I did so. How could he keep something like this from me?

Because he doesn't care about you, my mind answered. *He never did. He's using you. Because you look like her.*

What other explanation was there?

"I don't feel very well," I mumbled.

"What's going on?" Sophie asked, reaching for my hand.

No! No, I didn't need her diagnosing me, not right now.

"I'll be okay. Just . . . go on, all of you. I'll catch up with you later, okay?"

"No, I'll stay with you," Cece said. "Sophie, can you tell Todd?"

"No. Please. I swear, I'm fine. I just . . . I need to be alone right now, okay?"

"No way," Cece said, meeting my gaze with her own determined one. "Go on, everyone. Out. We'll catch up with you later."

Mercifully, they obeyed.

As soon as the door shut behind them, Cece turned toward me. "What's going on, Violet? And don't lie to me, I know it has something to do with that picture."

I sat back down on the bed, wishing I could disappear, wishing that a vision would come—anything, to get me out of this.

I swallowed hard before I spoke. "Cece, you've got to trust me on this, okay? You're my best friend, and I feel awful about it, but there are some things about Aidan—about Aidan and me—that I can't tell you. Not because I don't want to," I said quickly, seeing her eyes darken, "but because I really, really can't. They're not . . . not my secrets to tell." Hadn't Aidan said something like that about Jenna?

"Has he done something to you? Has he hurt you or—"

"It's nothing like that, Cee. It's just private, that's all. I can't explain it, but this picture—well, I need to talk to him. Now."

"You're scaring me, Violet," Cece said, her bottom lip trembling. "After what happened with Allison—"

"This is nothing like that, and I promise you I'm not going anywhere, okay? Honestly, I don't know what I'd do without you." Cece was probably the best friend I'd ever had, and I couldn't even tell her half of what was going on in my life. It wasn't fair!

"What can I do?" she asked, sitting down beside me on the bed.

"Go on to the dance, and tell everyone I'm not feeling well. Tell them I've got cramps or something."

She put her arm around my shoulder and gave it a squeeze. "Okay. But later tonight I'm going to want some answers."

I just nodded, knowing full well that I could never give her the answers she wanted.

Cece stood up, straightening her dress. "And for the record, you're a much better roommate than Allison was."

"Thanks," I murmured, my heart swelling with affection. "You look great, by the way." It was the truth. Her slip dress was a deep shade of burgundy, perfect with her skin tone. She wore a little black shrug over it, and her hair was twisted into a knot on the back of her head. "Very sophisticated," I added.

"Yeah, well, Todd better appreciate it."

"You really like him," I said, suddenly realizing that I'd been so caught up in my own crazy love life that I'd barely realized what was going on in hers.

Cece just smiled. "Yeah, I do. And my parents aren't going to like it, not one bit. Because he's white, you know? They're old-fashioned that way. They'll say there are plenty of black guys here at Winterhaven, and . . . well, anyway, I better go. You sure you're okay?"

"I'm sure," I said, trying to sound more confident than I felt.

"Okay, then. Good luck!"

"Thanks, you too."

As soon as she left, I locked the door behind her, promising myself that I'd ask her later if she wanted to talk more about Todd and her parents. I had no idea she had that kind of conflict going on inside that head of hers.

But now . . . I had to deal with this. I picked up the miniature again and glanced at it one more time, hoping that maybe I'd been wrong, that I'd somehow exaggerated the resemblance in my mind.

But I hadn't. The girl in the painting was still my long-lost twin.

I need to see you, I called out in my mind. *Now.*

I'm in the East Hall lounge, came his reply.

I grabbed my key and left, the hateful thing still clutched in my sweaty hand.

As soon as I saw him standing there, my anger began to burn out of control. He looked so cool, so casual. I wanted him to know how pissed I was—I wasn't even bothering to block my thoughts. Anger, humiliation, rage—it all spilled out of me, and he just stood there, watching me, looking totally indifferent.

"Not here," he said at last. "Follow me."

For a full five minutes I trailed behind him, down several sets of stairs and unfamiliar corridors. He opened one door, then another. A light flickered on, and the door shut behind us as I looked around.

It was a tiny room with a desk in one corner, a computer on it, and a daybed against the wall. Opposite the bed were bookshelves, piled high to overflowing. There were no windows, no lights except one overhead fixture.

"This is your room?" I asked, shocked at how bare it was, how simple and cell-like.

"I keep a room in the dorms, too. But yeah, I mostly stay here when I'm not in class or the lab."

Something dug sharply into my palm, and I remembered the reason I'd followed him there. *The miniature.* I opened my fingers, revealing it. If he was surprised to see it, he did a good job of hiding it.

"When were you planning on telling me?" I asked, my voice shaking.

Aidan shrugged, but it was clear he knew exactly what

I was talking about. "Never, if I could get away with it," he said, and I wanted to slap him.

"Oh, yeah? Why's that?"

"Because I was afraid you'd react just like this, that's why," he said, his arms folded defiantly across his chest.

"How else am I supposed to react? Look at this thing!" I thrust the miniature at him. "In case you didn't notice, she looks just like me."

He met my eyes, his gaze unwavering. "There's a resemblance, yes."

"A resemblance?" My voice rose a full pitch. "That's what you call it? She looks *exactly* like me!"

"I think you're exaggerating. Besides, what difference does it make?"

"Are you kidding me?" I sputtered. "What am I, like her stand-in or something? Do you pretend that I'm her *all* the time, or just when we're making out?"

"I think you need to calm down, Violet," he said, reaching for my arm.

I twisted out of his grasp. "Well, at least you got my name right. I am *such* an idiot. I actually believed that you . . . you . . ." I shook my head, unable to say it.

"I *do* love you, Violet. I know you don't believe me, but my feelings for you have nothing to do with her. I admit, at first I was intrigued. Listen to me, Violet—once I got to know you, it was obvious that you were nothing like her. Nothing. She was selfish and shallow—"

"Oh, yeah, so much so that you moved in with her. I don't buy it, not for a minute. It's been nothing but lies since the day I met you, hasn't it? I don't know what game you're playing—"

"You really think that I'm . . . what? Using you? Pretending you're her? C'mon, Vi, you can't possibly believe that." He actually had the nerve to laugh.

"What else am I supposed to think? I mean, you somehow forgot to mention that I look just like your ex? I'm supposed to think it's just a coincidence?"

He looked away, toward the blank wall, the muscle in his jaw flexing. "Look, I don't even know what it means, okay? I've been reading everything I can about *Sâbbats,* and I've found nothing to explain it." He shook his head before continuing. "All I've got is theories, conjecture based on legend."

"Like what?" I prodded.

"Reincarnation. For some sort of . . . I don't know, retribution?"

I felt the blood drain from my face. I was suddenly cold, so cold. "So let me get this straight," I said, struggling to keep the hysteria from my voice. "Now you're saying I don't just look like her; I *am* her? And that's supposed to make me feel better?"

"It's just one theory." He paused. "I have another."

"Go on." After all, it couldn't be any worse than the first.

"The other possibility is that somehow a *Sâbbat* is born with the face of a . . . of someone who was important to a vampire in his mortal life. As a form of bait."

"What do you mean, a form of bait?" And then it dawned on me. "You mean, to draw the vampire in so that the *Sâbbat* can . . . can kill it?"

He nodded, his jaw tightening. "Exactly. But like I said, it's all pure conjecture. I'm just cobbling together—"

"Forget it, I don't want to talk about this anymore."

"So you're just going to storm out instead, convinced that I'm some kind of asshole who only cares about you because . . . because what? Because you look just like my ex, one who's been dead for more than a hundred years?"

"Yeah, something like that," I muttered. I mean, if he'd told me from the start, if he'd come clean—okay, I wouldn't have believed him. Or I would have thought he was crazy or something. And yet, he'd had months to tell me, and he'd decided to keep it from me—would *still* be keeping it from me if it wasn't for Jenna spilling the beans.

Read my thoughts, Violet, he said in my mind. *Read them, and you'll know I'm telling the truth.*

"I don't want to get inside your head anymore," I said, knowing it was cruel, trying to be cruel. "I'm through with this."

"With me, you mean," he said, his voice so calm, so cool that I wanted to scream. "Just like that, you no longer trust me?"

"Don't you see?" I cried, pain tearing through my heart. "How can I ever be sure? How can I know it's *me* you love, *me* you want, and not just the memory of . . . of *her*?" I couldn't even bear to say her name.

He let out his breath in a rush. "Because I'm telling you so, Violet. Because I've never lied to you."

"Oh, no. You don't lie to me. You just omit things, important things. And you don't seem to realize that that's just as bad."

He flexed his hands by his sides. "If I do, it's just to spare you, to—"

"That's not for you to decide! Don't you get that?"

"This is stupid," he said, his voice hard. "All you have to do is breach my mind, read my thoughts, and you'll know I'm telling the truth. Why are you being so stubborn?"

I eyed him sharply. "Can you look me in the eye and tell me honestly that you couldn't manipulate your thoughts somehow if you wanted to? That you couldn't make me see whatever you wanted me to see?"

He swallowed hard, and I could see the indecision flashing across his features. *He's trying to decide whether or not to lie to me.*

"I could manipulate my thoughts if I wanted to," he finally said with a nod. "But I wouldn't do that to you, Violet. You know I wouldn't."

"No, I *don't* know that!" I cried. "I . . . never mind. I'm leaving now. I need some space, some time to think. I have to figure out what I'm going to tell my friends. How am I going to explain this? They know it isn't me in the painting. How did Jenna get it, anyway?"

"I have no idea, but you better believe I'm going to find out. Just tell them I found it at an antique shop or something. I bought it because of the resemblance, that's all."

Actually, that wasn't so bad. Jenna would know I was lying, but I didn't give a damn.

And then I had a horrible thought—the vision I'd had, the one where I'd seen me and Aidan in bed together. The bed had seemed old, really old-fashioned. Maybe . . . maybe my visions were shifting. Maybe I wasn't flash-forwarding to the future, but flashing back to the past. Maybe the girl I'd seen under him in that bed hadn't been me, but Isabel.

I *had* to know. "Did you ever . . . you know, with Isabel, after you were turned?"

"What are you talking about?" he asked, though I could tell he knew exactly what I meant.

"Don't make me say it, Aidan. Did you or didn't you? Once you were turned."

"I am not having this conversation with you. Not now" was all he said, and that was answer enough. I swallowed hard, trying to push the images out of my mind.

"Fine," I bit out, meeting his gaze. For the first time, I didn't feel that connection, that physical jolt I always felt when our eyes met. Instead his looked cold, distant—a pale, washed-out gray, totally empty of emotion.

It was happening, I realized. Just as he had warned, just as I had feared. Our feelings for each other were ebbing, replaced by the distrust of two natural-born enemies—vampire and *Sâbbat*. I no longer trusted his feelings for me, and he was willing to let me walk away.

This is what we'd come to.

And the worst part? I couldn't even summon the energy to care.

23 ~ Friends and Enemies

I sat at my desk, staring at the window, where gray sheets of driving rain pelted the glass. I had a paper due the next day in history class, and I was supposed to be doing the final edits on it. It was Sunday, and Cece had gone to an afternoon movie with Todd. Kate was with Jack, and Marissa and Sophie were off somewhere, surely having more fun than I was.

I dropped my head into my hands. I'd been sitting here for nearly three hours, and my paper wasn't going to get any more polished than it already was. If it wasn't for the rain, I'd go to the gym and do some practicing, but I didn't feel like getting drenched, and besides, the damp weather made my shoulder ache like crazy.

So now that I was done with the paper, there was nothing to do—nobody to do anything with, unless I managed to track down Marissa and Sophie. Not an easy thing to do, considering our cell phones had to stay in our rooms.

Deciding to check my e-mail, I went online and found a message from Whitney—dated three days ago. Had it been that long since I'd checked my e-mail?

> *Hey, Violet! I know it's been ages since we've talked, but I had to tell you the good news—I auditioned for a summer dance program in New York City, and I got accepted! Four weeks, starting in June. I'll be living in the dorms, but I hope we can hang out some. Maybe I could spend a few days with you and Patsy before it starts? Let me know ASAP if you'll be around!*
>
> *Love, Whit*

I stared at the screen, a little stunned. Whitney, in New York? I wanted to see her—I really did. But what if she wanted to meet my new friends? It's not like I could introduce her to them—I mean, I *could,* but we'd all be hiding something from her, and that just didn't seem right.

I'd have to figure something out. She'd been my best friend

for ages—the only close friend I'd had, really, for so many years. I felt like a total jerk even considering blowing her off. Of course, Gran had invited me to spend the summer with her in Atlanta, anyway, so it might not even be an issue. I hadn't yet decided what I wanted to do, but I had no real reason to stay in New York.

My cell phone rang, startling me. I reached for it with shaking hands, glancing down at the caller ID.

Patsy.

"Hey, Mom!" I said, trying to hide the disappointment in my voice.

"Hey, there. Just calling to say hi. Are you busy?" Since when did she just call to say hi?

"Just working on a history paper." Which was the truth, more or less.

"Oh, yeah? How's school?"

I twisted a lock of hair around one finger as I spoke. "The same. I'm doing really well."

"Good. Are you still upset about Aidan? You sounded pretty down in your last e-mail. I just wanted to make sure you're okay."

I'd told her that Aidan and I had broken up. I have no idea why, except that I knew she'd ask about him, and I didn't want to talk about him. *At all.* "Yeah, I'm fine. I'll get over it."

"I know it seems like a big deal now, but there'll be other guys. Still . . . I don't know, over Christmas the two of you seemed so into each other. Are you sure you don't want to talk about it?"

"I'm sure. How's work? Are you finished with that big case?" I asked, changing the subject.

"Not quite." I heard a doorbell ring in the background. "Uh-oh, someone's at the door," Patsy said. "I've got to run, okay?"

"Sure."

I heard a click, and she was gone.

As I put away my phone, I looked up at the calendar above my desk. Only two weeks till spring break. I was really looking forward to getting away from here for a little while, going to Atlanta. After all, the weeks since Valentine's Day had dragged on, one day no different from the next. I got up, went to class, then came back to my room and studied. Each night I went to fencing practice, then came back and went to bed, where I slept a dreamless sleep, and awoke to start it all over again.

My friends flocked around me, creating a protective circle, trying their best to distract me from what seemed like nothing more than a bad breakup. Kate had gotten a karaoke machine for Christmas, and we spent a lot of time holed up in Cece's and my room, taking turns with the mic. I reveled in the normalcy of it. When we weren't belting out tunes, we were watching DVDs or hanging out in the café.

Just normal stuff. Well, normal if you ignored the fact that Kate could pass around the mic telekinetically, and Marissa could somehow predict which song would pop up next, even with the machine set to shuffle.

Still, I saw Aidan every day, twice a day. First-period history and fifth-period anthropology. He no longer sat next to me, but I was always painfully aware of his eyes watching me, studying me. Most days I half-expected to hear his voice in my head—asking for forgiveness, asking to meet me after class, chastising me for abandoning my so-called training. Something. Anything.

But it was complete and total radio silence. A little unnerving, really, but by the beginning of March, I was getting used to it. And even weirder, I didn't have a single vision in all those weeks. Not one. I couldn't explain it, except that maybe I'd somehow turned off a switch in my mind, that part of my brain that operated my sixth sense. I convinced myself it was for the best.

But I couldn't help the anxiety that crept into my heart as spring approached. I tried to push it aside, but it was there, niggling at a dark corner of my brain.

Just because I wasn't still having the vision didn't mean it wasn't going to happen, just as I'd seen it. Maybe I'd made a mistake in cutting Aidan out of my life, or maybe that was just my hormones talking. At some point, though, we were going to have to talk about it, to plan for what was to come. *If* it was to come.

It was all so confusing.

A knock sounded on the door, nearly making me jump out of my skin.

"Miss McKenna?" It was Mrs. Girard. "Are you in, *chérie*?"

I hurried to the door, my heart pounding. "Is something wrong?"

"Of course not," she said with a smile. "Dr. Blackwell would like to see you in his office, that's all."

"Am I in some kind of trouble?" As far as I knew, I hadn't broken any rules recently. In fact, I'd been a model student these past few weeks.

Mrs. Girard smiled a warm, grandmotherly smile. "Not at all, *chérie*. It's just a chat he wants, nothing more."

"Oh, okay. Um, do I need to bring anything?" A stupid question, but my mind was spinning. What did Dr. Blackwell want with me?

"Nothing but yourself. It's chilly in the corridors, though. You might want a sweater."

Five minutes later I was standing with Mrs. Girard just

outside Dr. Blackwell's closed door, wearing my favorite black hoodie and making sure the wall was up around my mind, protecting my thoughts.

"I'm sure he'll be right with you," she said. "I've got to scoot off to a meeting."

"No problem," I murmured, wiping my damp palms on my jeans.

Almost immediately the door swung open. "Come in, Miss McKenna," the headmaster called out, and nervously I obeyed. This felt wrong, all wrong.

I closed the door behind me and took my usual seat across from his desk, tucking my shaking hands under my thighs.

For a moment Dr. Blackwell just watched me, his lips curving into a smile. "I hope by now you know you have nothing to fear from me," he said at last. "My students are, first and foremost, my priority."

I could only nod.

He steepled his hands, resting his chin on his fingertips. "I will be frank with you, and tell you upfront that I asked to see you because I am worried about Mr. Gray."

"What do you mean?" I asked. What was wrong with Aidan?

"I mean, Miss McKenna, that Aidan is in serious danger. Mortal danger, as you have no doubt foreseen. You have the gift of precognition, do you not? He must put aside his work on the cure immediately. I cannot say this any more plainly."

"I can't make him do that," I said, shaking my head. "His research is important to him. There's no way he'll stop working on it."

"He will if you tell him to. And I'm asking you to do just that." He dropped his hands into his lap and leaned back in his chair, frowning now. "Let me put it this way—Aidan will never survive to see a cure. If you care about him, if you want to see him live, then you must convince him to abandon his work at once."

And then I felt it—something weird, something intrusive. Like tentacles from Dr. Blackwell's mind reaching out into mine. He was trying to use some form of mind control on me. Focusing as hard as I could, I pushed back. Immediately I felt his retreat.

So I had the power to resist it, then!

"Do you really think Julius will kill him if he doesn't stop?" I asked, testing the waters, wanting to see just how much he knew. Because that was all Aidan had told him—that I'd had a vision that indicated Julius was behind the destruction in the lab.

"Julius won't. He'll make sure that *you* do, Miss McKenna. I thought you realized that."

A lump formed in my throat, and I couldn't speak. I'm sure the color drained from my face. *He knows I'm a Sâbbat—and he knows what Julius is planning. But how?*

"You must do as I ask," he continued on, his voice insistent. "There is no other way. I hope I can count on you. Aidan is like a son to me, and I cannot bear the thought—" He broke off, tears dampening his silver eyes. Removing his glasses, he wiped his eyes with a handkerchief he'd pulled from his pocket. "You must excuse me for getting so emotional."

"No, that's . . . that's okay." I swallowed hard, wanting desperately to get out of that office.

"I wish it did not have to be this way. But what choice remains? Aidan must never know we've had this conversation. I know you've learned to guard your thoughts. He would never forgive my interference, you see."

Again, I just nodded.

"Very well. I won't keep you, then. I hope you'll carefully consider what I've said. After all, his very life depends on it."

I felt it again, the tentacles reaching toward my mind. I tried to resist, but it caught me off guard this time and I couldn't quite focus my energies. I found myself nodding. "I will," I said, almost involuntarily.

"Good, good," he said with a smile. "I knew I could count on you."

Shaking off the uneasy feeling, I let myself out of his office and hurried back to my room, relieved to find it empty.

He knew. I paced back and forth across the room, more terrified than ever now. Was he somehow involved in Julius's plot? I shook my head, confused. Maybe Dr. Blackwell had discovered the plot himself and was just trying to protect his protégé; maybe I was reading way more into it than I should.

I felt the pull toward Aidan, felt an inexplicable desire to follow Dr. Blackwell's orders, to go insist that Aidan abandon his work. But I knew that the headmaster was manipulating me—using some kind of mind control, trying to bend me to his will. *Resist it,* I told myself. I had to follow my own instincts; they were usually right.

Weren't they? Oh my God, I didn't know, wasn't sure anymore. What if I was wrong—what if Blackwell had been telling the truth, and trying to convince Aidan to give up his work was the only way to save him? Nothing had prepared me for a dilemma like this. I didn't know who to believe anymore, who to trust. I felt alone and scared and . . .

And I have to tell Aidan. The answer came to me, just like that. I stopped pacing, tried to slow my racing heart. It didn't matter how angry I was at Aidan, how hurt I felt about the whole Isabel thing. My instincts told me to trust him, and that was exactly what I was going to do. I was going to ignore Blackwell's threats, and tell Aidan everything.

I took a deep breath, forcing myself to focus. After all, it had been a while since I'd used the telepathy.

Aidan? I called out.

No answer.

I know you can hear me. This is important. Meet me at the chapel, okay? Now.

I ran through the driving rain, clutching my raincoat around me. Twice my hood fell back, and twice I tugged it back into place, pushing wet hair from my eyes as I did so. I silently cursed myself for leaving my umbrella in my room. *Stupid.*

Breathless, I pulled open the chapel's heavy door and raced inside, hurrying down the aisle toward the altar. In minutes I was climbing up the stairs at the back of the chapel, dripping rainwater in my wake.

At last I reached the loft, dimly lit by several sputtering candles. Aidan's back was to me; he was just standing there, staring at the wall. His arms were folded and the same striped scarf he'd worn my first day at Winterhaven was draped around his neck.

"What happened?" he asked, his back still toward me.

"Blackwell," I answered, still trying to catch my breath.

He turned to face me, his arms still folded across his chest. "What about him?"

I spoke quickly. "He knows that I'm a *Sâbbat*. He knows about the plot—everything. I think he's . . . he's somehow involved."

Aidan shook his head. "Impossible."

"Just listen," I said, trying to catch my breath. "He called me to his office just now and told me that you'd never live to see a cure, that I had to convince you to stop your work. He was trying to control my mind; I felt it."

Aidan just stood there, his eyes narrowed. He didn't say a word in reply.

"You don't believe me?" I asked, my voice rising in surprise.

"I think you must have misunderstood, Violet." His voice was cold, clipped.

"I know what I heard, Aidan," I snapped. "And that's not all. He told me not to tell you about our conversation. Gave me some story about how you wouldn't like him interfering, but I don't believe it."

Again Aidan said nothing. He just continued to stare at me like I'd lost my mind.

"I swear I'm telling you the truth. I've never lied to *you*, after all." I had to get that dig in.

"You're implying, of course, that *I've* lied to *you*," he answered.

"Do we have to have this argument again? Lied, withheld information, whatever you want to call it, it's not important now." A shiver worked its way down my spine, and I realized I was scared. Terrified. All this time I'd thought Dr. Blackwell was protecting Aidan, keeping him safe. What if he was really leading him into some sort of trap? And what if I was a part of that trap?

Aidan ran a hand through his hair. "This doesn't make any sense. Blackwell's never been anything but supportive of my work. Why would he turn on me now, after all this time?"

"I don't know," I said, shaking my head. "Maybe I'm wrong. I hope I'm wrong."

"But you're never wrong, are you?"

I took a tentative step toward him. "So . . . what do we do?"

"Honestly, I don't know," he said, sounding exhausted. Defeated. "This is uncharted territory, even for me."

"I could try to coax another vision," I suggested. "You know, see if I can find out anything about Blackwell's involvement. Sandra's been trying to teach me how, though I haven't quite gotten the hang of it yet."

"That's a good idea," he said, looking hopeful. "Is there anything in particular that seems to bring them on?"

I searched my memory. "A lot of the time I'm thinking about you when I have one. But when it was Patsy, that time before her crash? I think it was because it was just about to happen."

The corners of his mouth twitched with a smile. "So, you're usually thinking about me when it happens, huh? Don't know if I should be flattered by that or offended."

"Probably both," I said.

"So"—he cleared his throat—"what kind of mental state would you say you're in at the time? Because you probably need to be able to get yourself there if you want to bring on a vision."

I shrugged. "I don't know. Confused, upset? That's usually how I'm feeling when I'm thinking about you."

His eyes narrowed a fraction. "That's just great, Violet. Thanks."

"I didn't mean it like that." I reached for his hand, taking it in my own. "But you know what's weird? I haven't had a single vision since . . . well, since we broke up."

"Broke up? Is that what you call it?"

"I'm just saying that they stopped when we stopped hanging out," I clarified.

He gave my hand a little squeeze before dropping it. "So you're saying maybe I'm some kind of trigger for you?"

"I don't know. Maybe." I shivered, wrapping my arms around myself.

"You're cold," he said, reaching for my raincoat. "Take this off; it's soaking wet." He helped me out of it and tossed it to the ground, then removed his scarf and pulled his dark gray sweater over his head.

"Here," he said, holding the sweater out to me. "Put it on."

My fingers trembling, I took it and pulled it over my head. It was soft, probably cashmere, I realized, and so fine a knit that I knew it must have cost a fortune.

"You were right, Violet," Aidan said softly. "I should have told you about Isabel. About the resemblance. But I hope you understand why I didn't."

I could only nod. The anger I'd felt toward him had dissipated, reduced now to a dull ache of disappointment.

"I didn't want to lose you," he continued. "Though now I realize it's probably better this way."

I flinched at his words. "How is it better this way?" I asked.

"Because it's dangerous to fight our natural instincts. After all, it's only a matter of time—"

"Till what, Aidan? Till we start acting like enemies? Till we start trying to take each other out?"

He closed his eyes, taking a deep breath before answering me. "I would destroy myself before I'd let myself hurt you, Violet. I've told you so more than once."

"Yeah, it's easy for you to say that now," I muttered.

He glanced up at the ceiling, where the square-cut window showed the sky beyond. "Look, the rain has stopped. You should go."

"Do you want me to go?" I asked, trying to hide the disappointment in my voice.

"I think it's best if you do," he answered, his voice soft, gentle. "Just promise me you won't turn off your inner eye. If a vision comes, tell me at once what you see. Just . . . reach out telepathically. Will you do that?"

I nodded, a painful lump in my throat.

"Are you going to be in Manhattan over the break?" he asked, reaching for my raincoat and shaking it out.

"No, I'm going to visit my Gran in Atlanta."

"Good. I suppose you'll be safe there."

Because what I'd foreseen happens *here*, at Winterhaven.

He held out my coat, and for a moment I just stood there, staring. I didn't want it to be like this between us. I wanted to tell him I was sorry; I wanted to say that it didn't matter that he'd kept the truth about Isabel from me. More than anything, I wanted to tell him that I still loved him.

Instead, I took my raincoat and silently shrugged into it without meeting his eyes.

"See you around, Violet," he said, his voice full of sadness.

"Yeah," I mumbled, trying to force back the inevitable tears. "See you around."

Some kick-ass vampire slayer I was.

"It was amazing, Violet! I wish you'd come with us." Cece was haphazardly pulling clothes out of her suitcase and tossing them onto the floor by her bed as she chattered on. "You wouldn't believe how many celebrities we saw."

I set my own suitcase on my bed and unzipped it. "Yeah? Like who?"

She rattled off a half dozen A-listers, including the lead singer of my favorite band.

"Cool! You're sure it was him?"

"I'm sure." She nodded. "Later on, I astrally projected to his hotel room."

My eyes widened with surprise. "You didn't!"

"He has a new tattoo," she said coyly. "Right here." She indicated a spot just below her left shoulder.

"Wow," I murmured, suitably impressed. "Do you do that often? Spy on celebrities, I mean?" I'd never really thought about it, but since she could go to anyone, anytime . . .

"Maybe," she said with a wicked smile. "Anyway, we really missed you and Kate."

"Sure you did," I teased. "How was the weather?"

Cece scooped up her clothes and walked to the closet, dumping them there in a heap. "It was perfect!" she called out. "Warm, but not too hot. Poor Sophie got a pretty bad sunburn."

"What?" I let out my breath in a huff. "I called her and warned her!" Because I'd seen it, the very first day of break—a quick vision of Sophie in pain, her skin red and blistered. I'd been trying to coax a vision about Blackwell, but somehow I'd gotten Sophie instead. "Why didn't she wear sunscreen like I told her to?"

Cece winced. "I think she forgot to reapply. Anyway, she's fine now. How was Atlanta?"

"It was great," I said, which was entirely true. It had been nice to spend some quiet time with Gran. We'd had lunch at the club, lounged by the pool. My seventeenth birthday had come and gone, celebrated quietly with Gran and Lupe, who'd made me my favorite cake—red velvet with buttercream frosting. I'd hoped to see Whitney while I was there, but our breaks coincided and she'd gone to the beach with her family. Still, all in all, it had been a nice trip. Relaxing, even.

"Well, it looks like you got a bit of a tan yourself. I swear, you were so pale you were starting to look like a vampire."

My heart skipped a beat. But then I realized she was just kidding; the word "vampire" was just a figure of speech to her.

"Anyway," Cece continued, "next time you have to go to Saint Bart's with us. Promise?"

"I promise," I agreed, just because it seemed like the right thing to say.

Cece sighed, collapsing back on her bed. "It's good to be back here at the 'Haven, though, isn't it? I mean, it just feels so much safer here."

My skin prickled all over. "What do you mean, safer?"

"I don't know. Just that here we're free to be ourselves. I mean, what happens when we all go off to college?"

I shook my head. "I don't know. I just wish I'd come here sooner."

"Yeah, I wish you had too," Cece answered. "Hey, you want to go to the café for a little while? I'm starved, and dinner's not for another hour."

"Sure." I was mostly unpacked, and hungry—all I'd gotten on the plane was a tiny bag of pretzels. "Want to call and see if everyone else wants to meet us there?" Kate and Sophie and Marissa—the whole gang. I'd missed them, I realized.

A half hour later, we were all tucked into a booth in the back, laughing and chatting. We decided to skip dinner altogether and had sandwiches there instead, followed by coffee and thick slices of cheesecake drizzled with strawberry sauce and whipped cream. I took a sip of cappuccino and watched my friends over the rim of the mug, warmth spreading through my veins.

Yeah, Winterhaven was probably the best thing that had ever happened to me. In less than a year's time, I felt like I'd finally found myself, found the friends I'd have for life.

And Aidan . . . well, I'd had plenty of time to think about him over the break. I wanted him back, wanted our relationship the way it was before I flipped out about the whole Isabel thing. The only question was, did he want me? I had to know, had to try . . .

"Hey, earth to Violet," Sophie said, waving a hand in front of my eyes. "You've got that dreamy look on your face again. A penny for your thoughts?"

"I'm not sure they're worth that," I said, laughing. "I was just thinking how glad I am to be back, that's all." Which was partly true. I *had* been thinking that, before Aidan crept into my thoughts.

"I'm glad to be back too," Kate said. "It took me two full days to remember that I had to actually get up and walk across the room to pick up my purse or my keys or whatever."

"My God, you are so lazy," Marissa said with a snort of laughter.

"Yeah, well, it becomes habit," Kate protested. "It's difficult having a gift that's so hard to hide."

"Hey," Sophie said, "not to change the subject, but are any of you taking the SAT prep course that starts this week?"

I'd almost forgotten about the upcoming SATs. Patsy had sent in the money for the prep course just before spring break. "I am. Do you know who's teaching it?"

"No idea." Sophie shook her head, leaning forward in her seat. "Don't look now, but Dr. Hottie just walked in."

"Dr. Hottie?" I asked, resisting the urge to turn around and look at the door.

"He teaches senior-level science classes," Cece whispered beside me, "and he can't be more than twenty-six. Fresh out of grad school."

"What's his real name?" I whispered back in confusion.

"Dr. Byrne," Sophie said. "As in, Byrne-ing hot. Get it?"

"C'mon, I gotta turn around," I pleaded.

Cece nudged me. "Oh, go on. Just be casual."

Totally casual, I thought, twisting my torso in my seat. The so-called Dr. Hottie stood just inside the door, chatting with a couple of students. I'd seen him around before, and they weren't kidding. He was definitely hot.

"Hey, you're blushing!" Cece said, and I quickly turned back around, feeling the heat in my cheeks.

"He only teaches really advanced classes," Kate said with a sigh. "So I have no chance of getting him next year."

"Oh, you better believe I'll be taking his class. I'll fill you in," Sophie offered with a naughty smile.

Kate nudged Marissa in the ribs. "Hey, you've gotten awfully quiet. Don't tell me you don't appreciate the finer points of Dr. Hottie?"

Marissa looked suddenly uncomfortable. "Yeah, I'm just . . . I don't know, something feels weird all of a sudden. Sort of off. I can't explain it."

I studied her face, my heart accelerating when I saw something that looked like fear in her eyes. "What's wrong?"

She closed her eyes for a moment, then opened them again. "I don't know that anything's wrong," she said at last. "But something's definitely not right. I think I want to go back to my room."

Suddenly the gaiety was gone. In silence, we gathered up our things and headed out into the cool night.

Not five minutes later it happened—my vision tunneled, my ears hummed. Next thing I knew, I fell to my knees on the concrete sidewalk. I vaguely heard my friends calling my name, felt someone tugging on my arm.

But it was too late; I was already gone, back down the rabbit hole.

24 ~ Mirage

I was in Manhattan—Central Park. It was dark; the sun had just set. I could see the city's lights all around the park's perimeter. There was a fountain about a hundred yards away, yet the area was strangely empty. A lamppost stood to my left, throwing an eerie yellow light across the pavement.

Two women lurked in the shadows. Beside the fountain two men were talking—Julius and Dr. Blackwell, I realized with a start. I moved closer, knowing I needed to hear. ". . . an all-school assembly," Dr. Blackwell was saying. "Everyone else will be engaged, and you can have him then. I'll summon them to my office just as the assembly gets under way—him, and the Sâbbat*."*

"Excellent," Julius said. Though I couldn't see his face, I could hear the glee in his voice.

"But afterward the Sâbbat *stays with me," Blackwell warned. "I won't have her harmed."*

Julius nodded. "That was our agreement." So it was a trade—me for Aidan. But what did Blackwell want with me?

"Violet, oh my God!" It was Sophie, trying to pull me to my feet.

"It's okay," Cece said soothingly. "She's okay. This is what happens when she has a vision."

"I think she's hurt," Kate said. "Oh, shit, she's bleeding!"

My knees burned, and so did my palms. I must have fallen, I realized. Scraped my knees and hands on the sidewalk. I tried to get up, stumbled, and fell back down again. Something was wrong. My vision began to tunnel again, pulling me back in.

Nothing like this had ever happened—usually it ended, and that was it. But this . . . my friends' voices sounded far away. The humming in my ears grew louder, then faded away. It felt like an iron band was wrapped around my chest, and I struggled for air, struggled to fill my lungs.

Aidan. I needed Aidan. I had to tell him what I'd seen. I needed him to pull me out of this before it sucked me down for good.

"Aidan," I managed to croak. "Get him. Please."

"I'll project to him," I heard Cece say. "If he can't hear me, then we'll send Kate once I know where he is."

"Hurry, Cece!" Sophie said. "I don't know what's going on, but her pulse is way too fast. She's having some kind of fit or something."

"We can't just stay here!" someone shouted. "We should take her to the infirmary."

"No!" someone shouted. Definitely Marissa. "Aidan will know what to do."

I squeezed my eyes shut, felt the ground sway beneath me. I felt the hot trickle of blood run down my leg, felt particles of cement abrading my hands. *Aidan, please,* I called out with my mind. *Please, help me.*

My friends' voices were back. "Oh, God, Cece looks dead. I hate it when she does this. C'mon, Cece, make it quick."

There was a loud gasp, and then Cece spoke. "He's in a classroom, a chemistry lab—"

"Go, Kate!" someone yelled.

"Violet?" *Aidan.* Had Kate found him, or had my telepathy summoned him there? I wasn't sure. I didn't know how much time had passed. I opened my eyes and his face swam into focus, but then I had to close them again, because everything went fuzzy.

"I . . . I don't know what's happening," I said, my voice a hoarse whisper. "It keeps trying to drag me back under."

I felt Aidan's cold fingers on my face. "Hey, c'mon, Vi. Snap out of it. Stay with me, love."

He cradled me on the sidewalk, my head against his chest. I felt his lips in my hair, on my temple. My blood stirred, and I felt myself swimming back to full consciousness, felt the band around my lungs loosen and disappear.

Suddenly the black edging my vision disappeared entirely. Sounds were normal now; I could breathe again. "What happened to me?" I gasped.

"A vision. What did you see?" Aidan asked.

"Not here," I murmured, looking up at my friends' panicked faces.

"Do you want me to . . . you know, check you out?" Sophie offered.

"No, I'm fine. Really." I rose, Aidan holding me by the elbow. "Whatever it was, it's passed now."

Cece glanced from me to Aidan, then back to me again. She nodded to herself, as if satisfied that I was in good hands. "We'll meet you back at the room in a little bit, okay?"

I just nodded, watching them all walk away.

"Where are you taking me?" I asked Aidan, knowing full well we weren't going to travel the normal way.

"To my room. Take my hand and close your eyes, okay?"

I closed them, all right—as tightly as I could. A few seconds passed, a hum and a pop, and there we were, inside his little room. The door swung shut behind us, and I heard a bolt slide into place before he led me to the narrow little daybed and sat down beside me.

"You're sure you're okay?" he asked, stroking my hair.

And then I remembered—the blood! I leapt up and ran for the door, my heart pounding. "Aidan, you've got to let me out. My knees and my hands—I . . . I'm bleeding."

He was beside me in an instant, reaching for my hand, drawing me back toward him. "Let me see."

I shook my head so wildly it felt like it might snap right off my neck. "No way. Don't you remember the last time?"

"Look at me, Violet. Look at my eyes. My teeth." He raised his upper lip. "I'm fine. I just took the elixir, not an hour ago. It's just a few scrapes, nothing serious. I can fix it."

I took two steps away from him, back toward the door. "What do you mean, fix it?"

"What do you think, that when I leave a victim lying on the street, I leave the puncture marks visible? Imagine the panic that would cause," he said with a laugh.

"But . . . but I saw the marks you left on that junkie's neck," I stammered.

"I fixed those while you were passed out cold on the sidewalk."

"You mean just left me lying there, and—"

"It only took me a few seconds, I promise."

I just stood there, blinking in confusion, more afraid than I wanted to admit.

"Please don't be frightened of me, Violet. I can bear just about anything but that. Come here." Again he reached for my hand, and this time I let him take it. He pulled me back to the bed and made me sit.

Kneeling before me, he gently pushed up the legs of my bloodstained khaki capris—my favorite little Abercrombie & Fitch lowriders, ruined now—till my knees were exposed.

"Maybe you shouldn't watch," he said, looking up, his eyes meeting mine. His weren't red, thank God, so I guessed I was safe. Still, I could see hunger in his gaze—something that looked a little like lust, and a shudder worked its way down my spine.

What is he going to do to me? I had no clue, but whatever it was, my eyes were staying open.

"Okay," he said, his voice deeper, rougher than usual. "But don't say I didn't warn you." He smiled then, a slow, sexy smile, and I watched in horror as his canine teeth elongated, if only slightly.

And then his tongue came out of his mouth, and he licked my wounds—literally. Once, twice his tongue made slow, soft strokes against my bloody, raw skin. Goose bumps erupted all over me, and it was all I could do to sit still. I clamped my mouth shut, grinding my teeth, trying to keep from making a sound.

Whatever he was doing, it felt like nothing I'd ever experienced before, and I didn't want him to stop—*ever.* He finished with my right knee and moved to my left, repeating the slow, sensuous licks before he reached for my hands and did the same to my hypersensitive palms. Every once in a while he'd pause and glance up at me questioningly, as if he were testing my response. The look in his eyes—the heat, the tenderness, all blended into something indescribable—stole away my breath. By the time he finished, I was reduced to a quivering mass on the bed, panting and squirming.

"Are you okay?" he asked softly, rising from his knees and sitting beside me on the bed. "Do you need to lie down?"

Yeah, I do.

"Here," he said, lifting me up and laying me back against the pillow. I closed my eyes and took a deep, calming breath.

"I hope I didn't hurt you."

I glanced down at my knees, at my hands, and gasped. The blood was gone, the scrapes were gone. Everything was just . . .

gone. My skin looked perfect, totally unblemished. As if nothing had happened.

"Okay, love," he said, brushing back a stray lock of hair from my flushed cheek. "Now you've got to tell me what happened."

Taking a deep, steadying breath, I told him.

"And that's everything?" he asked, lying beside me now, his arm tucked around me, my cheek resting on his chest—I could hear the faint thump-thump of his heart, his vampire heart, pumping the infected blood throughout his body. "Nothing else?"

"Nothing else. And then there was that weird reaction afterward, like the vision kept trying to suck me back into it, but couldn't quite do it. That's never happened before."

"That almost frightens me more than the vision itself," Aidan said.

I took a deep breath, then exhaled slowly, trying to calm my racing heart. "The next all-school assembly is Friday. Five days from now," I clarified. "It's coming, Aidan. Whatever it is, it's coming."

"It would seem that way."

I bit my lower lip, steeling myself for what I knew I must say. "We've got to tell them. There's no other way."

"Tell who?"

"My friends. Cece and Sophie and Kate and Marissa. All of them. We need them. Maybe Jack, too."

"We can't tell them, Violet. It's impossible for me to do so. It's against the laws of my kind."

"You told me about Blackwell," I shot back.

"Yes, and I paid a price for it."

"What do you mean?" I asked, an uncomfortable lump in my throat.

"I was sent to the Tribunal for that little slip," he answered, his voice hard. "I suppose it was Blackwell himself who turned me in."

"The tribunal? Like a vampire court or something?"

"Something like that, except there's no pleading your case. Punishments are simply handed down. My sentence was three days of torture."

"They . . . they tortured you?" I stammered, my stomach lurching uncomfortably.

He just shrugged.

"What did they do to you? I . . . I thought it was impossible to hurt you."

"My body will heal itself when injured," he explained. "But that doesn't mean I don't feel pain. Especially when an . . . injury . . . is repeated over and over again, every time it *does* heal."

Hate and revulsion welled up inside of me. More than anything, I wanted to harm the vampires who had harmed Aidan.

But this was a war, and we needed an army. "Well, there aren't any laws preventing *me* from telling them," I said. "Are there? Would you be held accountable if I did?"

"No," he answered. "I wouldn't. I guess you could call that a loophole."

Thank God. "We need their help, then."

"What are you suggesting?" he asked.

"A plan, that's what. With everyone's gifts combined, we can turn the tables on Julius and his allies. Lead them into our own trap."

"Blackwell would never allow—"

"Blackwell is the enemy, remember?"

"But according to your vision, he'll protect you. He won't let them harm you."

"Even if that's true, what about you?"

"Your safety has its price," he said somberly.

I shoved myself up to a sitting position. "No way. You're not going to . . . to . . . *sacrifice* yourself for me, Aidan. Forget it."

"I'll do whatever it takes to keep you safe, Violet," he said, his voice suddenly hoarse. "I've already stood by once, watching helplessly as a woman I cared for lost her life in my stead. It won't happen again. I won't let it. If taking my life will save your own, then I must have your word that you'll do it. I've taught you how."

I hit him then, on the chest. Hard, though he didn't even flinch. Again I struck him. "No, you hear me? I won't do it!"

In a flash he'd captured my wrists and was holding them immobile in his grasp. His head ducked down toward mine, his blue-gray gaze steady and firm. "Yes, Violet. You will. You must."

I swallowed hard, trying desperately to slow my breathing, to steady my heart. "It won't come to that. Not if you let my friends help us. I'm telling them everything, tonight."

"They'll think you're mad. You realize that, don't you?"

I shook my head. "No, they won't. And when Julius shows up here on Friday, we'll be ready. All of us. If I'm taking out any vampires, it's them."

Immediately he released me. "You don't know what you're saying. You have no idea what kind of danger you're putting yourself in."

"How is asking for help any more dangerous than facing them alone, Aidan? Explain that to me. We're sitting ducks either way."

"Not necessarily," he said, his eyes glittering. "You've foreseen the future, but we can thwart it. We can leave; we can disappear before Friday comes. If we're not here, there's no way it can happen as you saw it."

"What, and run forever? If we don't face them now, they'll just come after us."

He shook his head. "If Patsy hadn't gotten in that cab, she wouldn't have been in the accident. If your father hadn't gone to Afghanistan, he might very well still be alive. At least, that's what you've always believed, isn't it? Didn't you save Lupe from falling on the ice and breaking her hip?"

"This is different and you know it. Julius is after you, and Blackwell is helping him. That's not going to stop just because we're not around on Friday."

Aidan raked a hand through his hair. "Very well. You win. Tell your friends. Still, I believe that everything will happen as you saw it. I must have your word that if Julius has me and the only way to save yourself is to put that stake through my heart, then you goddamn better do it, do you hear me?"

I'd never seen him so fierce. "You have my word," I said, my voice a whisper. After all, it wouldn't come to that. It couldn't.

"Then go," he said, rising from the bed. "There's not much time before curfew. Tell my story, and see if anyone believes it."

I took his hand and rose to stand beside him. "Don't be angry, Aidan."

"I'm not angry," he said, though it was pretty obvious that he was. "Just promise me you'll stay away from Blackwell, okay?"

"What about anthropology class?"

"Just keep your thoughts protected."

I nodded, hoping he was right, hoping that Blackwell couldn't tell exactly what we were plotting.

"C'mon, I'll walk you as far as the East Hall lounge. Or should I take you there by other means? Much quicker, you know."

I shook my head. "I think I've had enough excitement for one night. Let's walk, okay?"

"You sure? How are those knees and hands?"

"They feel perfect, as if nothing ever happened to them." As soon as the words left my lips, something he'd said earlier struck me like a ton of bricks. "Wait, you said you took the elixir today. That's the only way you could stand being near me, with the blood and all that."

"That's right," he said. "What about it?"

"But . . . but doesn't that weaken *all* the effects of vampirism? Not just the hunger?"

He shook his head. "No. Even immediately after taking it, I'm stronger and faster than any human, and as you just saw, my healing capabilities remain unaffected, as do most of my psychic abilities. But yes, I'm somewhat compromised, far weaker than I would be otherwise."

I took a deep breath. "And how long did you say before it usually wears off?"

"About two weeks," he answered dully, and I knew then that he had already realized what was just beginning to dawn on me.

Five days. We had five days till Julius and his merry gang showed up, bent on vengeance, and Aidan's full range of powers wouldn't return for two weeks!

Still, my mind reasoned, even in his weakened state he could move faster than any human I'd ever seen, and with a few flicks of his tongue, he could totally heal some nasty scrapes and cuts.

But . . . if those were the powers of a weakened vampire, then what exactly were his enemies capable of?

We needed my friends and their combined powers, and we needed them badly. All I had to do was convince them.

25 ~ A Little Help from My Friends

"Yeah, that's real funny, Violet," Sophie said, a scowl on her face. "Why'd you call us all in here if you're not even going to tell us what's really going on?"

I sighed heavily, mentally exhausted from pouring out the whole story to them. "I *am* telling you what's going on. I know it sounds crazy, but—"

"C'mon, Violet, vampires?" Kate's voice was laced with sarcasm. "I mean, you really expect us to believe that?"

"Trust me, I thought it was just as crazy as you do. But . . . I've seen proof. And my visions—"

"Proof?" Sophie asked. "What kind of proof?"

"Remember when I got the weekend pass to visit my

stepmother? Well, I never made it to her apartment. I ended up in a dark alley instead, where a junkie attacked me. Aidan . . . well, he saved me. Trust me, I saw him in action that night and if there was any doubt left in my mind, that got rid of it real fast. I know if you really think about what I'm telling you, it'll all make sense."

I looked around at my friends' faces, hoping to see some sign of belief, of trust. Instead, all I saw was skepticism, even annoyance.

"Anyway, there's more," I continued, figuring I might as well just get it all out there. "It turns out that I'm some sort of vampire slayer, something called a *Sâbbat*. That's why Aidan and I can speak telepathically."

"Oh my God, she's lost her mind," Kate muttered. "He's brainwashed her or something."

"Even if there *were* vampires—even if they really existed—you think Dr. Blackwell would allow them here? At Winterhaven?" Sophie asked. "I mean, his gifts are pretty strong. I think he'd know if there were vampires masquerading as students, don't you?"

"Oh, Blackwell knows, all right," I said, nodding. "Considering he *is* one."

They all started talking at once.

"Shh," Cece said, quieting them. "Let's hear her out, okay?"

So I continued on. I told them about Julius, about his sect of Propagators, about my recurring vision, about Dr. Blackwell's involvement. "So we've only got till Friday, but the elixir has weakened Aidan; he won't be at full strength by then. Which is why we need you. All of you. With everyone's gifts combined, we can set a trap for them."

Kate stood up. "Okay, I think I've heard just about enough of this crap. What did he do, drug you or something? Is that what he does in the chem lab—manufacture mind-altering drugs?"

"I saw him once, just outside the window," Cece whispered, sounding slightly dazed. "I thought I must have imagined it."

"That's crazy," Sophie said, shaking her head. "You're on the fifth floor."

Kate folded her arms, glaring at me. "What, next you're going to tell us he can fly?"

I shook my head. "I don't know what he does. But he can somehow carry me across campus in . . . well, in a matter of seconds. I'm not sure if he's just moving really fast or somehow teleporting or what."

"He *does* move quickly," Sophie said, chewing on her thumbnail. "Even I've noticed that. It's like he's there one minute, and gone the next. I always thought it was kind of freaky."

Feeling like I was finally getting through to them, I went on. "And you know that thing you call the Aidan effect? It's really just nature's way of drawing prey to him. Making him seem more attractive than he really is, sort of weakening your reflexes around him. Not that he would ever hurt any of you," I added quickly. "Because he wouldn't."

"And you're saying Dr. Blackwell is one too?" Cece asked, her brow furrowed. "Maybe that's why we all think he's cool, even though he's actually a little creepy, if you think about it."

"He's got that whole 'grandfatherly' thing going on," Sophie said. "He totally reminds me of Grandpa Patterson."

Kate's gaze shot over to Sophie. "Hey, he reminds me of my grandpa too."

I nodded. It made sense—his grandfatherly appeal was probably what drew students to him, made them feel safe in his presence. "And all this time, Aidan thought Blackwell was protecting him," I continued. "But now it looks like he's handing him over to his enemies. This Friday, according to my vision."

I suddenly realized that Marissa hadn't said a single word since I'd started talking. She just sat there the entire time, totally silent. Just as I was wondering what she was thinking, her eyes met mine, and she nodded.

"Violet's telling the truth," she said suddenly.

Everyone turned to stare at her, eyes widened with surprise.

"You've got to be kidding me, Marissa," Kate scoffed. "You actually believe this crap?"

"Yeah, I do. What I don't understand is why you don't. Do you honestly think Violet would lie about something like this? Besides, I've got this feeling . . ." She trailed off, and I saw her shiver. "It feels like the truth. Like somehow I've always known, somewhere in the back of my mind."

I wanted to hug her. Who would have thought Marissa of all people would end up defending me against the rest of them? Tears gathered in my eyes.

"Well, I believe her too," Cece said, standing up and reaching for my hand. "I mean, is it really such a stretch? There's all kinds of weird stuff going on here at Winterhaven, including kids who can shape-shift. Are vampires really all that more out there?"

"Yeah, they are!" Kate protested.

"No, Cece's right," Sophie said. "I mean, why not? I wonder if I could sense it. You know, like an illness or something?"

I nodded, squeezing Cece's hand and then releasing it. "Probably. He says it's some sort of blood-borne infection, a parasite or something. Like malaria. Have you ever touched Dr. Blackwell?"

Sophie shook her head. "Not once. Never had a reason to."

"So what do we do?" Marissa asked. "What's the plan?"

I shrugged. "I don't know. I haven't thought that far ahead. Aidan didn't even think you'd believe me."

"I believe you," Marissa said.

"Me too." Cece.

"Yep, me too." Sophie.

That just left Kate. "I think I must have lost my mind, but yeah, me too."

"What about Jack—do you think he would help us?" I asked her.

Kate shrugged. "I could ask. He and Aidan spend a lot of time together. Who knows, maybe he already suspects it."

"Joshua!" I said, letting out my breath in a rush. I'd totally forgotten about Joshua, the shape-shifter. Hadn't he said that he owed me one—me and Aidan both? Now was the time to call in that favor. After all, he'd seen Aidan in action, seen the red eyes, the fangs. It wouldn't be that hard to convince him.

"Who's Joshua?" Marissa and Sophie asked in unison.

"He's one of the shifters. Aidan and I once saved him from some jerk who was bullying him, and in return he promised to help us out if I ever needed anything. Remember that time I was talking to one of them in the dining hall? The short, blond guy? Kinda cute? That was Joshua."

"So that makes, what? Eight of us?" Marissa held up her

fingers, ticking them off. "Against how many of them? Do we even know?"

"Julius, and two female vampires. Plus Blackwell. I think that's it."

"So we outnumber them two to one," Cece said. "That sounds like pretty good odds, right?"

"Yeah, but keep in mind that they're . . . well, vampires. They've got powers way beyond ours. And Aidan's weakened by the elixir."

"But you said you're some kind of vampire slayer," Marissa said. "What exactly does that mean, anyway?"

"That I can kill them. But hopefully it won't come to that."

Kate shook her head, looking skeptical. "You think we can just chase them away? A bunch of badass vampires on a mission?"

"I have no idea. All I know is that we've got to try." Tears burned behind my eyelids, blurring my vision. "I can't . . . I can't just let them kill Aidan. Or worse, make *me* kill him. Because that's their plan, you know. If you won't help, we'll have to fight them alone."

Sophie glanced down at her watch. "Uh-oh, guys, ten minutes till curfew. We've got to go. Just tell us what to do, and we'll do it."

"Let's all meet tomorrow, after sixth period. With Aidan.

I'll try and get Joshua to join us too. Kate, you talk to Jack. Do you know where the chapel is?"

"Ugh, that creepy old place?" Marissa said with a mock shiver.

"That's where Aidan and I usually hang out. It's private; we never see anyone else around there. I think it's as good a place as any to meet."

Sophie reached for the doorknob. "Hey, at least now we know where to find you two."

"Yeah, but if the chapel's a-rockin', don't come a-knockin'," Kate teased.

I laughed uneasily, but relief filled me as they filed out, all but Cece. Thank God they believed me. There was hope after all.

As soon as we were alone, Cece and I quickly changed into our pajamas and climbed into our beds. For the longest time, neither of us spoke, and I wondered what was going through her head.

Finally she broke the strained silence. "I can't believe you kept all this crazy stuff a secret for so long. I mean, weren't you going nuts?"

"A little. I'm sorry I couldn't tell you before now. It's just . . . well, they're Aidan's secrets, really, and if it wasn't a life-or-death situation—"

"No," Cece interrupted. "I totally understand. I just feel

bad that you've had to go through all of this alone."

"Well, I had Aidan. Some of the time, at least," I added.

"What was the deal with that picture? You know, the one Jenna gave you on Valentine's Day. I thought you two broke up over that."

I took a deep breath, wondering if I should tell her. *Why not?* "That picture was a painting of the opera dancer I mentioned. The woman he was living with when he was made a vampire, the one who got killed."

"But . . . but she looks just like you!" Cece stammered.

"Yeah, exactly. But he left that part out when he told me his story." My face got hot just thinking about it. Even now I couldn't entirely erase my doubts where Isabel was concerned. Just thinking about her made me angry.

"But what does it mean? Is it just some random coincidence, or . . . or what?"

I shook my head, staring at the ceiling, watching the shadows play across the plaster. "I have no idea. Aidan has some theories, but he doesn't know either."

"Well, I can see why he wouldn't tell you. I mean, I'm sure he figured that you'd think he only liked you because you looked like her, or something like that."

"Yeah," I said, wincing. "That's pretty much exactly what I thought when I found out."

"But now you don't?" she asked, sounding hopeful.

A slow smile spread across my face. "No, I'm pretty sure he likes me for me. At least, I think I am."

"But . . . but how's it ever going to work out between you two? I mean, he's a vampire and you're not. He's immortal, right? Or is that just legend stuff?"

"No, it's true. But he's working on a cure, remember? He thinks he's pretty close to getting it right."

"But if he doesn't?" Cece asked. "You're pretty much the same age now, right? What if it takes him ten or twenty years to cure it? You'll be that much older, and he'll still be, what? Sixteen, seventeen?"

"Seventeen. He's . . . he was seventeen when it happened." My chest tightened. There was nothing worse than hearing your own fears spoken aloud. "I just have to hope he finds the cure fast, that's all. Anyway, we've got Friday to get through first. One thing at a time." Because if things went badly on Friday, the rest of it was all moot, wasn't it?

Sweat broke out all over my body, and I shivered. *Don't think about it now,* I told myself. "We really should go to sleep," I said, my voice shaky. "It's going to be a long week."

"Yeah, I guess you're right," Cece said. "'Night, Violet."

"Good night, Cee."

* * *

"I think that's enough for today," Aidan said, folding his arms across his chest. "I've got some work to do tonight, but can everyone meet back here tomorrow, same time?"

There was murmuring, and heads nodded in unison. I think everyone was still a little afraid of him, and they hadn't even seen the fangs or the red eyes. Except Joshua, I realized, watching him pick up his backpack and sling it over one shoulder. Yet he didn't seem frightened. Not at all.

Neither did Jack, now that I thought about it. Then again, Jack had been working side by side with Aidan in the chem lab for years, so I guess he knew he had nothing to fear. If Aidan had wanted to hurt him, he'd had plenty of opportunity before now. Kate had said he'd barely batted an eyelash when she'd told him.

In fact, Jack was standing next to Aidan now. "Couldn't we aerosolize it somehow?" Jack was saying, and I sidled up closer, hoping to hear a little better. "We can lure them in here and then somehow release it into the air, maybe through the ducts?"

Aidan nodded. "That's not a bad idea. It'll help level our abilities."

Jack nodded. "Okay, I'll meet you in the lab right after dinner. I think it'll be easy to do; I'll just compress the molecules, and . . ."

I moved away, bored by the science-speak. Instead I retrieved my bag from the corner, trying not to look at the "gift" Aidan had presented me with when we'd first arrived at the chapel today.

A real stake, not like the blunt-end practice one I'd used before. This hawthorn stake—smooth and shiny—was sharpened to a deadly point on one end. Aidan had even crafted me a special holster-type thing to carry it in. Silly, really, because it wasn't like I could just walk around with the thing banging against my hip. This wasn't the Wild West.

"You need a jacket, Violet," Aidan said, beside me now. Jack was striding back down the chapel's center aisle, toward Kate. "You'll have to wear your raincoat or something long enough to cover it."

"What if it's not raining?" I asked, hating the sight of that thing.

"Doesn't matter. I want you wearing it at all times from now on. You can't allow yourself to get caught unaware, okay? I have to go to the lab now."

"That's okay, I have the SAT prep class right after dinner," I said with a shrug. "Though I was kind of thinking of just skipping it." There really wasn't any point in my going—it's not like I was going to be able to concentrate. The SAT seemed like such an unimportant abstraction compared to the very real danger that lay ahead.

Aidan shook his head. "Don't skip it. Just go on about your

business, as if nothing is amiss. We've got three more days to work out the details of the plan. You can spare an hour for your class."

"What are you, my mother?" I muttered.

"Besides"—his mouth curved into a beautiful smile—"according to your friends' animated conversation over there, someone they're calling 'Dr. Hottie' is the instructor. Dr. Byrne, I presume? You wouldn't want to miss out."

I looked over his shoulder to where Sophie, Marissa, and Cece were gathered, chattering animatedly, just as he said. Forget mortal danger; there was Dr. Hottie to discuss.

"You can hear them from all the way over here?" I asked, surprised. The entire length of the chapel separated us from them.

"Easily," he replied. "And that's with reduced capabilities."

"Which means Julius and his little harem will be able to hear us from even farther away," I said with a sigh. "Great."

"Exactly."

"Violet, you coming?" Cece called out.

"Be right there," I yelled back.

Aidan leaned close to my ear. "They're wondering if we're going to kiss good-bye."

Almost involuntarily, I licked my lips. It had been *so* long. "Are we?"

His head dipped down toward my neck, his lips brushing across the sensitive skin below my ear. Gooseflesh prickled my skin, making me shiver.

I heard him chuckle, and then he moved away. "I think I just scared them all half to death. Go on, so they don't think I've taken a bite."

Disappointment washed over me, and my cheeks grew hot. "Gee, thanks."

"No distractions, Violet," he said, serious now. "And don't forget your stake."

He held it out to me. I took it, surprised at how *right* it felt in my hands, despite my reluctance.

"Until tomorrow, love," he murmured in his best Lord Brompton voice.

"I'll be sure and give Dr. Hottie your regards," I said, shoving the stake into its holder and giving him my dirtiest look.

His eyes met mine for the briefest of seconds, and I could have sworn I saw a flicker of jealousy there.

Good.

26 ~ The Winterhaven Warriors

Friday began just like any other day. I got up, took a shower, brushed my teeth, got dressed, went to breakfast. All usual stuff, except for strapping on the stake. I found that if I tied a sweater around my waist and arranged it just right, it covered the entire stake and holster. Still, I wore my khaki Burberry trench coat, a Christmas gift from Patsy, when I wasn't in class. At least while I walked around, I had double the concealment.

We had six classes to get through before the plan went into motion, and then everything was carefully choreographed, right down to the last detail. Everyone had a job. Cece would project to Julius, or at least attempt to. Then she would report back on his movements. Once they were located, Joshua would move with the enemy, shifting into camouflaging shapes when necessary. Apparently he was entirely capable of doing that, as crazy as it sounded.

Jack was in charge of the aerosolized elixir, which he would release into the chapel once Julius and the females entered. Kate and Marissa would remain with me. I worried the most about this, because in my vision I'd seen both of them held against their will by the females. I made a mental note to talk to Aidan about that.

Cece would stay hidden in the loft, out of the way. From there she would project to Dr. Blackwell, to see what he was up to. If she needed to get a message to Aidan, she could do that via projection, too. Sophie's job was to keep an eye on Cece, to keep her vulnerable body safe while her astral self was away. After it was all said and done, there might be more for Sophie to do—assessing the damage, so to speak.

As to Aidan, he hoped to reason with Julius, to assure him that he was no danger to him and his kind. After all, apparently there were some pretty strict vampire laws, enforced by the Tribunal, and what Julius was doing was completely against those laws. Still, as a Propagator, Julius had always operated just outside the law. All that meant, really, was that he wasn't afforded the Tribunal's protection.

If nothing else, I hoped our show of strength would dissuade them. Beyond that, I wasn't really sure what to expect. If it came to it, I was prepared to do what I was supposedly born to do—with the stake. Mostly, I tried not to think about that. Aidan still insisted that if the plan failed and all was lost, I must put the stake through his heart. He felt certain that Julius would honor the agreement he'd made with Blackwell—my safety in exchange for Aidan's death.

There was no way in hell I planned on ending the day by destroying Aidan. I had faith in my friends, in our combined abilities. After all, what were three ordinary vampires against five psychic kids, a shape-shifter, a vampire, and a vampire slayer? Yeah, we had the better team, as far as I was concerned, and we had the foreknowledge to boot.

At least, that's what I kept telling myself. But what really bothered me was that I hadn't had any time alone with Aidan all week. Between classes, the SAT prep course, and our group training sessions, I hadn't had five minutes alone with him.

Somewhere in the back of my mind, a little voice was saying, *What if it doesn't work out? What if it really is Aidan's blood spilled all over the grass, just as I saw?*

What if we never had another chance to be together?

"Miss McKenna? Do you know the answer or not?"

I looked up from my notebook in confusion, realizing I was

sitting in Dr. Penworth's history class and that he was asking me a question.

"I'm sorry," I mumbled, feeling my cheeks burn.

Removing his spectacles, he shook his head in obvious frustration. "Someone else, then?"

Aidan, of course, was nowhere to be found. He'd skipped class, and I had no idea where he was or what he was doing.

The hours dragged by. I sat with my friends at lunch, but no one ate a bite. How could we? Everyone's face looked pale, pinched. Worry charged the air. Marissa tried her best to diffuse it, but considering she was pretty freaked-out herself, it was no use. Now and then Cece clutched my hand, whispering, "It'll be okay," as if she could make it so just by saying it.

A huge banner was strung across the wall. WINTERHAVEN WARRIORS ALL THE WAY, it declared in black and lavender block letters. Something about the boys soccer team; I think they were playing in the state championships. In the back, near the soda machines, some kids had started up a chant, their voices resonating throughout the crowded room.

"We are the Warriors . . . the mighty, mighty Warriors . . ."

Rah-rah, I thought sourly. I mean, what was a state championship compared to what we were about to try and accomplish? The game was completely inconsequential in the grand scheme of things, whereas *this . . . this* was life-or-death. *We* were the real warriors—my friends and I.

I looked at each of them in turn, hoping they knew how much they meant to me. Cece, her hand still clutched tightly in mine—hers dark, mine pale, both of them trembling. Kate, tucking her hair behind her ears, like she always did when she was nervous. Sophie, chewing on her lower lip. Marissa, picking at the hem of her sleeve.

Across the dining hall, Joshua's eyes met ours, and he nodded. He, at least, didn't look scared out of his wits. Jack seemed pretty confident too when he joined us at our table.

Still, the minutes dragged by.

Dusk . . . we had until dusk. Then what?

"Miss McKenna," Dr. Blackwell called out, just as the bells indicated the end of fifth period. "May I have a word with you and Mr. Gray?"

Here it comes, I realized. He's summoning us to his office, just like he said he would.

I glanced over at Aidan, fear making my heart race.

His gaze met mine. *Block your mind, Violet. Keep it locked tight.*

I just nodded.

Slowly, reluctantly, I made my way toward Dr. Blackwell's desk, Aidan keeping pace beside me.

"I need to speak to you both, tonight," he said tersely. "I hate to ask you to skip the assembly, but it won't take long. Please report to my office at seven thirty."

"Is everything okay?" Aidan asked.

"Everything's fine," the headmaster said with a nod. "Just a matter that needs to be discussed. Nothing to be alarmed about."

"We'll be there," Aidan said, and I was amazed at how calm he looked.

As for me, I couldn't even bring myself to speak. Probably for the best. It was all happening, just as I'd seen. Every last piece was falling neatly into place, and there was nothing I could do to stop it.

"They're here," Aidan said, and everyone looked up at once. "They've entered the grounds. I feel it."

If Aidan could sense them, then that meant they could sense him, too. Would they come straight for us? Or follow the plan and wait for us in Blackwell's office?

"Cece, can you find them?" he asked, and she nodded.

"I'll take her up to the loft," I said, my stomach clenching into a knot. "It's quiet up there." I rose from the pew, glancing back one last time at the group gathered in the chapel's first two rows. Everyone looked anxious, even Aidan. Taking a deep breath, I turned and made my way toward the stairs that led up, Cece following silently behind.

As quickly as possible, I arranged the blankets on the floor, along with a couple of tasseled pillows.

Cece looked around in amazement. "This is where you and Aidan hang out?"

I just nodded.

Her dark eyes widened. "What is it, some kind of love nest? What exactly do you two *do* up here?"

"Not what it looks like," I muttered, mostly to myself. "C'mon, you better get comfortable. We should get going with this."

Cece nodded. "Sorry. Don't worry, I'll be quick."

I held my breath, waiting for her to start doing her thing.

"The gatehouse," she said, not five minutes later. I'd been pacing back and forth the entire time, trying not to look at her. It freaked me out too much, seeing her lie there completely still and lifeless.

"It's just Julius and the two women," Cece added breathlessly, scrambling to her feet.

I reached for her hand and gave it a squeeze. "Good job, Cee. Okay, let's go."

I missed a rung climbing back down and almost slipped, mercifully catching myself just in time. In a minute or two, we were back in the main chapel, everyone staring up at us expectantly.

"The gatehouse," Cece said, out of breath. "Just the three of them."

Joshua rose. "I'm on it."

Aidan turned toward him, and I couldn't help but notice how worried he looked. "Make sure your thoughts aren't blocked, so I can hear them. My range is *way* better than a normal mind reader's," he added sheepishly. "I can relay messages to Violet telepathically. Just keep our channel open, okay, Vi?"

As *if* it were ever closed to him. Still, I nodded.

Joshua took off. No one spoke till the heavy door swung shut behind him.

"I'm not comfortable sending him out alone," Aidan said, pacing back and forth in front of the altar.

Marissa wrapped her arms around herself, as if she were cold. "He'll be okay. I . . . I feel pretty sure of it."

I stood and went to Aidan, taking one cold hand in mine. "Hey, come and sit down. Save your energy, okay?"

But really I just wanted him next to me, holding my hand, making me feel safe. Would any of us ever really be safe again?

An hour passed by, excruciatingly slow. Then another. The tension in the room felt like a living, breathing thing. Some sat, some got up and walked a circuit around the pews. Jack and Kate sat in the back whispering, their heads bent together. Without Aidan beside me, his grip firm on my hand, I might have gone mad. "Nothing, no movement," Aidan passed on to the rest of us via Joshua's thoughts.

Dusk was drawing near; the sun was making its slow descent toward the horizon, turning the sky a familiar purplish hue. The all-school assembly began—a peal of bells had marked it. Dr. Blackwell would be waiting for us now, in his office, but we weren't coming. No, we'd lure them to us instead.

Beside me, Aidan's body was taut, tense. *I should not have involved you all,* he said in my mind. *I should have just let them take me.*

Yeah, but it's not happening that way, remember? Julius doesn't want to take you—he wants me to kill you.

Do you believe in God? he asked me.

Yeah, I answered. *Yeah, I do.*

Then pray to him, Vi.

So I did. Fervently. We were in a church, after all. Maybe that somehow aided the connection.

Abruptly Aidan dropped my hand and stood up. "They're moving. They realize we're not coming to Blackwell's office, and they're on their way here. Joshua is following them."

Someone whimpered. It might have been me. Time seemed

to stand still, and I think I might have forgotten how to breathe.

"They're close now," Aidan said minutes later, looking toward the door. "Is everyone ready?"

Jack got up and strode off toward the back of the chapel. "I'm going up." He had fans set up to release the elixir into the air, through the vents.

"Me too," Cece said, following him. "C'mon, Sophie."

The rest of us stood, rigid and tense, facing the door. My hand moved to the stake against my hip, my fingers running over its satiny shaft. Marissa had a second stake tucked inside her jacket, and other weapons—freshly sharpened swords, some matches and lighter fluid—were stashed inside the chapel's lone confessional. Because if any vampires were slain tonight, their heads had to be separated from their bodies, and then burned. Every time I thought about it, I got woozy. If Aidan was still around, he'd take care of it. If not . . . well, then, my friends would have to help me.

Glancing down, I remembered my crucifix necklace—Lupe's gift—and pulled it out from beneath my shirt. For luck, I kissed it, then let it fall back against my shirt, in plain sight now. *Just breathe,* I told myself, then glanced over at my friends, wondering if they were as terrified as I was.

Considering what we were up against, Marissa and Kate looked remarkably calm and determined—almost fierce.

Aidan stood in front of us, his feet planted wide apart, his hands clenched into fists by his sides. This was it, then. The time had come.

The Winterhaven Warriors were ready for action.

27 ~ To Arms!

Not five minutes later, the double doors burst open and Julius strode into the chapel. He was well over six feet tall, with impossibly broad shoulders. His black hair fell to his shoulders, his dark eyes menacing beneath heavy brows. His nose was long, his lips full above a close-clipped goatee.

He looked exactly as I remembered him from my visions—tall, dark, and terrifying. A vampire in his prime, probably turned in his midthirties. Facing him, Aidan looked like . . . like a boy.

Oh my God, this was insane. What had I been thinking, bringing my friends here to fight him?

"Aidan Gray," Julius called out, his voice strangely melodic. "A church? What an odd place to find you. Have you come to make a confession?"

His black gaze slid around the room, lingering on me, then Kate, then Marissa. I felt his confusion, and I forced myself to focus, to invade his thoughts.

Hmm, which one is the Sâbbat?

It occurred to me then that we had a slight advantage—it could be any of us three, and I felt his indecision as he examined us each in turn.

Aidan took several steps toward Julius, his posture casual, nonthreatening. "It's been, what? Forty years? To what do I owe the pleasure, Julius?"

"We must speak, old friend. Alone. And what a charming place to do so." He spread his arms wide and turned in a circle, as if he were admiring the view. "An exact replica of the chapel at King's College, is it not?"

"It is indeed. I'm happy to talk, but they stay," Aidan said, tipping his head toward where Marissa, Kate, and I stood trembling behind him. All our calm determination had fled now that Julius stood before us, looking far more dangerous than we'd imagined.

Julius laughed. "I beg to differ, Aidan. We speak alone," he repeated.

As he advanced on Aidan, anger flowed through my veins, making my pulse leap and my skin flush hotly. Oh, man . . . I was going to take this vampire *down*.

Suddenly the two females appeared behind Julius, as if from nowhere. Instinctively, I took two steps backward, blinking hard. I was aware of a strange smell in the air, of the air becoming misty. *The elixir,* I realized.

The females advanced on us—me, Kate, Marissa. Aidan tried to move between us, but Julius cut him off. Suddenly pews lifted from the ground and blocked the females; a beam fell from the ceiling in their path, missing the advancing women by mere inches. They waved away the mist, looking slightly confused by it, and I wondered what effect, if any, the elixir was having on their powers.

Kate continued to move objects into their path as the three of us backed toward the altar in full retreat. I'd lost sight of Aidan and Julius; I had no idea who had the upper hand in that confrontation.

"Your mind tricks are useless against us, mortal," the taller female called out, her thin face pulled into a smile that looked more like a grimace. They continued toward us—slowly, as if they were enjoying the anticipation.

As they drew closer, I reached for my stake, realizing my

mistake as soon as I made it. Damn it, I had identified myself as the *Sâbbat.*

It's that one, the taller female said to other. I could hear her as clearly as I could hear Aidan speak in my mind. *We need to restrain the other two.*

What happened next was entirely a blur. Somehow I was outside, sprawled on the grass. A full moon had risen and its light illuminated the dusky sky. Not ten feet away, daffodils ruffled in the breeze. Behind me, one female held Marissa, another had Kate. They both looked terrified, but neither made a sound. In front of me, Julius held Aidan captive, one thick arm around Aidan's slender neck.

It was exactly like my vision. Stumbling to my feet, I reached for my stake.

It was gone.

"Looking for this?" Julius taunted, and then he kicked it toward me.

I lunged for it, grasping it in my sweaty palm as I skittered back, away from him.

"This is simple, *Sâbbat*. You take that shiny little stake of yours and you plunge it straight into Aidan's heart, or your friends die. Your choice."

"No," I said, shaking my head. "No, I won't." The stake

slipped from my hands, and I bent down and retrieved it, bile rising in my throat.

Now, Julius! one of the females demanded.

I heard Kate cry out in pain as her captor grabbed a fistful of her hair, pulling her head sideways, exposing her neck. Marissa's captor did the same, fangs poised over my friend's pale skin.

"Now, *Sâbbat*!" Julius commanded. "Now, or your friends die a slow and painful death."

"Do it, now!" Marissa screamed, her voice full of terror. I couldn't look at her or Kate. Couldn't look at Jack and Joshua, now standing at the edge of the scene, watching helplessly. Instead, I focused on Aidan. This was where reality had to veer from my vision; where we had to do something to change what I'd seen, to alter the outcome.

Aidan's gaze locked with mine, and he nodded, a faint smile on his lips. *Do it, Violet,* he spoke in my mind, his voice calm and soothing. *There's no other way. Go on, I taught you how . . .*

"No!" I screamed, tears running down my cheeks. Why was he giving in so easily? "I can't," I sobbed, my legs shaking so badly that I could barely stand.

Behind me I heard a horrible sound, an inhuman scream, and I realized it was Marissa. Turning in horror, I saw the female vampire's fangs buried in Marissa's neck. Marissa's whole body spasmed, her feet lifted clear off the ground.

"No!" Kate cried. "Make it stop! Violet, do it!"

Listen to me, Violet! It was all a lie, Aidan said in my mind, his voice now rough, angry. *I loved Isabel, I never got over her death. I never loved you; only her. You look just like her, and I used you, I—*

"Shut up!" I screamed, taking two steps toward him, pain slashing at my heart. I knew it was a lie, knew he was trying to manipulate me. Oh, God, I had to do it. I didn't have a choice. They were killing Marissa, and Kate would be next.

We had failed.

My entire body trembling with fear, I raised the stake high above my head. Anger and fear flowed through my veins, mixing into some new emotion, giving me courage. I took a deep breath, felt strength surge through my arm, into the stake, and—

There was a horrible growling noise, a snarl behind me, followed by a scream. I spun around just in time to see an enormous dog lunge at Marissa's captor, knocking the vampire to the ground. The other female released Kate, moving as fast as lightning toward the animal that appeared to be ripping out the female's throat.

It was chaos. Everyone was yelling; vampire and human

screams all intermingled with canine snarls. Julius had taken a few steps toward the attacking dog, dragging Aidan with him, but a thick, impenetrable fog—created by Joshua, no doubt—appeared out of nowhere, shrouding the scene, increasing the confusion. Somehow I had dropped my stake, and I looked around wildly for it, in a panic. Not a second later it flew straight into my hand. My fingers closed around the familiar smooth wood as I silently thanked Kate.

Now. I had to take advantage of the confusion. Without the slightest hesitation, I took a running start. Instantaneously the fog vanished, and I lifted the stake high, my grasp firm and steady. With an earsplitting shriek I plunged it down toward its target, as hard as I could.

Right into Julius's heart.

Before I knew what had happened, Aidan was behind me, taking captive the female vampire who'd held Kate only moments before.

"Violet, here!" he called out, and I knew what I had to do; it was easy this time. I raised the stake and plunged it down once more, straight through her heart.

The huge dog released the other female—the one it had been attacking so viciously—and trotted over to my side, prodding me with its enormous snout. Its thick, coppery-brown fur was matted with blood, but bright blue eyes met mine—intelligent, wolfish eyes, and yet they looked so familiar. A shiver of recognition rippled down my spine as the injured beast turned and limped off toward the bushes with a whimper.

But there was no time to think about it—I had one more vampire left to slay. The third time would be easy; thanks to the wolf, this vampire's throat was already ripped open, her eyes glassy, her breathing shallow.

"Her injuries aren't mortal unless you do it," Aidan said, though I needed no prodding. She'd hurt my friend; maybe killed her. I took great pleasure in raising my trusty stake a third time and plunging it down through her heart.

And then I collapsed in the blood-soaked grass and cried—deep, gulping sobs. Someone yelled for Jack to get Marissa to the infirmary, and fast. I was vaguely aware of activity around me, of Aidan carrying away the slain vampires, presumably to separate their heads from their bodies and then burn them.

Familiar voices surrounded me—my friends, checking on one another, cleaning up the mess. I wanted to get up, to help. But all I could do was lie there—weak, entirely drained—and cry.

At some point Aidan returned, lifting me gently from the grass. "Shh," he whispered in my ear. "Everything's going to be fine."

But how could it be? How could anything ever be fine again?

"I'll be back in a few minutes," he called out over one shoulder. "Close your eyes, Violet. We're going the quick way."

Swallowing the painful lump in my throat, I did as I was told.

28 ~ The Queen of Hearts

I woke up on Aidan's daybed, blankets pulled up to my chin. Beside me, Aidan sat in a chair watching me, his gray-blue eyes unblinking.

"What time is it?" I asked, yawning, feeling as if I'd been drugged. I'd had a terrible nightmare.

"Almost eleven," he answered, his eyes never leaving my face.

I shook my head in confusion. There were no windows in his room; it was disorienting. "At night?" I asked, stretching my arms out. I felt stiff all over, sore in places that weren't usually sore.

Aidan raised one brow. "Eleven in the morning. You slept through the night."

I sat up abruptly, panic washing over me. "I'm going to be late for class!"

"It's Saturday," he said, amusement in his voice. "You've just woken up in my bed, and your first thought is about being late for class?"

I shook my head, trying to clear the cobwebs. "How did I get in your bed?"

"I brought you here. You needed to rest."

My bare legs brushed against soft, silky sheets, and I started in surprise. "What am I . . . where are my clothes?" I peeked under the covers and saw that I was wearing nothing but one of Aidan's T-shirts and my own panties. Oh, crap—what had happened? What had we done? If I got caught in his room . . .

And then I saw it, in the corner. A pile of clothes—*my* clothes, covered in dark, dried blood. Aidan reached for my hand just as it all came back in a painful rush—the events of last night.

Oh my God. The nightmare . . . it had been real.

"Shh, just let it come," he said. "It'll only hurt for a moment."

I'd killed three vampires. *Killed* them. I'd enjoyed it too, I realized with horror, remembering the sense of . . . of *pleasure* I'd felt when my stake hit its mark. I glanced down at my hands, remembering the blood there, the—

"It's your destiny, Vi," Aidan said, interrupting the downward spiral of my thoughts. "You can't fight it. Besides, they would have killed your friends."

My friends? More painful memories came flooding back. Marissa . . . her lifeless body lying in the blood-soaked grass. "Marissa," I breathed, barely able to speak. "Is she . . . is she dead?"

"No, she's in the infirmary, recuperating. She's going to be fine."

"But . . . but how?"

"The damage wasn't fatal. We put some blood back in her, healed the wounds in her neck. She'll be weak for a bit, a little anemic."

"But Nurse Campbell . . . what did you tell her? I mean, how did you explain—"

"Oh, Nurse Campbell is aware of . . . the situation. She's a gifted healer, you know. Anyway, Marissa will recover. Jenna's injuries are a bit more complicated, but she'll recover too."

"Jenna?" I asked, my heart accelerating.

"Jenna Holley."

"What . . . what about her?" Jenna hadn't been there.

"She's in the infirmary recuperating from injuries too," he said, reaching up to brush a stray lock of hair from my burning cheek. "We should go check on them later."

And then it hit me. *The dog.* Oh my God, the dog. But that didn't make sense; it was impossible. That meant she was . . . what? Some sort of shape-shifter? Or a . . . a . . . "Werewolf?" I whispered.

"I believe she prefers to be called a lycanthrope," Aidan offered. "A vampire's natural enemy, though it would seem Jenna didn't get the memo."

I nodded, unable to speak. She'd saved us. Somehow she'd saved us all. *But why?* She wasn't our friend; she owed us nothing.

"What about Blackwell?" I asked, finding my voice again.

"No longer a threat" was all Aidan said in reply. He rose from his chair, his legs long and lean in a pair of frayed jeans, his skin pale against a rumpled black T-shirt. He was barefoot, I realized. I'd never seen him barefoot before.

"Are you feeling well enough to get up and get dressed? Cece brought you some clean clothes, there on the bed. She's the one who undressed you last night, by the way."

I breathed a sigh of relief.

The barest hint of a smile tipped the corners of his mouth. "Anyway, if you're well enough, the headmaster wishes to speak with you."

So Blackwell was still around, the traitor. "How can you stand to look at him, after what he did?"

"I think you'll find there have been some changes at Winterhaven," he said cryptically, reaching for a pair of sneakers and slipping them on. "Should I leave while you get dressed?"

"No." No, I didn't want him to leave my side—not now, not ever. "Just . . . just turn your back or something."

With a nod, he turned toward the bookshelves, his hands thrust into his pockets while I reached for my clothes. Luckily Cece had remembered a bra, since I wasn't wearing one now. Moving quickly, I shed Aidan's shirt and put on my own stuff. "Okay," I called out, zipping up my hoodie. "Ready."

Aidan turned around to face me, a sad, almost bittersweet smile on his face. "Before we go"—he cleared his throat, looking uncomfortable all of a sudden—"I just wanted to make sure you understand . . . those things I said last night, before Jenna struck. Surely you realize . . . you know why I said those things, right?"

As painful as it was, I allowed myself to remember. When Aidan had said those hateful words, I'd known exactly what he was doing—and why. Still, I'd gotten angry; I'd felt myself grow stronger, more sure of my abilities. I'd been poised to strike—I *would* have struck if Jenna hadn't attacked when she did. Whether I would have struck Aidan or Julius, I'd never know for sure.

But Jenna's appearance had changed everything. It had

been the point where reality had veered away from my vision—it was the new element, the one that allowed me to believe we could change the outcome.

"Of course I know why you said those things," I said at last. He would have sacrificed himself for me, for my friends. "Did you *really* think I'd believe it?"

In reply he reached for me and drew me to him—roughly, almost violently. I felt his lips in my hair, his fingers biting into my shoulders, as if he'd never let me go.

But then he did. Releasing my shoulders, he took a step back, his gaze meeting mine. I held my breath, the familiar frisson of electricity passing between us, making gooseflesh rise on my skin. Relief washed over me. *It's still there.*

Raising one hand to his lips, he kissed his fingertips, and then pressed them against my heart. Something about the gesture said more than any words could, bringing tears to my eyes.

I stood outside that big carved-wood door as I had so many times in the past, only this time Aidan stood by my side. I was scared—terrified, really. How could Aidan trust Dr. Blackwell again? He could be plotting against him still, at this very minute, summoning some other sect of rogue vampires to Winterhaven, some other killers who operated outside vampire law.

At last the door swung open, and I took a deep breath.

Squeezing Aidan's cold hand in my own, I stepped inside and waited for the big leather chair behind the desk to swivel around.

It did, and all I could do was gasp.

"Good morning, Miss McKenna," Mrs. Girard said cheerily, her hair perfectly coiffed. "I'm glad to see you looking so well."

My mouth fell open, but no words came out before I snapped it shut again.

Mrs. G. just smiled. "If you'll take a seat, *chérie,* I'll explain it all to you."

Nodding, I sank into the chair before me. Aidan stood behind me, his hands resting on my shoulders.

"Where's . . . where's Blackwell?" I stammered, finding my voice at last.

"Gone," she said simply. "I am headmaster now. Acting headmaster, technically, though I'm certain the board will quickly make the appointment permanent."

"He's gone, or dead?" I had to know.

Mrs. Girard looked me square in the eye. "Dead. I'm only sorry I didn't learn the truth in time to foil their plot and spare you the trouble."

"Are you saying that you're . . . you're one of . . . of them?"

"A vampire? Yes, *chérie*. I am."

I twisted in my chair, looking up accusingly at Aidan. "She's one too, and you didn't tell me?"

"Please, Miss McKenna," Mrs. Girard said, and I turned back to face her. "You must know that he could not tell you. It's against our laws to do so, and the punishment would have been severe. Only I could tell you such a truth without punishment, and I had no cause to do so. Until now, of course."

Remembering the three days of torture Aidan had endured as punishment for telling me about Dr. Blackwell, I just nodded, swallowing hard.

I'm sorry, I said to Aidan. *I shouldn't have accused you—*

No, I understand. But just know that she is very powerful, more so than Blackwell was. Much more so.

In other words, we should be cautious.

"But yes, I am a vampire, and Aidan Gray is perhaps my greatest handiwork, my most valuable creation. I could not possibly let Blackwell destroy that, not when Aidan offers our kind such hope."

She turned you? I asked him, completely stunned. *Mrs. Girard is the vampire who did this to you? But I thought you didn't know—*

I didn't. Not until last night, while you were sleeping.

"Anyway, Miss McKenna," Mrs. Girard continued, unaware that Aidan and I were having our own private little conversation, "I want you to know that you are safe here. Blackwell was a fool—weak and easily manipulated, it would seem. Winterhaven was meant to be a safe haven, a nurturing environment for those in need of one, even a *Sâbbat*. That Blackwell violated that tenet—well, it's unconscionable. I hope you'll choose to stay on. For now, at least, despite the recent unpleasantness."

"But . . . but I thought you weren't allowed to . . . you know, harm one of your kind. Won't the Tribunal—"

She waved one hand in dismissal. "Oh, have no fear about that, Miss McKenna. You see, I *am* the Tribunal. Chairwoman, at least."

I nodded, trying to digest that. The kindly Mrs. Girard, chair of some merciless vampire court? *She was part of the group that tortured you?* I asked Aidan.

She's the one who ordered it, he answered.

"Anyway, you *will* stay, won't you?" she asked, watching me closely, as if she was trying to gauge my response. For the first time I noticed that her eyes were as pale and washed-out as Dr. Blackwell's. How had I missed that?

I cleared my throat before I answered her. "I'm not going anywhere. All my friends are here, and Aidan . . . well, Aidan and I . . ." I trailed off, not quite sure what to say. She was the headmaster now, after all, and I'd just spent the night in his room. Surely that was grounds for expulsion.

"Mr. Gray has explained your feelings for each other, Miss McKenna. I offer only one warning—you are a *Sâbbat*, a powerful one, if last night is any indication. I've known several throughout the centuries, and every last one possessed a deep, internalized hatred of my kind. It's safe to say that your current feelings are an anomaly, and it's likely that your feelings will change as you come of age. If that happens, if your presence here begins to pose a threat to Mr. Gray and myself, I'll have to ask you to leave Winterhaven."

"My feelings aren't going to change," I said, shaking my head. I loved him entirely, with all my heart.

Nor mine, came Aidan's voice in my head. *I am yours, heart and soul.*

Mrs. Girard smiled, looking more like someone's elegant grandmother than a powerful vampire. "I hope you are right, *chérie*. Truly, I do. Perhaps you'll prove to be the first of a rare new breed, a *Sâbbat* who can see inside a vampire's heart, who can tell the good from the evil. That might prove useful for our kind. Some vampires are far less monstrous than many mortals are, you know."

I thought of the mortal monsters who had executed my father, and nodded in agreement.

"I fear that a war is brewing amongst our kind. Perhaps someday . . ." She trailed off, sighing heavily. "Never mind. In the meantime, Mr. Gray will continue with his work. Perhaps he'll find his cure before it's too late. I'm a romantic, you see.

Perhaps it's the Parisian in me," she said with a shrug. "Either way, we can only hope for the best. So, if there's nothing else, I think you've some friends in the infirmary who would be pleased to see you."

I just nodded.

"I'm happy to see the true spirit of friendship thrive here at Winterhaven," Mrs. G. continued. "Vampire, lycan, shape-shifter, *Sâbbat*—all coming together as friends, despite their differences, despite their natural instincts. It's a rare thing, isn't it? If only the rest of the world could take notice. Ah, well. Our secrets must remain safe, no matter how enlightened." She stood then, showing us both to the door. "Enjoy the rest of your weekend. I should get back to work."

I took Aidan's hand and followed him out. "Thank you, Mrs. Girard," I said, turning back toward her one last time. "I . . . I promise you have nothing to fear from me."

She just smiled. "Time will tell, won't it, *chérie*? Oh, and, Mr. Gray? Please see that Miss McKenna finds her *own* room tonight."

My cheeks flamed as she closed the door.

"That went well, don't you think?" Aidan asked, then bent down and kissed me lightly on the lips.

I was suddenly so overwhelmed with emotion that I could only nod. At once the world seemed a bright, happy place. I had my friends—plus one, if you counted Jenna. And after yesterday, how could you not? And I had Aidan. A lump formed in my throat as I looked at the boy beside me, pale and beautiful and loving and kind, even if he *was* a vampire.

As to the future—well, I supposed that Mrs. Girard was right, and that time would tell. Still, I had to believe that our feelings for each other wouldn't change, even when I came of age; that Aidan would find his cure; that someday he'd be mortal again, before it was too late for us.

And if not . . . we'd cross that bridge when we came to it. I wouldn't think about it now—I couldn't.

Still, there were so many questions left unanswered. Why had Jenna come to our aid? How had she even known about Julius and the attack? Were there other Propagators out there, and would they come after Aidan too? And what about the other two *Sâbbats* who were out there somewhere? Girls like me, born to slay vampires. Did they know their purpose yet? Could I find them, these sisters of mine, if I tried? Did I even want to?

"Shall we go to the infirmary?" Aidan asked, interrupting my thoughts. "To see your friends—*our* friends?" he amended. "They're waiting for us."

Tears welled in my eyes—happy tears—and without warning Aidan pulled me into his arms. I laid my cheek against his heart, listening to the steady thump-thump, breathing in his familiar scent. He was cold, so cold. And yet I didn't mind, not one bit. Cold was the new hot, I told myself, then laughed at my own cleverness.

"Let's go," I said, leaving the safety of his arms and starting off down the corridor.

"Forget walking; let's go my way," he said, his voice full of mischief. "The fast way."

"Fine," I said with a grin, feeling suddenly brave and adventurous. I reached out my hand, and he took it firmly in his. "Only this time, my eyes stay open."

ACKNOWLEDGMENTS

There are so many people who helped make *Haven* a reality—where to begin?! First of all, I'd like to thank three amazing authors: Charlotte Featherstone, Lori Devoti, and Caroline Linden. Your insightful comments and critiques were invaluable as I wrote (and rewrote!) the manuscript. I owe a huge debt of gratitude to Dr. Michael Davis, professor of Biomolecular Science at Central Connecticut State University, for his aid in crafting a "scientific" explanation for vampirism (and for not laughing at the request!). And thanks to his wife, Kate Rothwell, for offering up his expertise.

Big thanks and hugs to my generous beta readers, Sonya Russell and Carey Corp. You both rock! Thank you to my agent, Marcy Posner, for her continued guidance, support, and friendship. I'm so glad to have you in my corner! An equally enthusiastic thank-you to my editor, Jen Klonsky, for making this a better book, and for being so much fun to work with.

Lastly, heartfelt thanks to my family—Dan, Vivian, and Eleanor—for . . . well, everything.